Brian Mc

To Answer The Peacock

Copyright

This novel is entirely a work of fiction. The names, characters and incidents portrayed in it are the work of the author's imagination. Any resemblance to actual persons, living or dead, events or localities is entirely coincidental.

Published by High Hold Books
www.brianmcneill.co.uk

First published in Great Britain by Black Ace Books 1999 ISBN : 1-872988-32-6

Paperback Edition © 24.08.2020 ISBN : 978-1-913957-00-1

Elaine Greene, in memoriam

This story could never have come to fruition without the generous and unstinting help of:

Raymond Riou, The Menzies family, Eric Bogle, Hunter Steele, The Scottish Arts Council, Sally Davis and Jacqueline France.

The Breton tours my original group, The Battlefield Band, did in the 1970s were the seed of *To Answer The Peacock*. The ambivalence I'd always felt about nationalism was put into stark relief by the power of Brittany's traditional music; a brilliant, crystal-clear expression of a culture, once heard, never forgotten. So when the time came for my busker to explore the contradictions around Celtic independence with a tale of love, loss and confusion, Brittany seemed the only possible place to start.

The actual story didn't begin until an anarchic visit to Tasmania (Longford Festival—unforgettable! Why can't I remember more of it?) years later. Why that utterly foreign landscape provided the trigger escapes me, but my usual pattern of monomania followed for the rest of our Antipodean tour. I remember writing the fest-noz scene while waiting for Rudolf Nureyev to finish rehearsing in Wellington, New Zealand, and creating the mythical island of Colrhanna while walking round Lake Bullen Merri, a crater lake in Victoria—a place as unlike the Scottish Highlands as any on the planet.

I can only hope my various hosts will belatedly forgive the strange, preoccupied Scottish ghost who sat at their tables.

Brian

1

STREET

I WAS ON my haunches, ready to tally up, when the shadow fell over the caseful of coins and robbed them of their shine. Someone was standing close behind me.

Cops? Please, I thought, not more cops. Was Rennes going to be Paris all over again? With one hand I picked up my fiddle and bow from the warm cobblestones, with the other I thrust the money I'd already counted into my pocket—and then the stink reached down and told me who it really was. As I rose I heard the muttered word.

"Salaud!"

I turned. He was young, probably younger than I was—and somehow that made it worse.

"Salaud," he hissed again, "thief!"

The accusation was a hoarse croak that barely had the strength to escape from the matted mess of moustache and beard, but there was no mistaking its anger. A greasy hank of hair hung across his face as he swayed before me, but when his head lolled to one side it fell back and showed me his eyes—dull, glazed over with the effort of trying to focus his hate. The brow above the left one was a yellow and black bruise, fastened in place on the filthy skin by a web of bloody streaks. At the sight of it, pity almost overcame my wariness—but not quite, for I knew from bitter experience how unpredictable this kind of drunk could be. At first he'd contented himself with a few shouted oaths from the other side of the square, but the bottle which had been half full when I'd first seen him was empty now. Determined to take no more chances, I drew my belongings further out of reach.

"Espèce de con!"

This time it was a snarl—and the sudden flaring of his nostrils doubled the warning. The grab was half-hearted, the hand slow, ready for violence but unused to it. As I batted it away I thought it might be better not to understand French.

"I'm just making a few shillings, friend. Why don't you leave me alone?"

I held out a coin. He gave no sign of hearing or understanding, but this time he moved like lightning. Brows furrowed, he examined the coin with both hands, then polished its dullness on his sleeve. I watched it disappear into a ragged fold of jacket—and only once it was safe did he remember how much he hated me. He spat at my feet and began to shuffle back towards the fountain by the far wall, muttering, shaking his head, brandishing the empty bottle. Slowly, I let myself relax, bending to pack away my things as I watched him—but as he sat down amid his pile of possessions my relief died, for I saw what I'd missed before.

A bow, sticking out from the tattered knapsack. Beside it, wet from the fountain's spray, a fiddle.

He was a busker too—and he had to a right to be angry. I'd stolen his pitch.

I crossed the square in my turn. The aggression had left him now, but the paranoia which had replaced it was no less extreme. As I drew near he cowered away, wrapping the jacket tight round him, hunching chin down over chest. I dug into my pocket and brought out a handful of the change I'd been so anxious to keep from him a few minutes before. As I dropped it into the hat that lay beside him, I nodded at his fiddle.

"Here, I'm sorry. I never saw it."

The indecision was pitiful. The eyes registered the money, but he was too frightened now to lift it. His mouth worked. He gripped the ragged lapels tighter and turned further away from me, waiting for the kick, the blow. I lifted his sodden violin from the puddle and held it out to him. It might have been a good instrument once, but now it was a wreck—no amount of filth could cover the cracks and cigarette burns. There were only three strings.

"You should dry it. It won't play if it's wet."

One eye looked up. Hesitantly, the arms began to loosen their straitjacket grip. He stared at my face as though he'd never seen it before—and then, as his gaze shifted, I realised I was still holding my own instrument. A longing came into his eyes. When he reached out again, it was towards my fiddle, not his. The grimy hand nearly closed on the ribbon of the silver St. Christopher that hung from the scroll—but I was fast enough. I thrust his own violin back at him. He scowled, spat. I backed off until I was out of his reach, then turned and walked away—my rudeness had been accidental, I'd made it good as best I could. It was time to go, before his mood changed again. What could I do to help him anyway? I'd enough problems of my own without—

Halfway across the square the sound of his fiddle stopped me. I turned.

He was sitting cross-legged on the fountain steps, scraping the almost hairless bow across the untuned strings, shaking his head from side to side in pathetic imitation of a jolly fiddler. The sound was an eerie mockery of music, the open-mouthed grin an insane parody of merriment. Pity returned to me, only to be driven out by a familiar stab of fear.

Was that me, a few years down the road?

The thought scared me. For four years now, ever since leaving Scotland behind, I'd been a busker—a professional one, if that word meant anything, making my living on the streets of Europe. Trouble with the law had pushed me into the life, but I'd quickly discovered how much I loved it, and I knew I'd never be anything else.

But there was no escaping the one hard fact—it wasn't a job which came with pensions and cosy retirement schemes...

So was that my future? A stretch of pavement to rule from a wet stone step, a doorway to sleep in? Madness? Even though I was strong now, I'd been near madness once—near enough to fear it more than anything. I knelt, let the ritual of putting away the fiddle banish the thought. And then I lifted the case, turned my back on him and lost no time leaving the square.

I strode off down the narrow street of mediaeval half-timbered houses that would lead me back towards the town centre. The city of Rennes was giving them a facelift, sanitising its heritage, renovating the crumbling facades for tourist eyes, and hammer and drill soon drowned out all other sound, musical or otherwise. For that I was grateful, and I was thankful for the shade as well, for the afternoon sun was hot enough to work its usual paradox, sticking my wet shirt to the small of my back and my dry tongue to the roof of my mouth. When a waiter appeared from one of the nearby cafés and began weaving through the scaffolding, my eyes followed his tray. The single frosted glass on it seemed cruel, a mockery of my thirst, intensifying all the grimy city tastes I'd collected in the last few hours. Just one beer, I thought, one really cold beer...

But I marched on, for I could afford neither the time nor the cash. I had a deadline, and since leaving the north my luck had been doing its best to stop me keeping it.

The place I was headed for was Concarneau, a small town on Brittany's south coast. I'd planned to make my way there from Germany at a leisurely pace, working just enough to make ends meet—a week's busking, I'd figured, would be ample to take care of petrol and give me enough for a few days of simple living. Or at least, that had been the theory...

It was the run-in with the Paris Metro cops which had changed everything. Six hours in their *gendarmerie's* carbolic stink had been bad enough, but the fiddle case which had been full of money when they took me in had come back empty when they let me go—and argument would have been suicide. And then the next day, just past Chartres, my aging Fiat decided I'd ignored its overheating long enough. The new radiator had been ruinously expensive—doubly so, for I'd had to wait a day and a half for it to reach the village where I'd broken down, and there was nowhere to busk.

The upshot of it all was that I was in a near-penniless state which only the street could cure—and though my one morning in Rennes had shown me how generous the Bretons could be, I knew it was going to take a long time to get enough money together for my needs. It was worrying, but not as worrying as the fact that I was already three days late. Tonight I'd phone—I *had* to phone. I turned into an alleyway, hoping to avoid the press of people and find a short cut to the main shopping street, the Rue d'Orléans. As I walked I reached into my back pocket for the letter which had found me just before I left Germany.

It was from the woman who had given me the St. Christopher. Her name was Elly. She was thirty-seven years old, she was Dutch, she was calm and beautiful—and she was a problem.

For nearly seven years now we'd tried to force the love we felt for each other into some kind of permanence. We'd tried living with each other, we'd tried living without each other, and neither option had left us satisfied. More than a month in one place left me feeling shackled, more than a month without me left her feeling abandoned. It seemed insoluble, but we'd been apart now since early spring, and the letter's arrival had brought home to me how much I missed her.

I stopped beside a bright swathe of anti-nuclear posters and read the few lines again. She was spending a couple of days in Brittany, she'd rented a cottage, miles from anywhere. Did I want to come for a while, talk things through? The phone number was a bar in Concarneau. I'd left a message to say I'd arrive by Sunday the 20th of July, and today was already Wednesday, the 23rd. I put the crumpled envelope away again, cursing myself. When the troubles with the cops and the car had started, I should have phoned again, but I'd put it off—I'd feared it would sound like an evasion, an excuse. But if today's takings didn't give me enough to fill the tank, I'd do it. I had to. If I didn't...

I turned the corner and felt instinct override the familiar arguments.

A street without cars. A pedestrian precinct.

And a prosperous one at that; boutiques, *parfumeries,* cafés—it looked right. I cut through the crowd to the next intersection—and *smiled* with satisfaction when I reached it. Better than just right, much better—a bywater of the main Rue d'Orléans concourse, a nice little carless crossroads, shaded by a cluster of tall shrubs planted in concrete pots. It was a natural place for people to stop—and the shrubs were a double bonus, for as well as offering me shade, they'd give privacy to those who preferred to open their purses discreetly. Nearly four now—no time to lose. I opened the case, lifted the violin and started to play.

And within five minutes I knew I had a gold mine.

Women.

If the world was really split according to the myth of the sexual divide, then no busker would be crazy enough to choose the male half for an audience. It's not a question of generosity—both sexes have that—it's a question of accessibility. Men rule their world by subduing it, women by gauging it—and gauging it means they perceive more of it. Men take stock of their environment as and when they need to, but women judge to a fine point how and where they fit into things, they continually assess and reassess the relationships between themselves and their surroundings. It doesn't make them better or worse than their male counterparts—but it does mean that they pick up stimuli faster, that they're better at perceiving the new.

And on the street, that simply means that something out of the usual stands more chance of being noticed, of making its living—and here, it was obvious that the living could be very good indeed.

For the kind of women who were bending to drop money into my fiddle case were doing it with a dainty sideways swivel of the knees, dictated by the tightness of their skirts and the height of their heels. Sophisticated, older women, droves of them—and with money to burn. I'd struck it lucky.

It wasn't hard to see what was drawing them. The boutiques surrounding me were devoted to fashion, but there was none of the usual scramble for a share of the almighty teenage purse. Across the four corners, Louis Vuitton and Hermès challenged each other with umbrella and handbag, and two old-fashioned dress shops gave themselves airs and tried to think of themselves as couturiers, competing with understated refinement, the single gown in each of their windows unsullied by the mention of anything as vulgar as price. And as far as the eye could see in every direction, the stylish displays craned forward to beckon—gloves, hats, shoes, jewellery, make-up to create mystique, perfume to perpetuate it, luxury lotions to pamper from bath to bedroom. One word came irresistibly to mind. *Cornucopia...* Every window was a horn of plenty, every doorway practically a command to dally.

I played. The case filled quickly, and the fact obviously had nothing to do with my music. I was a fixture, a talking point, just like the wares in the windows. To some of the women I was an excuse to peruse the shoe shop beside me, to others the shoe shop was the pretext, and I was the object of scrutiny. I could see them speculate, trying to classify me. What was I? Just another beggar, or something more exotic, a *fin de saison* special offer? Worth a closer look? The ones who decided I was used my case to get it—and buy themselves a few coppers' worth of admiration at the same time. A franc for the chance of showing off a pretty pair of ankles, a neck as yet unlined by age—it was a bargain with flirtation thrown in free. Once it was done they smiled with satisfaction at their own daring, snapped their handbags shut, and went on their way.

I didn't mind. It was harmless, and as the perfumed coin rained down into my case I enjoyed them in my turn, and not just for their money or their looks. I liked the care with which they took their expensive ease. They were painstaking in their perusal, unhurried in their search for a lavish bargain, sure in their judgement of what suited. Older or not, they were no less devoted to fashion than they'd been ten years before, or twenty—but it was all less frenetic now. They'd learned discrimination, and this clever little corner knew how to help them exercise it, how to emphasise the fact that there was as much to look forward to as to look back on—plenty of well-tailored elegance to show *madame* how striking she could still look, cashmere, silk and lace to promise her tomorrow's finesse—but no jeans shops to remind her of yesterday's waistline. The single dress in the window would make her ten years younger if she wanted to surprise, or ten lives older if she wanted to seduce.

I played. I watched—and wondered what the men made of it all. The odd briefcase went by, but hurriedly, as though its owner knew he had no place here without a chaperone, and when the waiter I'd seen earlier passed me again, en route to his home base at the next corner's café, he frowned, as though he held the territory's sole franchise for unattached masculinity. But a few signs of male independence did exist, albeit with suitable discretion. Brass plates announced the presence of *M. le notaire* or *M. le médecin* in the sober grey upper storeys. Did they only come out after dark? I smiled at the fantasy as I looked up into the first floor apartment opposite. Through the open window I heard a man's voice answer the telephone and saw a striped cuff reach up to draw the blind. It lingered long after the job was done, and I wondered—was I being listened to, or were the women being watched?

The answer came immediately. A shapely pair of legs sauntered past me. As soon as they disappeared round the corner, the hand vanished—and I smiled at my own vanity. An audience *and* money, that would be too much to expect... I stopped, put the fiddle down and knelt to gather the take—a hundred, and ten, and twenty, thirty... As I counted the coin, my eyes found the St. Christopher. Had it finally worked, changed my luck? Were things going right for me at last?

And the minute I stood up again, I knew they were.

In front of me stood two boys and three girls, each with a

shiny black violin case.

Now, any good busker knows how to capitalise on kids—but ten-or-eleven-year-olds who were musicians as well, and fiddlers to boot, that was a heaven-sent opportunity. Immediately, people began to stop, intrigued by the confrontation. Within minutes I was surrounded by a semicircle of expectant faces.

Once more I played. A set of reels, fast and flashy—*The Devil's Dream,* and an American tune, *Whisky Before Breakfast.* A slow air and strathspeys. A hornpipe called *Wrapped Up Tidy...*

At the end of each piece—for I kept them short, to milk the situation—the children applauded, all except the sixth, the one I hadn't noticed arriving. His violin case was different from the others, one of the beautiful old morocco leather ones I'd always wanted, and he held it in front of him with both hands, shyly. I was reaching him, though, his eyes told me so—he had an insight into my music. I always knew when someone did, when they understood from the heart, when it was more than just entertainment. But I resisted the temptation to play just for him, for the longer I could keep all the children, the better business would be.

So I played *The Four-poster Bed.* Irresistible—when the bow's heel beat out the rhythm on the fiddle's pine top, their faces broke into smiles. The next step was *The Sow's Lament For The Tatties*—and as always, the bow's imitation of the pig's voice worked its rough magic. Except for the one boy, they laughed out loud. My success delighted the crowd beyond measure; their applause, the strong, respectful tribute of adults, joined the children's—and the money rolled in. But as I struck up again I heard exclamations of annoyance.

At first glance the middle-aged man who pushed through from behind looked like a salesman or a clerk, but I knew he was the children's violin teacher by the proprietorial look he gave them, and by the professional appraisal he gave my stance and hands. He was perhaps in his early forties, bearded in the square-cut Breton style with no moustache, balding at crown and temple. He'd been handsome once, and muscular, but the body had run to seed and the face was sad, its heavy features sagging with the kind of permanent tiredness that comes from late nights and empty bottles. His crumpled suit was at once too tight and too youthful, and his striped shirt cuff identified him as the man I'd seen earlier, at the window. This was the connoisseur of shapely legs.

He lifted his wristwatch, a public registration of his annoyance—and his pupils hung their heads in guilt. It was only a small cruelty, but it angered me. I could see he expected me to stop playing, and when I didn't, he smiled. It was a defensive smile, a smile for hiding things, but it was no more successful than the tight waistcoat was at hiding his paunch. Behind it I could see him weigh up the pros and cons of confrontation. Quickly he rounded on the children.

"Time for work, *mes enfants,*" he said loudly. He turned back to me. "And you, sir. I'm afraid I'll have to ask you to move. The childrens' lesson, you understand."

I stopped. His rudeness nearly made me take the bait, but in the end it wasn't worth the argument. When someone asks me to leave I always do, for I hate the thought of my music annoying anyone, and I had enough cash now, or nearly. I saw the plate in the doorway beside the shrub pots as he began to shepherd the children away. *G. Berolet & Son. Violins. Sale, repair & restoration.* A carefully cut piece of card was attached to the bottom. *P. Berolet. Superior instruction in violin and viola.* Reluctantly, the children picked up their cases.

But the crowd didn't like it. There was a loud muttering, and someone booed. He looked surprised, hurt even, that anyone should challenge him. He appealed to them.

"They'll hear, upstairs!"

A female voice protested. "There'd be nothing wrong with that! Bet they'd learn as much from him as from you, friend! If you can do better, let's hear you!"

The chorus of agreement jarred him. The shoulders tensed, annoyance deepened the lines on the tanned brow—and then someone laughed. The last of his ease vanished. Anger raked the flabby figure into pompous rigidity—and suddenly the playboy cut of the suit wasn't just wrong, it was ridiculous. I waited for the put-down.

"Doing better, *madame,* has nothing to do with it. Real musicians—*classical* musicians—do not beg in the street."

The crowd's contempt was voluble, a long collective jeer. I thought he was going to erupt, but another voice held him in check:

"Philippe, Philippe, the lady is right. You mustn't see these matters in such a rigid way. The gentleman plays very well. Let the children listen a little longer. The lesson can run late."

The cultured voice came from an older, more comfortable version of the same man. He was dressed for business, with a smartness his son would never achieve. His suit was dark and plain, but it had been well cut and he knew how to wear it. When he lifted his hat and bowed to me, I saw the full head of hair—and felt a brief sympathy for the teacher. To be corrected by his father in public—particularly a father like this one, particularly in front of children he had to teach...

It was the final blow to his dignity. As the crowd applauded the older man, the younger took the only refuge he could. As I listened to the father's courteous voice I watched the return of the son's armoured smile.

"Your violin. Scottish?"

"Yes. John Carr, Falkirk. Eighteen ninety-seven."

"May I...?"

I only hesitated a second; I trusted him instinctively. I handed him the instrument. He took a few steps to the side and held it up to the light to read the label inside. The crowd, their imagination caught now, pushed past me and closed in on him—was he going to pronounce it valuable? A hand caught at my sleeve. I turned. It was the boy, the one who had listened so attentively.

"Mister?"

Hearing him speak English startled me. The accent was well bred, but with a rural edge. West Country?

"Where does the pig's voice come from?"

The naiveté of the question was a second surprise—I'd taken him for older. There was a bright orange tag on his shirt. Nick. His name, I wondered, or a designer label?

"If you play the strings behind the bridge," I said, "instead of—"

Someone shoved me from behind. I turned as voices were raised.

"Hey! *Salaud!* What are you—"

"Attention! Le violon!"

As the crowd scattered I lost sight of the boy. I heard incoherent shouting, a woman's scream and a volley of curses. I fought my way through the mass of bodies to the front—to see the old man being helped up from the cobbles by his son. Then a noise from behind spun me round.

Ragged jacket, blood-stained face...

Him! The beggar, my adversary from the square! He must

have come from behind, from the steps—

And then I didn't care where he'd come from—all I could see was the filthy hand and what it held.

My fiddle.

Somehow he had grabbed it... Automatically I reached out to the instrument, but the old man's arm stopped me. He was breathless with the shock.

"No. He might damage it. Let me, I know him." He brushed dust from his sleeves and walked forward. "Pigez, give me back the violin. Now."

The matted head shook. The fiddle went further away into the jacket. He squatted down on the cobbles.

And spat, noisily.

The sound triggered the crowd's disgust. They roared at him. He snarled back like a dog. There was a chaos of abuse and a waving of fists as the people recovered their courage, a sound of running feet as even more came to investigate. The old man, his authority fully returned now, held up his hands for quiet.

"Pigez, give it to me. Nobody will hurt you. We won't—"

"Attention les flics!"

The crowd parted to let two policemen through.

"What's going on here?"

Everyone tried to speak at once.

"A thief, officer, he—"

"—when I was examining this gentleman's violin."

"—shouldn't be allowed, the likes of—"

"It's mine! He stole it from me!"

The pain in the hoarse cry stilled every voice. Slowly the words sank in. My fiddle—all I had in the world, and he was claiming it belonged to him! This time it was a policeman's hand that stopped me, the burlier of the two. He misread my intentions completely.

"Easy, now. We'll have no brawling here"

His eyes took in me, then the caseful of coins. "Licence?"

"What? What d'you mean?"

By the time I understood him his expression had changed to one of disgust. "I thought so. Don't come the innocent—you need a licence to beg in this city, and fine you know it. Damn layabouts, you're all the bloody same." He turned to the old man. "Whose fiddle is it?"

I saw red. I shouted at him. "It's mine! I've had it for years!"

The drunk roared at all of us. "*Menteur!* He's a liar! He took it from me!"

He looked up—and the conviction in the mad eyes stopped me dead. It had animated his face, given him back his youth—he believed what he was saying, there was no doubt of it. My hesitation was enough to convince the cop of his course of action. He waved at the crowd.

"Move along now, excitement's over." He turned to his partner. "We'll sort this out down at the station. Get that one, Jules." He grabbed me by the wrist. "You, come with me."

He began to pull me away. In desperation I appealed to the old man.

"Help me—explain to them! I have to get to Concarneau, tonight! I have to!"

The old man tried to speak, but then the noise from the pavement made nonsense of explanation. The other policeman had lifted his quarry by the lapels, but he'd underestimated the beggar Pigez's new-found strength. The ragged figure broke away, the fiddle swung out at arm's length—and suddenly I knew that once more everything had changed in his mind.

My instrument was a weapon, now—*and he was going to hit the cop with it!*

This time I wasn't to be stopped. I broke free, ran forward and lunged, but all I caught was a handful of sleeve. Pigez kicked at me but I held on. A staggering ballet began that whirled all of us across the cobbles. A police kepi rolled away, someone's foot sent my case flying, and the crowd screamed as their money showered back over them. I managed to get a hand to the fiddle, and then a fist hit me squarely on the side of the head. At the same time the policeman I'd evaded caught me by the neck. The fiddle flew out of my grip, and then we all crashed to the ground—but when I managed to get up again I was free of all hands.

It was then that I saw my violin. It was lying a few yards away. The chin rest was gone and two of the pegs had been sheared off. I ran to it, but as I picked it up, a body crashed into me. Once more the instrument went flying—but this time right over the concrete flowerpots that held the shrubs.

"You can come—"

I heard the dissonant crash on the stones behind, the awful sound of splintering wood.

"—the easy way—"

It couldn't have survived a fall like that. No instrument could.

"—or the hard way, son. All the same to me."

As he spun me round, red rage filled me. I hit out as hard as I could, felt fist connect with bone, and watched him go down like a ninepin. Then another body slammed into me and a blue serge arm came round my throat.

The last thing I saw before my head hit the cobblestones was the English boy's face, screwed up in fear.

2

AUTHORITY

"RIGHT, YOU. UP."

I got to my feet. There was no point in arguing—once they've got you inside a police station there never is. I felt my gut tighten in anticipation.

As soon as we'd reached the basement, I'd known what was coming. First, fingerprints upstairs, then paperwork in the squad room, but no statement. A whispered conference in the corner had dispelled the atmosphere of official rage—and then all of them had carefully avoided looking at me. A pale youngster had brought me down here and left me to contemplate my own stupidity while I waited for the inevitable. Hardly a word had been said since the arrest.

Until now.

There were three of them. The ones on either side were both huge, probably the two biggest they could find in the station. They had brutal faces, dark and Gallic. The middle one was incongruous between them, short and stocky, sandy-haired, more like an English country parson than a French policeman.

"Time you learned some respect, son."

The venom squeezed out past the cigarette at the corner of his mouth. I stared at the row of lockers.

"Some manners. High time, don't you think?"

"I've nothing—"

He slapped me twice, hard. "Don't talk back to me, son."

As I grabbed the table beside me for support, the lit cigarette came down on the back of my hand. The sharpness of the hurt sent me stumbling forward until our faces almost touched.

He enjoyed the first punch. I saw it in his eyes before it caught me in the stomach. It was hard enough to double me over, but even before I felt the pain bite, the other two were hauling me back up for their turn. I managed to get an arm free to cover my face, but it was useless—a knee butted me in the groin, and this time the agony was immediate. Tears stung my eyes as I tried to yell, but the cry found no breath. A flurry of sharp jabs jarred my head back against the locker door—and the next thing I knew I was on the floor. I felt my mouth fill with blood, but what I tasted was fear. Dizziness came. I tried not to vomit—and then a regulation police boot came into view and self-preservation took over. Turn! Away! Anything else, no matter how bad, but not the fingers!

I got them out of reach just in time. The heel came down hard. It only raked the back of my hand, but the pain was incredible. I screamed. A fist yanked me up by the hair.

"I thought I told you to get *up.*"

The boot caught neck and shoulder and sent me crashing back through a forest of chair legs.

"I'll teach you to hit a cop, sunshine. I'll fucking well show you!"

"If I might have a word, detective Lemercier? And I'm sure Serpin and Greuz have business elsewhere."

The voice was pleasant, as though the speaker had just interrupted a Bible reading instead of an assault, but there was no mistaking its authority. There was silence, then sounds of furniture being pushed out of the way, doors opening. As a fresh wave of nausea hit me I heard a low exchange of voices, brief and acrimonious, then more doors, a running tap. I tried to get up, but the stab of pain in my stomach folded me over again, and I fell forward among the chairs. Once more the pleasant voice came.

"Anyone who hits a policeman is either crazy or just plain bad—or has a very good reason. Let's assume you're neither of the first two, Mister Fiddler. Tell me what happened."

He waited for his answer. The tap stopped. I heard metal-heeled footsteps. I tried to speak, but it hurt too much.

"Ah, I see. Very well, we'll do without the story. Doesn't matter, comes to the same thing anyway. You can nod your head?

Good. Here."

A cloth, cold and damp, fell over my neck, and I found myself staring at a pair of shiny black brogues. I pulled the towel to my bleeding mouth and wiped it, then tried to look up, but it was even more painful than speaking. I caught a glimpse of a hand holding a computer printout as my head sank back.

"Alexander Fraser, born Stirling, U.K., 6.4.57. University degree, ex-teacher, last known occupation itinerant musician, no fixed abode. Convicted 1986 of wife's manslaughter, refused to appeal although advised to. 1989 witness, multiple murder case in Holland, cleared of involvement. Counterfeit money scandal, German police, investigated but not charged, see separate file. No knowledge of whereabouts since."

The recitation paused. When the voice began again its tone was somewhere between annoyance and amusement.

"Short but impressive. No stranger to excitement, are you?"

I said nothing. I couldn't.

"Two stars on your file, Mister Fiddler, means they think you're violent. *Agent* Gourong can vouch for that, can't he?" A locker door squeaked open. "We have a mutual acquaintance. Wolfgang Meyer."

I stared at the spots of blood on the worn stone. Meyer was a high-ranking Austrian policeman who'd become something more than a friend. What could he have to do with this?

"I've met Meyer at conferences. He doesn't approve of vagrants punching policemen any more than I do, but he's a good cop and I respect his judgement, so this is how it reads." Again the black brogues approached. "The *Boches* say you're the next best thing to a psycho, Meyer says you're not, it's sour grapes because you washed some of their dirty linen as publicly as possible. I don't give a toss either way, but I want one thing crystal clear. *Hitting policemen is something I will not tolerate, no matter how brainless they are.* Meyer's note on your dossier bought you a phone call, and that phone call's bought you a short walk out of here because he says you're on the side of the angels. But if I ever catch you at anything like this again, those gorillas can have you and good luck to them."

I coughed up more blood onto the stones, but this time I got the words out.

"Where's my fiddle?"

The laugh was ironic. "Meyer was right, he said you'd care

about damn all else. Upstairs, at the desk. This came with it."

An envelope landed beside my head.

"No knowledge of whereabouts since." The voice emphasised each word separately. "That's what the file says, and that's exactly the way I want things regarding you. Understood?"

I nodded, fighting back the dizziness.

"You disappear back into the woodwork. You get to hell and gone out of this city. Now. Tonight. Understood?"

The room swam as I collapsed again onto the flagstones.

"If you're caught so much as walking on the wrong side of the street anywhere in Rennes," he went on, "never mind busking without a licence, the sky will fall on your head like a ton of bricks. Is that clear?"

This time he didn't bother waiting for an answer. He bent to retrieve the bloodstained towel.

"It's not hard to understand, Mister Fiddler. You hit one cop, you hit every cop. Policemen are just like everybody else, they'll go outside the law to protect their own if they have to. Now when you're ready, get yourself out of here. Nobody'll bother you."

The towel landed on the bench by the wall.

"You're not going to charge me?"

"If we were, you wouldn't have a mark on you."

The brogues marched to the door. I forced my head up.

"Why did you stop them?"

He didn't turn. I saw a lot of silver at the shoulders as they went out into the corridor.

"This used to be my station. When I'm around, it runs by the book."

The door clanged shut. Slowly, I made it up onto all fours.

*

It took me hours to make it to Concarneau, and when I finally slowed down in the town centre, the big car which had been behind me most of the way swept past. I felt a long sigh of relief escape me; the white glare of its headlights in the mirror had almost been the last straw. I pulled into the wide market square and reached for the ignition, but the Fiat's engine beat me to it—a final cough, then it spluttered and died. I smelled petrol. No surprises there—according to the gauge it had been running on air for the last half hour.

The silence roared in my ears. I waited, trying to tell myself I'd be all right, but I knew I wasn't. I opened the door, hoping the fresh air would save me, but the rotting sea smells were worse than the car's fumes. Again I gagged. Afterwards I hung over the sill, exhausted. How many times now? Five? Six? I'd lost count. Somewhere round the corner a lone reveller sang his way home. It was past midnight.

I got out as slowly as I could. For the first couple of steps I was in danger of falling over, but I made it as far as the quayside and levered myself down onto a bollard. The ancient walled citadel of Concarneau loomed before me, a mountainous mass guarded on all sides by the harbour's water, its dark stone blocks pointed up by the brilliant spotlights at its gate. It was called the *Ville Close,* in her letter Elly had told me.

I looked at my hands. The cigarette burn was an ugly red brand on my left, but the right was worse, a swollen mess. Gingerly, I removed the bloodstained strip of shirt which had been my improvised bandage. The police boot had torn almost all the skin from its back, and the scab was half-formed, ugly with blood and pus. Better to leave the bandage off, I thought, it'll heal faster. Then I remembered my scream, and the bitterness filled me again; how long would that take to heal?

I forced myself up. The bar where we were supposed to meet was called *Ty Couz Soiz,* in the Avenue de la Gare. I went back to the car and lifted the fiddle case. Up the hill, she'd said...

I found it in minutes—and wished I hadn't. The shutters were up, the darkness inside was total, and the white envelope pinned to the door had my name on it. I tore it open.

Alex,

I don't know where you are or what's happened to you, and I can't face another day of this. I'm going south on my own. If you really do want to talk, I'll be home in a month or so.

Elly.

Even as the feelings came, I knew they were unfair.

Anger—at her, at the world. Everything I'd been through, all for nothing! Why couldn't she have waited? The fiddle case under my arm, I marched back down the hill towards the harbour, aware of nothing except hurt. Along the quayside the gulls scattered and the cats slunk out of my path. I let my rage possess me, cut me off from the world. Directionless, I forced myself forward.

How long it lasted, how long I walked before exhaustion stopped me, I have no idea, but when I came to, I found myself slumped on a stone step, hemmed in by the narrow walls of the *Ville Close.* Away to my left I could see the brightly lit archway that joined old town and new, but I had no memory of passing through. I rose, turned instinctively away from the new, began pushing deeper into the narrow canyons of the crumbling walls, following the winding street further into the citadel's heart. I neither knew nor cared where it took me—the walls were the middle ages, there were cracks and crevices, I would hide in them... I came to an opening and saw steps. Safety? A tower, a refuge? I scrambled halfway up, but the effort was too great and I collapsed against the wall, sobbing for breath, fighting for balance. Only desperation forced me up the last of them. I staggered out into moonlight and different air—and found myself looking out to sea.

Not a tower… I was on the citadel's ramparts.

The prosaic sight of the fish quay had no place in the confusion of my brain. At first I couldn't understand any of it, but slowly normality reasserted itself. The wind brought me the generator's hum and the distant sound of traffic, the arc lights showed me fish boxes, rubbish skips. I sat down on the wall's uneven top and stared at it all, trying hard to believe in the twentieth century.

The fullness of reality was harsh. I'd survived this far, but I was very nearly at rock bottom, and Elly's going was the weight that could break me, deep inside me I knew it. I had no friends here, no money—and I couldn't work. At the thought of the fiddle the pain welled up again. I stared at the case which lay beside me—dented and torn from the fight, barely whole. I hadn't yet found the courage to look inside, but if the instrument was as badly damaged as I thought, I doubted if it would ever play again. What could I do?

Suddenly, the pain in my hand doubled in intensity, stabbing at me. I thrust it into the torn pocket of my jacket—and found the envelope the policeman had dropped beside me on the locker room floor. I fumbled it open and stared at the name on the headed paper. Berolet? Who was Georges Berolet?

And then I remembered—the old man, the violin teacher's father... I forced my eyes to focus.

Mon ami d'Écosse,

My sorrow at your misfortune is only exceeded by my anger at myself. Without examining your instrument it is impossible to say if it can be saved, but it may be possible—my son is an expert in restoration. Bring your violin to me. There will be no charge—I feel responsible for the whole affair, and the repair is the least I can do in recompense for my own stupidity.

Please do not think of the money as a gift—it is no more than you would have earned had you been allowed to play on without interruption.

Georges Berolet.

A five hundred franc note...

The kindness of a stranger was almost too much. I sat there, holding the two pieces of paper, shivering—until the spark of self-preservation came. I forced myself up, lifted the fiddle case.

Tomorrow. I couldn't open it now—the morning would do for fears about the future or bitterness at the past. Now, only the present mattered, only survival. One step at a time; first win through this night.

Slowly, I began to take in my surroundings. There was an amphitheatre of sorts behind me—trees, a glassy slope. The bottom of it was sheltered by the walls, and I could see no wind ruffling the grass. Fresh air... Better than the car, at any rate. I'd fetch the sleeping bag and the blankets.

It took me a long time to make it back through the old town. Exhausted, I paused inside the gate, wondering if I could drive the car at least part of the way back, until I remembered there was no petrol in her. I came out into the cold light of the market square, searching for the familiar battered blue body—and froze, for I heard her before I saw her.

Someone was trying to start my car.

Puzzled, I took a few tentative steps forward. *My* car? A quick glance round the square confirmed what I already suspected—there were only a few other cars there, but they were all newer than mine. The Fiat was a rust-ridden ten-year-old, worthless. A kid, a joyrider? As I speculated, the would-be thief gave up and got out.

And saw me. We examined each other across the square's empty expanse. All I could make out was a white shirt and dark glasses.

I was tempted to make straight for the car, but something about him warned me. I didn't know what why this was dangerous, but I was sure it was—and now the emptiness of the square was a threat. The distance between the two of us was immaterial—I was so weak that if I were alone with this man I would be at his mercy. I began to walk back down the quayside at a tangent to him. On the edge of my vision I saw the figure beside my car, watching me. When I quickened my pace, he began to move as well.

In seconds we were both running—him easily, aiming for the point that would cut me off from the dark side streets, me at a snail's pace, limping past the lobster pots that lined the waterside. After the first few steps I knew it was only a matter of time before he caught me, but simple fear kept me going—it could only be money he wanted, and the five hundred franc note in my pocket was all that stood between me and starvation. I stumbled on, hearing him gaining. Could I make the corner?

Round it I saw three streets. Which way? Voices to my left decided it. With the last of my breath I pushed myself round another bend—to find a man and a girl standing at the open back of an old Citroën van. It was half-filled with big black plastic bags. The man was holding one in his arms, ready to add it to the van's load. I shouted.

"Help me! Someone's chasing me!"

The girl made no reply—and then we all heard my pursuer reach the corner, only a few yards behind me. I spun round.

The sunglasses made him faceless. I took in the rest of him—black hair, long sideburns, rolled-up shirt sleeves. As his left forearm came up, I saw a tattoo—an indistinguishable purplish shape beside a mermaid. There were letters beneath, C-O-L-... And then my attention focused on the metallic gleam at his fist.

Brass knuckles. The sight of them seemed to anger the man with the plastic bag. When he dropped it and took a step forward, I saw how big he was. My pursuer did as well. Although the sunglasses hid his eyes, I knew he was calculating the odds—and then suddenly he was gone, back round the corner. The big man made to go after him, but the girl stopped him.

"Non, Patrik! You can't take the chance!"

Reluctantly, the big man stopped. The running footsteps receded. As I sat down in the open back of the van, my saviour turned to me.

"Do you want the *gendarmes?"*

"No! No police!"

The panic in my voice silenced him. He knelt down beside me. The girl came into the light. She was blonde, bulky in a man's leather jerkin.

"Why was he chasing you?"

I shook my head. I hadn't the breath to speak. She saw my bloodied hand.

"He needs a doctor, Patrik."

"No! No doctors, no police," I said, quickly. "I'll be all right."

I heard the big man's voice change, subtly. "Why so afraid of the *flics,* friend?"

Before I could stop him he jerked my face up and examined it. I heard the girl's sharp intake of breath.

"Is that anything to do with why you don't want them?"

I said nothing.

Her voice was urgent, now. "Patrik, be careful!"

Something in me broke—I had to be alone, I couldn't take suspicion or kindness or pity. I took hold of the fiddle case and tried to stand, but my legs gave way beneath me. I felt the big man catch me, and for an instant everything swam. I don't know how long it took before I heard his voice again:

"Do you have a bed somewhere?"

The tears welled up in me again. More strangers, more charity!

"Where will you sleep?" he demanded.

"The old town. I'll be all right."

"And if your mysterious friend comes back?" He took a step nearer. "You're not Breton, are you, or French? Where do you come from?"

"Scotland."

They talked. I couldn't understand the language. Breton, I guessed. What was happening? Again the big man knelt by my side.

"A Breton can find room for a Scot for a night or two. We'll take you home. It's not luxurious, but it's safe. Celts should stick together."

He bundled me into the van, ushered me up onto the mound of plastic bags. After he'd heaved the last one in behind me, the voice found an edge of humour.

"Try not to bleed too much over the posters."

*

Two things brought me halfway back from sleep, two things which opposed each other and belonged to each other as well—a heavy, sweet smell, and a tune, half-hummed, half-sung. Both had some meaning for me, I was sure. Eyes still shut, I waited for a clue as to their significance, but then the pain came to claim me—the ache of my hands, the different rawnesses of bruised face and ribs. It was clarity and confusion at once—I knew it was right that I should hurt, but I didn't know why. I struggled to work it out—and then, through the pain, the smell named itself; lavender. The tune began again, a low female voice. A drinking song—a French drinking song, finally it came to me. The lavender memory broke indignantly through to counter it.

Boyhood. The violin lesson... The genteel poverty of Miss Lettie Chisholm's Bridge of Allan drawing room... Her grey head, its elegant shingled hairstyle fifty years out of date, nodding gently to the hesitant rhythm of a never-ending scale...

And her nine-year-old pupil, concentrating furiously, smelling the bowl of lavender pot-pourri, one eye on his music, the other on the sampler that hung behind her on the wall.

Strong Waters Grieve The Lord.

What does it mean, Miss Chisholm?

The slow smile, the measured stirring of the teacup.

Some day, Alexander, you'll know.

Were you happy, Miss Chisholm, teaching the violin from behind your lace curtains? Were you—

Violin and teacher... The faces changed before me. One by one, the degradations of the previous day began to crystallise. Before I could succumb to them, I fled into wakefulness.

The high eaves above me were the source of the smell. The lavender was suspended in sheaves from the roof's middle, on long wire loops.

But why were the bunches hung like that? To dry? But they'd dry just as well against the wall... Scurrying noises answered the question and puzzled me more at the same time.

Rats, definitely. Where was I? Bracing myself against the pain, I forced myself up on one elbow and looked.

A bare wooden floor, twenty feet or so square, made of massive planks, unpolished and dusty, bounded on three sides by walls of unplastered stone... There was no fourth wall, the floor simply ended. The space behind was mostly shadow, shot through with thin shafts of brightness, some from shuttered windows in the walls, some from a roof that had seen better days. The truncated floor's far end gave me what I needed to work it out—the top rungs of a ladder. I was in the loft of a barn.

I got to my feet. The mattress I'd slept upon was the only sign of human occupancy, there wasn't even a lamp. I walked to the edge of the wood and looked out.

I was about fifteen feet up. Another loft, the twin of mine, was about twenty-five feet away, and the space that separated them held a mountain of black plastic bags. Animal feed? Hay? I'd seen hay baled like that often enough... But a few of the top bags were torn, and the protruding edges showed me paper. One bag had been dumped away from the rest. There was a long brown smear across it—blood, dried… Mine?

Yes, it would be—I remembered the previous night's joke. The bale had been my first bed, in my benefactors' van. Posters, he'd said. But how many vanloads were here? As I wondered, the menacing jungle noises of the rats, stilled by my stirring, began once more. The voice came again.

"Cheval-iers de la tab-le rond-e, goût-ons voir si le vin—"

The rhythm of it was uneven, and as I reached the nearest window I heard the digging sounds that punctuated it. The shutters made no noise as I pushed them open.

There was almost no day left, but the summer dusk had a scent of its own—a compound of parched earth and resinous wood, of hot things waiting patiently for the night's freshness. A different freshness came up to me through it, a greenness.

The ground beside my barn was a hollow, a small glade that unfolded out onto the bank of a fast-flowing stream. Someone had taken great pains with it, walling it off, moulding its contours into the vegetable garden I could now see. The girl who had helped rescue me the night before was standing in the middle of it, surveying the long brown seam of earth that led to the wicker basket of potatoes at her bare feet. A watering can was filling from a standpipe behind her, and her arms were filled with vegetables, huge bunches of them—carrots, celery, lettuce, onions. Her mop of blonde curls spilled out from behind a carelessly-tied headscarf that was the largest garment on her, for the yellow bikini she was wearing had been designed with a different kind of water in mind, and it was tiny. The body it showed me was long and willowy, small-breasted and fashion-model slender, covered from the shoulders down with sweat and streaked with grime—but when she turned I saw the smile on her face. It was beatific.

And although it wasn't meant for me, I felt myself respond to it, smile in return; Mother Earth, dressed for the beach at St. Tropez. But there was nothing ridiculous about her—the aura of satisfaction was too deep. I turned away, back into the smells of cooling wooden shingles and lavender, lest she see me, lest her trance be broken.

And then I stopped. Breath left me.

The shape of the fiddle case was obvious beneath my clothes. Once again all the hurts, mental and physical, descended on me, draining me of strength. I looked round the three walls, then back at the absent fourth one—and felt gratitude touch me. Bare as a cell, but still open. And for now, at least, it seemed to be mine. It would do.

As I lay down on the bed and turned my back on the instrument case, the lavender smell seemed to intensify. That was a good piece of the past, a memory to welcome. And the innocence of the girl's smile was evidence of a good present. As if in agreement, her jerky song began again.

I listened, using it to check myself from any thoughts of the future, and closed my eyes.

3

LANGUAGE

"...AND THEN I decided to come back to the car for the sleeping bag..."

I paused. It was all too surreal—the Friday morning paper on the dresser, the sun on the kitchen's stone flags, the smell of baking, the marmalade-coloured cat on the long table, lying on a pair of motorcycle gauntlets. What had such domesticity to do with me? I realised they were waiting for me to go on.

"...and the rest you know," I finished awkwardly.

Of the three people watching me, the man Patrik—my saviour of two nights before and the person I had automatically tagged as my host—was the first to react. He nodded gravely. He knew how much of an ordeal the retelling had been, I could see. And the girl did as well. The serene smile I'd glimpsed in the kitchen garden was gone, replaced by obvious anger on my behalf, an emotion that gave a hard edge to the strong lines of her beauty.

But the third face, that of the small middle-aged man sitting rolling his cigarette in the corner, that was more difficult to assess. Somewhere along the line it had acquired a professional inscrutability—but the rest of him, crop-headed and compact, all wiriness beneath the tattered leather motorbike jacket, gave him away. I'd spent enough of my youth in Glasgow's east end to know a hard man when I saw one. And there was something else familiar about him as well, something I couldn't quite put my finger on...

But whatever the familiarity, he was suspicious of me, I knew it. Why? Was there something to be protected here? Something illegal, perhaps? Patrik stood up, went across to the window. He was less bulky than he'd seemed in the darkness of Concarneau's back streets, but there was still well over six feet of him, lithe and well-muscled. He ran a hand through the fine black hair that covered his long, angular head as he turned to me again.

"And you're sure," he said, "that you never saw him before, this man who came after you?"

Despite its politeness, it was a voice used to getting answers. The girl stood, bread knife in hand, its purpose forgotten. The little man went on rolling his cigarette.

"Absolutely," I said.

"The letters on his arm, C-O-L, they mean nothing to you?"

I shook my head, watched him ruminate.

"Col... *En Anglais,* 'collar', yes?"

I nodded.

"It makes no sense," he went on. "Part of another word, perhaps—Colette, maybe, a girl's name, or Colmar, the town. But that takes us no further. And the motive? Theft?"

I looked down. "Neither the car itself nor anything in it would be worth the trouble," I said.

In the kitchen's warm comfort, the admission shamed me. I reached for my coffee to cover the embarrassment, slowly—but not slowly enough. The girl read the change of movement, knew I was trying to avoid pain. Anger quickly ruled her mobile face.

"Bastards," she muttered, "bastard cops, bastard French."

The vehemence of it took me by surprise, but neither of the other two responded to her. She flushed, then turned quickly away, busying herself at the big range. Something raw had been prodded, I knew. Something private? Between her and Patrik? Were they a couple? He seemed easier round her than she did round him... My eyes went back to the corner. Or was it a communal nerve that had been touched, one that concerned Mister Inscrutable as well? I caught Patrik's eye upon me again, and my sense of shame returned—my speculation was impertinence. These people had taken me in out of kindness, their domestic arrangements were none of my business. Again I hid behind my coffee cup. When I put it down I found Patrik's eyes once again mapping out the destruction of my face.

"You said the *flics* in Rennes didn't get a chance to finish what they started, my friend." He gestured at my bruises. "Could your assailant be something to do with that, perhaps? A bit of unofficial revenge?" He turned to the small man in the corner. "They never give up, do they, Prosper? Not once they're crossed."

A curt nod was his only reply. I said nothing. I didn't believe it, but perhaps it was possible. Certainly I had no better answer.

"But who knows?" he went on. "Perhaps a mugger, or just a crazy, Concarneau's as full of them as anywhere else. Anyway, you're all right now? Nose OK? No ribs broken, nothing like that? No teeth? Teeth can be the devil, the only time I've ever been worked over I lost two. You're sure you're all right?"

Once again I was aware of the girl's eyes. The anger in them had been replaced now. By pity. That decided me.

"Completely sure, thank you, you've done more than enough. Look, if you'd be kind enough to give me a lift back—"

He laughed, gently, and waved the notion away with the same easy authority I remembered from Concarneau.

"Nonsense! I wouldn't hear of it! First of all you're in no fit state to go anywhere, second, we've yet to check on your car, and last, we've never had a guest from Scotland before and it would be rude of you to refuse. So if the rats in our barn don't trouble you too much..."

He ended the sentence with an open-handed gesture of welcome—and then the voice lost its jokiness and took on a proprietor's formality.

"I'm sorry that such misfortune has befallen you in our country, Mister Fraser."

He meant Brittany, not France, I knew—and the tone was odd, almost regal, as though responsibility for the place was his. Something made me want to see how the little man in the corner reacted to it, but this time I really did turn too fast. The pain caught at my ribs like a vice, nearly made me black out. When my vision stopped swimming, I was firmly back on the chair again, with Patrik's steadying hand on my arm. The only thing I could see was the girl's face. Anxiety had robbed it of its beauty entirely, given it a child's open-mouthed expression of shock. Once more, it was Patrik who took charge.

"That's settled then; you stay. Until you're recovered at least, and then as long as you like after that."

Again it had the air of a decree, but the tone of it told me I wasn't the only audience. Who else was being addressed? The man called Prosper?

The subject was closed by the arrival in the yard outside of the van which had brought me here, an ancient Citroën with corrugated sides, the kind the French call a *saladier.* A red-haired boy was at the wheel. He smiled and waved a greeting. Patrik returned it.

"Good, René's on time. Mister Fraser, I must ask you to excuse us, we have work to do."

As the girl took off her apron Patrik turned again to the corner. "You'll join us, Prosper?"

"In a moment."

A rough voice, rustic, a voice more used to farmyard than office. As the kitchen door closed he looked directly at me for the first time, then went back to the careful rolling of the next cigarette. Why hadn't he smoked any of them? I watched it go into the same thin, battered tin as all the others. It was several minutes before he spoke.

"Your French is excellent. For a foreigner."

"I studied languages."

"Ah, that would explain it."

He stood up, looked out of the window at the others—and then turned abruptly. "Ar wespedenn a drenv ho skouarn!" he exclaimed.

I stared at him, bewildered. "I don't speak Breton."

He sat down again. "I know that," he replied, beginning the next cigarette. I saw a smile touch his lips. "Now."

"What did you just say?" I asked, still puzzled.

"I told you there was a wasp behind your ear."

Why...? And then I got it—if I'd reacted, he'd have known I spoke the language. A test—but why should he need to test me? I felt an edge of annoyance.

"What's going on here?" I asked.

My question hardly seemed to register. Carefully, he licked the cigarette paper along its length, then sealed the seam and tamped the ends. Only then did he reach across to the table and pull a sheet of paper from the bundle by the cat. He held it out to me; a handbill, in French and Breton. It was vaguely familiar to me, but it took a few seconds to work out why—and then I had it.

The anti-nuclear posters I'd seen in Rennes, this was a miniature of them. I remembered the graphics—a futuristic building, caricatured as a rat. I read through the French; in nine days' time, on the fourth of August, a huge government facility was due to be opened at a place called Kergorff, west of the town of Douarnenez. The list of its purposes was chilling—nuclear reprocessing and dumping, toxic waste incineration. The organising committee of the PSB called upon people to come and stop the opening. Now I understood the mountain of posters in the barn. But who were the PSB....?

The logo at the bottom told me. The Partie Séparatiste de Bretagne.

Nationalists...

Prosper's ironic smile returned as he read my reaction. "The international image of Breton nationalism hasn't changed, I see—a mixture of yobs and yokels blowing up television transmitters, a few pseudo-intellectuals to eke out the numbers, a handful of students lobbing grenades they'll never learn to aim properly."

No, I thought, it had been more than that—some of the groups had been highly effective, I remembered. Hadn't there been bank robberies and gun running, aircraft blown up? Links to ETA, the Basque terrorists, and to the IRA...? I watched his back as he looked out of the window. Patrik was opening the doors of the barn where I'd slept. The ironic voice began again.

"We are a new party, Mister Fraser, we believe in ballot boxes rather than bombs, but that doesn't mean that Paris will play any fairer with us. Which brings us back to the subject of yourself. You're either exactly what you seem to be, or the French police have become a great deal more intelligent. Sending a non-Breton speaker to infiltrate us, yes, that would be subtle."

I was irritated, now. "And exactly what is it that I 'seem to be'?"

He nodded at the figure of Patrik. "Exactly what he likes, exactly what he doesn't need. Another waif, another stray, another bird with a broken wing."

Nathalie and the boy René appeared, carrying one of the bales of posters between them. From the way they strained, the weight of the thing was obvious. Behind them came Patrik, the same burden perched easily on one shoulder. Again Prosper's rough voice came, matter-of-fact now, the irony gone.

"Patrik Riou is the best hope Brittany has ever had," he said, "of getting rid of the kind of people who did that to your face.

The first real leader—brains, charisma, not a vice in the world, political instincts like radar. Never budges from a real principle, always negotiates to advantage, never uses violence, never lets it be used against him without gaining from it. Civil disobedience to the absolute hilt, no prison yet—but when it comes he'll take it like a lamb, and our vote'll double." He turned to me. "You know about prison, don't you?"

I didn't reply. How did they know...? But no matter how, I knew why he'd told me—it was a way of establishing control, of getting the psychological upper hand, of saying *I know your secret.* And then, as his eyes stayed calmly on me, I understood why he was familiar.

The cigarettes.

The smell of prison never quite rubs off. How many men in Barlinnie had I seen building their roll-ups with the same calm, secretive efficiency? This was just one ex-con recognising another, the biggest freemasonry in the world. As his eyes moved back to the scene outside, I wondered how much time he'd done, and where.

And why.

Outside, the van was full now. As the red-haired boy closed the back doors, I saw Patrik's arm land lightly across Nathalie's shapely shoulders. Her smile was brief. Acceptance? Obligation? A dislike of display in front of strangers? It seemed a far cry from yesterday's beatific survey of the vegetables.

"Waifs and strays," Prosper began again, "broken wings."

Did he mean the girl as well? The hard voice went on.

"The likes of you are always going to be around. There's a hint of the *curé* about him, the priest. Draws cripples. Perhaps that's part of his appeal."

"Why are you talking to me like this?"

My voice betrayed my dislike, brought a quick smile of triumph; blood drawn.

"So you'll know my eyes are on you." he said quietly.

The resolve rose in me again; I would leave, get myself away— Before I could speak, he rounded on me.

"He's the boss, make no mistake. He knows I'm talking to you now, but his word goes. You stay here, you keep out of the way of business. Maybe you talk to him, keep his mind off things, there'll be enough on it till this—" He gestured at the handbill. "—is over."

Outside, I heard the doors of the van's cab slam shut, and saw Nathalie walk round to the open back and place herself gracefully on one of the bales. Prosper's voice hardened even more as he watched her.

"And you keep your hands off the meat, no matter how tempting it gets. If you don't, I'll know."

Meat... As she closed the doors on herself, I felt my anger rise on her behalf. "What makes you think she'd be interested?" I said, tightly.

He stood up, stubbed out the cigarette on a saucer. "She's twenty years old."

He walked to the door, not bothering to look at me. The cat slunk away as he reached for his motorcycle gauntlets.

"Be another twenty at least before she stops thinking with her cunt."

4

QUESTIONS

THE NEXT DAY, the question came.

"So do you believe in nationalism, then, Alexander? For Scotland?"

Patrik and I were in the Citroën van, on the way back to Concarneau to see to my car. I hesitated.

"No."

Even to myself, the monosyllable sounded blunt, and I knew it wasn't the whole truth; but to explain...

I'd always been wary of *isms,* particularly political ones. No matter how lofty the ideals, there was always a subordination of self involved, a bowing to the wishes of the herd—a herd whose rhetoric, for all its visions, its fine talk of majorities and prosperities and solidarities, was designed to attack or exclude some other herd. The only person I'd ever been prepared to exclude from mass visions of the future was myself—I wasn't one of nature's joiners. And political nationalism—exclusion by race, or by lines drawn across some paper representation of the real world—that had always struck me as the least sensible *ism* of the lot, and for Scotland especially. What would a Scottish nation in search of an independent future be? Could it ever leave behind the grievances of the past? Unless it could, I could see nothing in independence. I had a vision of a narrow-minded rump state held together by rhetoric and resentment of the English, a tartan banana republic which was nothing more than a distinctive accent grafted on to a collective paranoia.

And yet, perhaps I was wrong... I was a Scot, undoubtedly. The place had stamped out the mould of me and filled it with all its improbable contradictions, a hot and viscous mixture, unable or unwilling to cool beneath the hardened shell the world saw. I couldn't escape being one of Scotland's sons, I'd learned that—but to me, like so many others, she was a mother best loved from a distance. I forced myself to speak.

"Breton nationalism isn't something I know much about."

He noted the evasion, and simply began to talk.

First he told me about himself, about dropping out of university in Paris, coming back to Brittany to buy a share in the fishing boat which was now his main living, and fighting to keep the smallholding which had been in his family for three generations. His conversion to nationalism had come from a simple event. His mother had tried to supplement their meagre income by applying for a job as an office cleaner, but because she spoke no French, only Breton, she was refused. At that point he knew, he said, that the French political system could never be other than repressive, and he began to study Brittany's history.

And a familiar history it was; a people and a culture first conquered, then systematically degraded until only two alternatives remained—complete assimilation or complete destruction. Over the centuries the pressure had been kept up in the name of kings and republicans alike, by force of arms and by decree, until the inevitable point had been reached where the adoption of France's tongue and France's habits became the only method of survival and the only ladder of advancement. It was exactly the same tactic England had used with the Gaels of Scotland, Ireland and Wales, a long-term variation of the old game of divide and rule.

First beat your enemy, then humiliate him, then promise him hope for his children—but only if he dresses them in the conqueror's garb. It was as effective as it was cruel; nothing kills a culture more surely than the perpetual theft of its offspring.

He told the story well, factually, without romanticising—and there was hardly any need to vilify, for the harsh facts spoke for themselves. And he knew Scotland's history as well, and used it to draw me out, asking me if the memory of the Highland Clearances was still strong, asking me if the English were still blamed, if the new devolved parliament would make a difference. My interest was caught. Before I knew it I was telling him of the clan chiefs who had sold their own people on to the emigration ships to free the land for sheep and profit, telling him that I believed that the real dividing line across the north of the British island wasn't the Scottish-English border, but the fault line that separated highland from lowland, that divided the English and Gaelic languages. He nodded in agreement.

"And the language, it will survive? Your Gaelic?"

"It's not my language. I'm a lowlander, an English speaker. But yes, it will. They've given up trying to kill it, now."

"They haven't given up here. They'd like us to believe they have, but it's a lie. I can still remember the signs in the school playgrounds. *No spitting or Breton spoken.* There's enough who'd bring that back." He turned to me. "Do you think it's wrong to fight that?"

"No, fight injustice by all means."

Our arrival at the main coast road ended the conversation. As we waited at the junction, ready to edge into the heavy traffic, the cars roared past us—holidaymakers' cars, loaded with half-naked children and beach balls, towing tent trailers and boats. The strand beyond was like a suntan lotion advert, silver-sanded and brown-bodied as far as the surf, bright with parasols against the afternoon's glare. Patrik's voice came again, no longer calm.

"Look at them, the summer plague. This is all we are now—a cheap holiday for France's cities, a place to dump their nuclear nightmares."

He turned to me. His pleasant face had been given character by the sudden vehemence, its sharp lines pulled into harsh relief by the stubborn jut of his jaw. It was a face that reminded me of bare Scottish hillsides and hard Welsh valleys, a face to be peered at across Roman walls and Norman ramparts. A Celtic face...

"My country deserves better," he said simply.

The silence that followed lasted until we reached Concarneau, and then, as our descent into the town began, he relaxed. The cause was easy to see—his posters were everywhere, on walls, on trees, on lamp posts. How many people did he expect to attract, I asked. Between ten and twenty thousand, he replied—and now it was his turn to read my face. He laughed.

"You shouldn't be so surprised, Alexander. Political apathy is only caused by meaningless politics. If the issue is real, the people will be there."

"Can you stop this nuclear dump being opened?" I asked.

"We can be seen to try," he said quietly, "and even if we fail, it will translate itself into votes."

"Isn't that a little cynical?"

He shook his head. "Not in the least. We're a new Breton party, different from any of our predecessors or competitors, fighting openly and democratically on a Breton issue. And we won't be doing it from behind a row of uniformed thugs with riot shields, or from some office hundreds of kilometres away in Paris. We'll be there in the front line, showing the people exactly the kind of leadership they can expect from us when we're elected. We will fight every ship that dares to dock at this place, we will fight every truck that tries to deliver this filth. What could be less cynical than that?"

As we parked in the scruffy streets behind Concarneau's market hall, I mused on the statement. A populist, a man of the people, was that how he saw himself?

If he did, within minutes of leaving the car I saw reason enough to justify it. Inside the first hundred yards, we must have stopped at least two dozen times—everyone, young and old alike, wanted to talk to the young prince of the PSB, to touch the hem. As we walked he held a handful of small badges, enamelled lapel pins with the party's initials, and as he handed them out he talked and laughed and listened. No matter was too small for his attention, no question too big. He stooped to hear problems about sewers and social security, he accepted good wishes and assurances of attendance at the demonstration, he declined glasses of Muscadet from the pavement cafes. When asked, he offered sage advice on everything from the artichoke harvest to the local team's half-backs, and when we reached a benchful of old men, tobacco-stained and shirt-sleeved, surrounded by the caged songbirds which were their passion, he let himself be drawn into a vigorous debate, half in Breton, half in French, that ranged from the price of fish to the merits of budgerigar over canary. Charm, charisma, pragmatism—he seemed to have it all; even the previously silent birds sang for him. As we left the old men laughing chestily at his joke that the best bird song would, of course, be in Breton, the tribute from the cages seemed no more than his due.

And as we came out of the side streets into the main square, I admitted to myself that I was impressed. His whole manner seemed easy and genuine, free of that cloying mixture of the glib and the greedy which characterises most politicians. Was it real, I wondered—and if it was, could it last, could it survive the compromises that came with the acquisition of power? Because power would definitely come to Patrik Riou, I knew that—I'd never seen a more natural politician. Small wonder that Prosper, the cold little adjutant, set so much store by him.

And as though thought could make flesh, suddenly Prosper was there, stone-faced and leather-jacketed. I saw that we had reached the spot in the market square where I had abandoned the Fiat. But it was gone. Where?

Prosper nodded to Patrik, then addressed me with a curt affability that was only marginally warmer than our last encounter.

"Your car. The ignition was ripped out to hot wire her. If there had been fuel in her she'd have been long gone. I got René to tow her up to his father's garage."

"I do my own repairs," I said, levelly. "I've no money to pay for a mechanic."

"That won't be necessary. René's one of us. We're always glad to help a fellow Celt on his way."

Said without inflection, but still an open reminder that he wanted me gone. He turned to Patrik.

"There's a problem at the printers. We have to go to Douarnenez. Now."

Some unspoken message, unreadable to me, passed between them, but before Patrik could reply, Nathalie appeared, squeezing through the avenues of parked cars, laden with plastic bags from the market. Again Prosper took the initiative.

"We should go alone," he said, easily. "Just the two of us."

For the merest second, I saw Patrik's ease vanish, a quick flash of emotion cross his face—and then he was in control again.

"Obviously," he said.

Anger, I thought, in the tense silence which followed—that was what I had seen... Oblivious of the atmosphere, the girl walked up to us, smiling. Before she could speak, Patrik put his arm round her.

"Something's come up, Nathalie, Prosper and I have to go. Look after our Scottish friend for the afternoon. Take him to Carnac, perhaps, eh?"

This time the silence was merely clumsy—and the situation became clear to me. Prosper was no ordinary subordinate. He had given Patrik an order.

I looked at Nathalie. What place did she have in the scheme of things, this girl? Was there some kind of personal tug-of-war over her? Or was she just a handy way for Prosper to show he was the real boss? Her face was reddening with embarrassment at being so obviously dismissed. Prosper reached out and took the shopping bags from her.

"Good meat," he said, handing them to me. "Spoil in this heat if you're not careful."

Meat, again... A repetition of yesterday's crude warning. I felt my anger flare, turned away to Patrik to hide it.

"Go with Nathalie, Alexander," he said.

For the first time I heard vulnerability in his voice, a longing that slipped through all the competence. It was obvious that he was very much in love with her. His voice recovered its normality as he went on.

"She'll look after you."

But as we faced each other in the square, I knew that what he really wanted to say was the exact opposite.

*

Carnac...

Row upon row of *menhirs* and *dolmens*, time-worn standing stones, incomprehensible now except as some massive neolithic celebration of the linear, a homage to the straight line in the same way that Stonehenge was a paean to the circle. The largest Celtic monument in Europe... How had it all been done? And in the name of whose God? As I surveyed it all in the dying light, I didn't care. All I knew was that I was in a church.

But a desecrated church. A tatty green wire mesh fence separated most of it from a litter-laden car park and a shabbily modernistic 'visitor centre'. Apart from that, the only other offerings the twentieth century had left here were the rusting dinosaur hulks of two lorries, and, on one of the cottages opposite, a satellite television dish. As we stood, watching in silence, a sports car came along the narrow road at breakneck speed, stereo pumping at full blast, its cargo of teenagers screaming with laughter. Brakes squealing, it stopped at the junction just long enough for us to read the Paris number plate.

And that was what finally let out her anger—the anger which had smouldered, under its cover of polite small talk, for the whole of the hour-and-a-half drive from Concarneau.

"The French," she said contemptuously. "They cheapen everything they touch."

I let it stand briefly before replying. "Breton teenagers would be different, would they?"

She shook her head. "No, of course not. We've learned, haven't we? To cheapen." She waved at the visitor centre, the satellite dish. "How much respect do you see here for our culture, our traditions?"

"And you think a free Brittany would change that?"

She must have heard the scepticism in my voice, for her reply was defiant. "It would be a start! Patrik says—"

She stopped short, caught unawares by her own saying of his name, by the pain of confronting the real source of her anger. When she saw in my face that I'd seen it, the frustration came flying out.

"Damn! Damn him!" She wandered a few steps away, then stopped abruptly. "I'm sorry," she said, "you're a total stranger, with enough worries of your own. You don't want mine."

"Maybe a total stranger's what you need," I said.

She gave me a quizzical look, then sat down on the road's raised verge, facing the long lines of stones. She threw her head back and let out a long breath that began as explosion and ended as sigh.

"What can I tell you? When I first met Patrik Riou I was a dewy-eyed virgin of eighteen," she said, "and I was bowled over. What girl wouldn't be—gentle, kind, matinee-idol looks. And principles. God, yes, principles—more than anything else I think it was that." She laughed, shaking her head. "Sometimes now I could scream, he's got so many damn principles, but then..." She kicked at the dust in front of her. "Ever since I was a little girl I promised myself I'd fall in love with a hero," she said softly. "The problem is, heroes have causes."

"And you're not in love with the cause?"

"Oh, don't get me wrong, I'm a nationalist, it runs in the family. Patrik and I would never have met if I hadn't been." There was an odd, wooden inflection to her voice as she said it—and then she shook her head. "No, I believe in what he's doing, I help when he lets me. It's just..." She shrugged. "What happened today, he does that a lot now. Keeps me at arm's length."

"And you think that's because he doesn't love you?"

As the silence grew longer, it was on the tip of my tongue to tell her how wrong I thought she was, but she spoke first.

"No. But it's left me with enough time to wonder how much I love him. Being a hero's lover is wonderful, but being a hero's wife..." Again the self-deprecating laugh came. "I'll carry his spear in the battle," she said, softly, "but I'm damned if I'll polish it."

"Is that what he wants? Marriage?"

She nodded as she rose, brushed the dust from her skirt, and walked over to the wire fence. Her voice changed as she looked across the long rows of stones, became softer.

"So what was it all, then? A cathedral?"

That she saw the place in the same way I did brought an odd spark of comfort. Before I could answer she went on.

"What would it feel like to be a Celtic god and know that you'd been forgotten, that no one knew your name any more?"

Another car passed, left its petrol fumes hanging in the warm darkness. She breathed in the smell.

"Ah, the conquering religion's incense." A fond smile came to her. "My father used to bring me here," she said, "when I was little, before they gave it all to the tourists. He was already old then. I was the child of his old age, his Benjamin. He used to sit me down on one of the *dolmens* and tell me stories. About the Celts. Romantic stories—nonsense about how they sat here round their fires with their backs to the moon, wrapped in their cloaks with their bronzed women, waiting for the dawn."

Nonsense or not, the longing in her voice brought the words close to poetry. A breeze came. She lifted her mop of blonde hair to let it cool her neck and turned the smile to me.

"Ridiculous, isn't it? But that's how I saw Patrik, if I'm honest. The king of the Celts, the warrior chief." The smile took on pain. "I can't explain it better—he just seemed so pure."

I didn't know whether I should say it, but in the end I did. "It would be hard to be pure around the likes of Prosper."

Again the silence was long.

"That's just it." she said, finally. "There's always going to be a Prosper, isn't there?"

She looked up at me, wanting to be wrong, to be contradicted, but we both knew she was right. I stood there, awkward because I had no comfort to give her—and then, before either of us could say more, another carload of teenagers came roaring past, and this time the headlights caught us standing together at the side of the road. The shouts that came made it clear that they thought we were a couple, headed for the seclusion of the *menhirs* for the obvious purpose. I looked away, embarrassed, until I heard the laugh in her voice.

"I don't think either of us needs a lover right now, Alexander, do you?"

She turned away, headed back towards the van, then stopped. When she spoke again, her voice was fierce, determined to be happy.

"No. I know what we need." She turned to me. "Music. Wouldn't that be good?"

I felt the bitterness rise in me—no god, Celtic or otherwise, could shield me from the hurt.

"Yes," I lied.

5

DANCES

THE RHYTHM WAS insidious, hypnotic, all-pervading—the rhythm of the village, of the field, a one-two-three-hop that was the clatter of the threshing mill, the swing of the sower's arm, the paced arc of the harvest scythe. And the dancers doubled its vitality. Linking hands, they moulded it into an sinuous chain of movement that was a hundred legs long, a headless and tailless dragon that kicked up the dust with one endless, shuffling step. I stood, feeling it all beneath my feet, watching the simple grace of the swinging arms, the perfect marriage of music and movement—and I was glad that I had lied to the girl.

Here, surrounded by rhythm and melody, the thought of my broken fiddle was painful, yes, as I'd known it would be—but I'd forgotten that music could heal as well as hurt. It had been right to come.

To the *fest-noz*, to Brittany's village dance.

Few events I'd seen in my life had seemed as right, as calmly certain of their own worth, as this humble celebration in the village of Autun. From my vantage point by the churchyard wall, I looked round. So simple—a field, big enough for a few hundred people, a rough podium of pine planks, a few basic lights, a single microphone.

And two young boys, beardless and earnest, wearing traditional velvet waistcoats and broad-brimmed cowboy-like hats, one with a *biniou*, a small, high-pitched bagpipe, the other with a *bombarde*, the piercing predecessor of the oboe.

The *sonneurs*, the players of the music.

And such music; raucous and raw—music made from harsh reeds, music full of unbridled modal jumps, music that moved people's hearts by making them move their feet. I watched the two boys revel in their control of it, stamping out the time, tossing the tune to each other with confidence and abandon. One would play a segment of melody, the other would join in with its last note and repeat the plaintive line, then the first would steal the lead back again. And never was the precious rhythm lost, never did the dancing dragon have to cease the steady coiling of its tail. I leaned back on the trunk of an ancient oak, smelling the dry perfume of the churchyard's wild roses, won over entirely, touched as I had rarely been by any music.

And listening to the harsh insistence of the tunes, I felt my kinship with them, those two boys up on their rough stage. For where did my own music came from, if not from the same Celtic roots? Didn't it touch the same emotions, serve the same purpose? Music to bind people together in dance, music composed by individuals to give communities voice... If my fiddle was whole again—no, *when* it was whole again, I told myself fiercely—I would learn some of their music. This music without a single leaden note in it, music—

"Music that could only be made among mountains."

Startled, I turned to find her holding two glasses of white wine.

"That's what my father used to call it," she said.

"And was it your father who taught you how to read minds?", I asked.

"No," she smiled. "That was the Muscadet. *Hiermad.*"

I smiled. My first word of the language, Brittany's universal toast, she'd taught me it earlier.

"Hiermad," I said, and drank.

The wine made a bitter freshness in my mouth, a cool antidote to the dust whipped up by the dragon's tail. As I watched her drain her glass, the tune came to the long, searing crescendo that was its end. Applause came as the two boys vacated the makeshift stage. She joined in, dropping her glass in her enthusiasm. I bent to retrieve it.

"So tell me about him, then," I said as I rose. "Your father."

She hesitated, then said, slowly. "My father was called Yann

Gwernig. He was a poet and a patriot, and this was his village."

"Your village as well?"

She shook her head. "No, we moved before I was born. I'm a big city girl, from Vannes." Saying the name seemed to relax her again. "You'd like Vannes, I should take you there."

She stopped. Her voice took on the measured tone of quotation.

"Vannes is an old turtle, lapping at the sea. You wait till it sleeps, then you creep under its shell and live in its shade."

Who was she quoting? Her father again? I wondered, for by the end of the lines her voice had again found its wistful edge. But before I could ask, she gestured at the scene around us.

"So what do you think of it? My Brittany?"

"I love it," I said simply.

"Wouldn't this be worth fighting for?"

"Yes, but who would you fight?" I said. "Your argument's not with the French, it's with the twentieth century."

She smiled, then reached into her skirt's pocket and took out one of the PSB badges I'd seen Patrik giving away in Concarneau.

"Unbeliever or not, I claim you for a free Brittany," she said. "Honorary membership, I'll win you round yet."

She reached out. As she pinned it on my shirt pocket's flap, it glinted in the reflected light from the stage. A fluttering came from the branches above us—a magpie. She looked up.

"Ah, brightness brings a thief!"

The bird surveyed us, then took off again in a flutter of black-and-white wings. She laughed, easily.

"*Kenavo,* Pigez!"

Pigez… The beggar's name... When I spoke, I tried to keep my voice even.

"What you just said, what did it mean?"

She knew something was wrong. "Goodbye, magpie," she said, hesitantly. "*Kenavo* means goodbye, Pigez means magpie. Alex..."

It petered out. When she saw I didn't want to explain, she simply gathered my empty glass and took my arm.

We walked round the edge of the site, along the arc of makeshift stalls that sold *merguez* sausages, beer, and the rough honey liqueur called *chouchenn*. The dancers and their friends milled round us, drinking, chatting, fanning the dust from each other. And as we reached the wine stall, a new sound pulled my attention back to the stage.

Three elderly ladies were gathered round the microphone. Their faces were lined and strong, and the sober black of their dresses was in stark contrast to the fine white lace of the elaborate raised coiffes on their heads. As their song gathered pace, they linked arms. High and flat-toned, fluid, fast and precise of diction—the energy of it caught me, banished the bitterness of the beggar's name. And because it used the same question-and-answer lines that the instruments had, within minutes the dancers had begun once more to form themselves into the dragon.

"What are they singing about?" I asked.

When she didn't answer I turned to her. Her cheeks were flushed.

"This is the simplest of the dances," she said quickly, "an *An Dro.* Would you like to try it?"

"Tell me what they're singing."

She blushed deeper and looked at the ground. "They're singing about the girls of Vannes, who are so beautiful and pure. And about the fishermen and the heroes who will fight over them when they return from across the sea."

Our eyes caught each other for a long moment, and then she laughed, sadly. "Can't escape him, can I?"

I said nothing. It was her turn for courage, now. As she stared at the dancers I saw the defiance I'd seen at Carnac return to her eyes, the fierce determination not to lose her joy. She rounded on me.

"Do you want to dance, then, or not?"

The question took me by surprise. Dancing... My discomfiture loosed the tension in her. Again the explosive sigh came, then a rueful smile, a smile of confession.

"Actually, I don't want to either," she said. She paused. "To tell you the truth, I've had a glass too many. I'm a little drunk."

It was an odd intimacy, but a real one, a gesture of trust. As I took the empty glass from her, I knew we were friends.

*

And over the next three days, back at the farmhouse in the hills behind Concarneau, that friendship grew.

Circumstances conspired to let it—no Prosper, no Patrik. I presumed their absence was to do with the anti-nuclear rally and wondered again if my original guess was right, that Patrik was keeping Nathalie away from some sort of danger, but whatever the reason, she seemed glad enough of the respite. And for my part, as the bruises of the police beating in Rennes went down, I found myself anxious for work. While I waited for the car I needed something to occupy hands and mind, for as the hurts of my body began to dissipate, the hurts of my situation began to close in on me again.

Elly...

My fiddle in its still unopened case...

The thoughts were never far away, but while Nathalie let it be subtly known that she was there to help, to talk seriously if I needed, she was intelligent enough to see that I was no confider by nature. She knew about the fiddle, and that something had gone badly wrong between me and someone close to me, but she never once pressed me. And I was happy to leave the territory of her and Patrik unmentioned.

It was the unspoken agreement of our days together, the social contract which gave them their ease.

We talked. Of history—not grandly, but of its small mysteries, of why the aurochs, the wild ox, had died off, of whether the Celts had been pushed to the seas at Europe's edge or drawn to them, of whether they'd been dark or fair or red-headed like René, the smiling teenager who'd taken my car off to repair it. On the first evening there, he arrived to deliver fresh fish—and I discovered that his mechanic's skills were only a sideline. He was a history student. When he saw I was interested, he spent a patient hour grounding me in Brittany's past. I learned of the loss of independent status to the French state in the sixteenth century, of the 1675 *Bonnets Rouges* peasant uprising, of the founding of Lorient, just along the coast, a port purpose-built to trade with the east, hence its name, L'Orient. It was fascinating, all of it, and, once his shyness was banished, told with an authority that belied his nineteen years. I liked him immensely.

But other than René, it was just the two of us, Nathalie and myself, and when we tired of history, smaller things dictated our days—mundanities like the lavender in the barn, how she had collected it in the hope of learning how to make perfume. Or the garden, how she had never known how happy it could make her just to grow a simple potato. More than anything else, it was these personal revelations which put the confessions of Carnac into context; whatever else her drawing away from Patrik was, it was no wholesale rejection of either the domestic or the overtly feminine. Only once, indeed, was his name mentioned at all. When I expressed surprise that he hadn't phoned, she told me with a chilling directness that he wouldn't, for as often as not the phone was tapped.

That apart, the only politics we indulged in was a little light sparring, and when we did, it was on a narrow ledge of half-serious banter, with neither of us hitting out too hard in case the other should fall off. Why did she sing her drinking song as she gathered the vegetables, I asked—it was French, wasn't that giving in to them? Why had I learned so many languages, she countered, and ignored Gaelic? When neither of us had an answer, which was often enough, the silence was a comfortable safety net. Without the trust we'd found at the *fest-noz,* none of it would have been possible.

So for three days, that was how it was—the two of us, working side by side in the quiet glade between the stream and the house. She gathered the vegetables and milked the solitary cow in her St. Tropez bikini, I chipped away with hammer and chisel at stones, trying to make them fit the kitchen garden wall that I'd taken it upon myself to repair. Both of us knew there was unhappiness near, but for those three days we made a calm that held it at bay—a calm which we both wanted to continue. Even when René returned with my expertly rewired car, the unspoken agreement between us was that I would not leave immediately.

The evening of the third day was a blissful quiet, the sun stippling patterns on the green mosses of the barn wall, the blackbird's song a melodic echo from the woods behind the stream. As I planted the last of the wall's fallen stones in place and turned to survey my handiwork, the satisfaction I felt was immense. For the first time in days, the ache in my muscles had no root in the humiliation I'd undergone in the police cellar, and I knew that the sweat running down my back was the forerunner of a pleasant lassitude.

I would use it, I decided, this peace. How long was it since I'd read a book? Tonight I'd find one and enjoy it before I slept, up in my barn bedroom. I examined the thought—odd, to have leisure again, to decide how to use it... As the resolution grew in my mind, Nathalie came round the edge of the garden, barefoot, skirt kirtled up round her mud-streaked thighs, vegetable basket in hand.

Yes, I thought, I would do that. She came up to me, smiling—and then, just as both of us were about to speak, we heard a rustling of leaves from across the stream.

A stag.

The stillness felt as though it would last forever. He stood as immobile as the *menhirs* at Carnac, velvet-sheened and massive, regal. Erect, proud-antlered, he watched us from the wood's edge, his dark eyes calm with the knowledge of his sovereignty. Every echo in the glade seemed to deepen as we waited.

And then a noise came from behind us—and he was gone, crashing away through the trees, back into the safe darkness of his kingdom. I turned.

A blond man was standing beside the garden gate. I heard a muttered imprecation from Nathalie as I examined him; white short-sleeved shirt, blue trousers....

Blue *uniform* trousers. I looked down. Black brogues...

Him? The one who'd saved me from the worst of the beating in Rennes? I wasn't absolutely sure until he spoke, and then the voice put it beyond doubt.

"Well, well, Mister Fiddler. And just what the hell are you doing here with my little sister?"

*

"Patrik Riou is an honourable politician!"

"Patrik Riou is an extremist."

"You're a liar! How much do the French pay you to lie?"

It was the kind of fight where there was nothing to win and only dignity to lose. Siblings... But as they fought, brother and sister, I could see how alike they were physically—and how different mentally. He held the centre of the arena they'd made of the farmhouse kitchen, dogged as a bear, uncompromising. She circled, whisky glass in hand, baiting him. It was ugly to watch.

"I didn't come to argue," he said.

"Then why did you come? Brotherly affection?"

The sneer made him hesitate just long enough to give her the initiative. She turned to me, her eyes alive with rage.

"Let me tell you about my wonderful big brother, Alexander! Christian Gwernig, Mister Career—every new promotion brings him a whole lot more baseball bats for his thugs, more tear gas to play with, more electric shock machines! What are you this week, Christian? Still head of the anti-terrorist squad? Or have you been promoted to *Monsieur le President's* arse wiper by now?"

He ignored the obscenity. "I've never seen an electric shock machine in my life," he said, quietly.

The reply that came back was icy with vindictiveness. "Not personally, no. You're far too well-organised. Delegation saves so much time."

That stung, I could see. The following silence was charged, as she looked to see how best she could wound.

"You're a disgrace to our father's name."

I heard anger finally touch him. "Don't bring that into this."

"Why not? He was ten times the man you are—and Patrik is as well. You must know he's gone or you wouldn't dare show your face here. How did you know—got him tailed, have you? Got the phone tapped, as usual?"

"I came to warn you. If you—"

Her whisky glass exploded against the wall behind him. "Either show me a warrant or get out! Now! If you're still here in five minutes I'm calling our lawyer."

She stormed out. I looked down, numb—such rage, such ruthlessness... And such loyalty to Patrik, as well—she might doubt, question, but God help anyone else who did; she was still there, carrying his spear. Her brother and I stood in the shattered silence she'd left behind, surrounded by the incongruous peace of the summer evening noises, the buzz of the insects, the lowing of the cow. Finally, I saw him recover at least some of the authority I remembered from the cellar in Rennes. He walked across to me, glass crunching beneath the soles of the black brogues.

"Was I wrong about you, Mister Fiddler?" he said, softly, gesturing at the badge she'd given me. "Are you part of this crazy circus here? Some psycho bomber I should have locked up for life when I had the chance?"

"No."

That much I owed him, but loyalty to her kept me from saying more—to explain would be to collude, to take his side against hers, and I would have no part of that. I watched the immobile mask of his face—a policeman's face, one that would never give anything away, like Prosper's. And then he nodded, brusquely.

"Okay, let's say your guardian angel's still in credit—but on one condition. If you've the slightest influence here, then get it across to her that my warning's serious. She's running around with some very heavy people now. Riou's—"

"I don't believe Patrik Riou's a terrorist," I said, quietly.

"Perhaps not, but he's not surrounded by choirboys—you'll have met Prosper, I suppose. And some of the other types the orders filter down to are no better than animals. Maybe Riou's hands are clean—"

He stopped, flushed to the roots of his hair as he realised he was simply recycling the accusation which had just been thrown at him. When he began again, his voice held real anger.

"This business at Kergorff, the nuclear dump they can't win it. But if this demonstration goes ahead, a lot of people are going to get hurt. I don't want that, and I'm going to stop it if I can. Keep her away from it."

He turned on his heel and made for the open door.

"Your father," I said. "Who was he?"

Wherever the impulse to ask had come from, I knew it was dangerous. He stopped at the doorway, turned again.

"Christ, you push your luck, don't you," he said, softly. He came back into the room. "How does a Breton poet finance himself if he's too lazy to work, Mister Fiddler? Inspiration doesn't pay the rent, so he takes three of his friends and sticks up a petrol station in Lyons in the middle of the night." He came right up to me, the anger reddening his face. "And for the lousy four thousand francs in the till, he frightens an old woman to death. And because he's stupid enough to leave his prints all over the place, he gets arrested."

He paused. I watched him fight for control.

"And when he can't face the music he tops himself. And every stupid bastard the length and breadth of Brittany calls him a patriot."

He turned and walked off into the darkness.

*

She wasn't anywhere around the farm buildings. I spent an hour trying to find her in the woods, shouting, shining a torch, but to no avail. Eventually I gave up—she wasn't hurt or lost, I was sure of it. She just wasn't ready to be found.

And by first light, my own involvement in the episode—in this whole household—seemed increasingly bizarre. This place had been a safe haven, yes, and I was grateful, but what could I contribute to it now?

For I was compromised, irredeemably—if I wanted to stay I was committed to a lie, albeit one of omission. If I told Patrik or Prosper that Nathalie's brother had been the one who rescued me in Rennes, their suspicions of me as a police informer could only come back with redoubled force. And if I didn't tell them, and they found out later, it would be worse.

So yes, it was time to go. If she asked me to stay, I would—but only until the others got back. And if she didn't ask me...

And somehow, making that decision gave me the courage for another. I looked round at the garden, at the stillness, at the colours washed in the clear dawn light. I was alone. There would never be a better time; it might as well be faced now.

I went into the barn, past the diminished mound of posters, scaled the ladder to my loft haven and found the fiddle case. My hands reached down to open it, but then I thought better of the impulse. No evasion. Let it be seen in the full light of day. Carrying it carefully under my arm, I went back down the ladder.

And as I came back out into the yard, she was there—dishevelled and weary, her bare legs a mass of scratches and cuts, her cheeks striped with dried tear tracks. She stared dully at the fiddle case, then looked up at me.

"You're leaving?"

"Not if you want me to stay."

In the long silence, I saw suspicion come to her, then fear. "Why are you going?" she said, her voice rising. *"What did he tell you?"*

The shout was desperation and anger in equal measure. I hesitated far too long for credence, no matter what I said. A look of pure pain crossed her face, and then she distilled the rest of her rage into armour.

"It was an accident! They never meant to harm the old woman, she died of a heart attack when they blindfolded her. He was a good man, my father—a man who loved his country! He only took part because they were desperate for money to print their manifesto! And when he couldn't live with what happened he paid! With the only thing he had," she finished bitterly.

"It's not for me to judge," I began, "it's—"

But her anger's guard was up now. "I have to go," she said, turning away. "To Patrik. I know where he'll be. He has to know about this."

"Nathalie—"

"Just go," she said, over her shoulder.

*

I drove for an hour or so along the coast, sore of heart, my thoughts a maze, and then pulled over at a deserted inlet that was fringed with a golden scrap of beach.

I had been dismissed, so why did I feel as though I'd deserted? I was sorry we hadn't parted on better terms, but there was nothing to be done about it now. And anyway, wasn't it better that she went back to her warrior chief, to carry his spear? How much longer could it have lasted, anyway, our playing-at-peasants idyll? I stared at the quiet wash of the sea, the folded up deck chairs awaiting the tourists, the empty rowing boats nudging each other in the slight swell—and frowned. I was only putting it off, I knew.

I lifted the fiddle case from the seat beside me and got out of the car.

I settled myself on a bench at the beach's edge and laid the case on my knees. I could be cold about this, I told myself, rational—if wood and glue couldn't be repaired, then another instrument would somehow have to be found. She was just a fiddle...

But even as the thought came, I knew it was a lie—she'd been through everything with me, even prison, and no matter what the future held, I couldn't imagine life without her. I could only hope the damage wasn't too bad. I closed my eyes, sprang the case locks and prised open the lid.

It was the smell that told me something was wrong—an expensive smell, instrument polish. I opened my eyes.

What the hell...

No wreckage. A grey cotton bag whose shape filled the case. I lifted it, opened the drawstrings. The polished smell intensified as I drew out the instrument inside.

A polished brown violin. Whole, in perfect condition.

I held it up to the light. It was a beautiful instrument—spruce top, maple back. Italian, I could tell by the style. But where was my own?

A car pulled up behind me. I heard a family begin to disembark, loud with self-congratulation at being first to the beach. As their jollity spilled out onto the sand, I checked the rest of the case. Nothing else had changed. The top compartment still held two spare strings and a crumbling block of resin, the bow was my old, cheap faithful. I reached into my makeshift wallet, a rip in the lid's tatty green velvet lining; passport, driving licence, birth certificate... Nothing had been disturbed. My eyes came back to the pristine violin. I peered into its f-hole, looking for the maker's label.

A date; seventeen twenty-three.

A name—surely it didn't mean anything, that name was on half the junk fiddles in Europe! Gently, I put the violin back down in the case and lifted the grey bag. There was something else inside it—a long envelope, open. I drew out its contents.

A document, old and brittle, dated 1948. I read the headings.

Age...

Value...

It was a certificate of provenance.

A little girl, naked and clutching a huge rubber ring, ran past me, yelling. As she plunged into the sea, her mother's indulgent laugh followed her.

"Hold on to it, *chérie!* Hold on!"

She made a gripping motion with her hands.

Involuntarily, I did the same.

If the document was real, I was holding a Stradivarius.

6

FORTUNE

WHO THE HELL had switched my fiddle for a Stradivarius? And why?

By mid-morning, after another hour of directionless driving, the questions had so gripped my brain that I was a danger to traffic. I stopped in the grey suburbs of Lorient, opposite the iron gates of a naval base. With the fiddle case under my arm I found a bar, ordered coffee, then pushed my way through the sullen clientele of off-duty sailors. The back room was just far enough away from the racket of pinball machine and jukebox to let me think.

Only one thing made more sense now—my would-be assailant in Concarneau. Stealing a ten-year-old Fiat made no sense—but if he'd thought there was a Stradivarius in the boot... And he'd transferred his attentions to me the minute he'd seen what I was carrying. No, he was no simple mugger—he'd been after the fiddle case.

And if that surmise was right, it meant that the switch of fiddles had taken place some time between my arrest and my release; at all other times the case had been in my sight, beside me on the car seat. No, I corrected myself—during the fracas itself I'd lost sight of it. But the exchange would have had to take place in plain view of dozens of witnesses—not likely, I decided.

Which left the prospect of the police station. I turned over the possibilities. Bent policemen, setting me up as the scapegoat for some robbery? Or revenge for me hitting the cop—a more sophisticated revenge, because their first one, the beating-up, had been thwarted? Set me up with a stolen violin, catch me with it, watch me go down for ten years or so? A sobering chain of thought... I felt the cafe's dark confines begin to close in on me. Prison again? I'd never be able to stand it, I knew. But I reassured myself—no policeman, crooked or otherwise, would use as prime a piece of merchandise as a Stradivarius for something as petty as that. And if something like that was the case, why hadn't they kept better tabs on me? I hadn't been watched, I was sure—and anyway, it was too elaborate, it didn't gel, not with the mindless brutality I'd encountered in the place.

I drank the last of my coffee and speculated. Nathalie's brother? Christian Gwernig, the not-so-secret policeman? But to what end would he plant it on me? To somehow discredit the PSB? But he couldn't have known that I would meet, and be offered hospitality by, his sister... That couldn't have been engineered, surely.

But what about the PSB itself?

I stared down at the empty coffee cup. What if I was wrong about the tattooed man in Concarneau? What if he had nothing to do with this? Or worse, what if the PSB had planted him? The swap could have been done at the farmhouse, very easily—the case had been left unsupervised in the barn loft for days on end. Nathalie? I put aside our painful parting and considered it coldly—and dismissed the notion. And after another minute's thought I struck out Patrik as well, no matter what kind of people he dealt with for his political ends. I had never met two individuals who were, in their different ways, so patently honest.

But Prosper, that was a different matter.

Very different. If there was the slightest political advantage to be had from stitching me up, then Prosper would be there, needle in one hand, lead weights in the other—and the case against me would be so seamless I'd go down for ever.

No, I very much hoped it wasn't Prosper...

But for the life of me, I couldn't see what possible advantage could be gained from such a thing. In fact, I could see nothing at all—and I would continue to see nothing, I realised, until I knew the history of this violin which I had been so rudely given. That was the key. But how was I to find that out?

And then it came to me. I knew how. There was one person who could help. I rose. The fiddle case tightly under my arm, I pushed my way back through the crop-headed sailors, paid at the counter, and came back out into daylight.

Two hours to Rennes.

*

"Certificates and labels can be easily counterfeited, *mon ami.* Antique violins—perhaps not so easily. But it is not impossible. So let us see."

Jeweller's loupe to his eye, Georges Berolet held up the violin that called itself a Stradivarius—and as he began to examine it, I could no longer bear to watch. I looked away instead, round the fine room that would have given me so much satisfaction if I'd come here under different circumstances—the neatly racked rows of instruments, the shelves of music books, the smells of wood and rosin. Still the old man did not pronounce. I closed my eyes—and heard the click of heels through the open window.

The women, the well-dressed women I'd played for, stalking the chic windows below in the afternoon heat...

Where was the old man's son, I wondered, the irascible violin teacher who had watched them from here? Only seven days had passed since then, but it seemed a lifetime ago... I opened my eyes to see the loupe came down again. The instrument followed, placed in its case with gentle firmness.

"Without experts, without scientific analysis, impossible to say definitively—but if it is a falsification, it is the best I have ever seen." He looked up at me. "Yes, my friend, I think this is a real eighteenth century Italian violin, very probably a real Stradivarius. And if it is, then it would be worth somewhere in the region of perhaps a quarter of a million British pounds. What do you want me to do with it?" He paused. "Are you suggesting that I sell it for you?"

The calmness of the last question was chilling. I looked round the room, at the rows of violins and violas, searching for an answer. To ask me was ridiculous—as if I would know what to do with the damn thing!

"The police," he began, tentatively. "They would—"

"No, not the police, Monsieur Berolet," I said evenly.

His head nodded in grave acceptance. Further explanation was unnecessary—he knew as well as I did that no policeman would ever believe that this instrument had come into my possession by honest accident. But a quarter of a million... The old man brought my confusion firmly to an end.

"So. What can be done? It is evidently not a previously undiscovered instrument—if it was, there would be no documentation. And an instrument with such documentation cannot go missing unnoticed." He shrugged. "The police, however, are not the only ones who can make enquiries."

It was the offer I'd been hoping for. "You would be prepared to do that?" I asked. "If I leave it here with you?"

He shook his head. "No, my friend, that is the one thing that must not happen. A documented violin by a master maker, worth several million francs? In a dealer's shop with no bill of sale? No, I have no wish to spend my declining years in either jail or litigation."

"So what should I do? Put the thing in a bank?"

I saw a quick shadow of disappointment pass across his face. Why? He rose, went across to the rack of bows on the far wall, selected one, then turned and lifted the Stradivarius from the case. He thrust violin and bow at me.

"Here. Play it."

The force behind the words was unexpected. Puzzled, I took the instrument and put it in the playing position under my chin. Tentatively, I began a scale.

"No!" he said, openly annoyed now. "Play it—play one of the fast airs, the dance tunes you play in the street!"

Still mystified, I obeyed. Hesitantly, I tried a reel, *The Fallen Angel,* and despite my clumsiness, the lilt of it came out. I played it twice through, then stopped. The old man grunted his approval, then went across to the row of books on the shelf beside his desk. He pulled out a thick volume and flicked through the pages until he came to what he was looking for, then read aloud.

"Antonio Stradivari, 1644-1737, maker, Italy. Perfected the Cremona violin. The finest of the Italian master craftsmen, his instruments—" He looked up gravely, no longer quoting. "—the Tuscan, the Dolphin, La Pucelle et al, famed for their sweetness of tone, thought to lie in the unique varnish." He snapped the book shut and laid it on the desk. "It says nothing there about banks," he said, aggressively—and then he turned. As he gestured at the room's instruments, his voice recovered its gentleness. "Violins have been my life. All my days I have sold them—expensive ones, cheap ones, good and not so good—but always to players, always to be played. A violin does not belong in a bank vault, it belongs in a violinist's hands! No instrument has ever been knowingly bought or sold in this shop for the purposes of mere investment."

The passion with which he said it touched me—and let me see just how much I liked this man. And how much I owed him—not once had he even hinted that my story might be false, not once had he tried to wash his hands of me. He had even, yet again, offered me money when he had learned of my circumstances. Now he laid his hand across mine on the violin's neck.

"You miss your own violin, that is right and proper—it was a fine instrument, and you were bound to it. I will search for it," he said. "I know every shop in this *département*, honest or otherwise, which might handle such a violin. But in the meantime, this instrument sits well in your hands. Until we find its real owner, you will make a fine steward for it. It has music in it and you have music in you."

He paused again. Still I didn't understand.

"You have no money, you refuse more of mine," he said. "Very well. A week ago, if you had had no money and an instrument in your hand, what would you have done?"

*

Vannes... What had Nathalie called it? An old turtle of a town, drinking from the sea. Well, the turtle's back was going to get wet soon—as I walked into the centre along the quayside, I heard the distant threat of thunder. At the first peal, the beach-clad people around me began loudly checking their bags for waterproof hats and plastic jackets.

"*Attention,* Louis! It's coming!"

"Eugénie! Jeanne! Take your raincoats, do you hear!"

The tourists, I thought. It was Patrik's description I remembered now—the summer plague... But against the heaviness of my heart, the innocence of their concern was soothing.

And the town itself helped lift my spirits as well, for as I explored I could see that it was a busker's paradise. The day before, after seeing Georges Berolet, I'd left Rennes, because I knew there would be police trouble if I tried to play there—but this was no second best. In the old streets that sloped up from the harbour, I found the perfect mix—open markets, holiday crowds with time on their hands, congenial corners by the dozen. The summer plague would bring me good business. And yet...

I wandered for hours, eying the trinkets, the tawdry souvenirs, the beach toys, before finally facing the truth that Georges Berolet had articulated so well for me.

The first law of busking. No money equals no food and no bed.

I'd refused handouts, I'd left the physical comfort of Patrik Riou's farmhouse, I'd spent the previous night in the car, and I had barely the price of a meal in my pocket. I had no choices left. The thunder rolled in heavy agreement. With an outward calm which was totally false, I stopped in one of the streets near the cathedral. Beneath a tall half-timbered gable, I opened the case and took it out.

It. A Stradivarius, on the street. It was the world turned upside down.

And as I lifted her, I knew that I was afraid. It wasn't the price tag—since talking to Georges Berolet in Rennes I'd barely thought of that. I turned her in my hands, surveyed the fine back. No, I realised, it was the instrument itself. It was the fear rooted in the maker's myth, bred in the bone of every musician who had ever lifted a violin.

Was I good enough to play a Stradivarius?

There was only one thing to do. I pushed the case out in front of me, put my chin down on a quarter of a million pounds, and brought up the bow. *The Fallen Angel,* I thought, the tune I'd played for the old man the day before, I'd play that and another couple like it. Get a few reels behind me and the fear would go. I'd—

A fifty-centime coin landed in the case. I looked up—and felt a very different emotion grip me.

I felt like a fraud.

A thin man in a battered flat cap was smiling at me, a baguette loaf under his arm. His tiny dog was straining at the confines of its makeshift string leash, nosing at the envelope.

The document envelope. The envelope which proved that the instrument I was holding was worth several million times what he had just given me. I stopped. I simply couldn't do this, it was dishonest. But then the world turned again. I saw disappointment come to the thin man's eyes, then frustration—and I almost laughed.

He felt cheated, yes, but for all the wrong reasons—he'd paid his money and got no tune! Aggrieved, he took the greasy cigar stub from his mouth and shouted at me.

"Alors, joue!"

I played a few bars of something, I don't know what. He grunted and walked off, dragging the barking dog behind him—and somehow, the ridiculous paradox of it made everything right. The worst was over. The Italian violin and I were ready for each other.

There were a few false starts, misunderstandings that tested patience—a tuning peg that kept slipping, an awkwardness of grip because there was no chin rest. And there was one slightly more serious disagreement—I was used to steel strings and she was strung with expensive gut ones. A different touch of bow was needed to compensate, a stroke foreign to me, lighter and more even than I was used to. It took an hour—an hour of undignified squeak and scrape, an hour of dirty looks and tilt-of-the-head sympathetic smiles from my public. But once I'd mastered it, we began.

When all's said and done, no fiddle is more than a contract between wood, wire, gut and air, regulated by that humblest of lawyers, the hair from a horse's tail. But it's the injection of technique—the business of fingers and wrists and forearms, the how, when and why—that brings the dividends, those seductive devil's bargains called expression and style.

Never before had I been in a situation where my technique wasn't equal to an instrument's capabilities.

First of all, the variety of tones in her was staggering—from a bell-like clarity of the bass register to a sweet, singing treble on the top string, and in between, if she was played softly, a nutty, almost muted resonance, a falling-off between notes that could easily have been mistaken for the cadences of a child's voice. I listened to it all in awe. What skill did it take to make such an instrument, what magic?

But for all the sonorous tone, it was a mysterious magic to me. I had almost no control over her. The slow airs I wanted to make expressive came out pompous, the waltzes rang where they should have lilted. In my hands she seemed to like her music loud and majestic—Scottish pipe marches, for instance, or the neo-classical Irish Planxtys. I played as many of them as I knew, glad to have established a link with her obvious strengths. But there were other cadences which I wanted to pull from her, and which I simply could not find. Was it me, I wondered, was it the cheap Scottish bow? After two hours of playing beneath the thunder's growl, she was almost as much of an enigma to me as she had been when we started, and the crux of the problem was simple.

The clarity and sweetness came when *she* wanted them to, not when I did, and that equation was the wrong way round.

But all the same, as I looked down into the case, I saw that we'd made enough of a deal with each other to pull in money. Maybe as much as four hundred francs, good... And it was a double victory, really, for in my absorption with her I had ignored my audience completely. Eye contact with people as they pass catches their interest, makes a personal bond—without it, a great deal of cash walks right past. So I'd been lucky to earn as much as I had—but it wouldn't do to go on like that. I'd have to pay more attention.

And heartened by the success, I did. For the next four hours, in the close heat of the still-threatening storm, I worked the street with something nearer my usual style, playing with as much vigour as my rapidly-tiring bow arm and the idiosyncratic fiddle allowed. Even though I knew some of it wouldn't feel right, I tried every side of my repertoire, from the pyrotechnics of *The Mecklenburg Reel* to the humorous tune I'd done so well with in Rennes, *The Sow's Lament for the Tatties.* The humour came off, the flashy stuff didn't; this was a violin which had no trouble distinguishing the clever from the effective.

But I got by and more, emptying the case's coin into my pocket from time to time, and as the shadows began to grow longer and the crowds dispersed, I congratulated myself—a workmanlike shift on the street, even though I could feel how exhausted I was. When the last pedestrian disappeared round the corner, I put the Stradivarius down in her open case, and leaned back against the wall to look at her.

Amazing, yes—and alien. And demanding and unforgiving. And beautiful.

And when it came down to it, she couldn't play a strathspey worth a damn.

Where was the wildness? Where was the bite?

I went on staring at her, lying there, pristine and sleek in the dilapidated case with the ripped lid. Again, the thought of the

Scottish fiddle I'd been stupid enough to lose swamped me—the quiet warmth she'd brought to the airs, the raw excitement she could generate as we pumped out the reels together. Where was she? If she was even halfway whole, I wanted her back on my shoulder again—and if she was dead...

A shout from the gable above made me look up—a window, right at the very top, a teenage couple, grinning, obviously naked, glistening with sweat.

"Hey, you make nice music, mister," the girl shouted.

The boy's voice was loud with bravado. "Nice music for fucking! All afternoon! Here!"

I saw the hand's throw—*God, no!*

Half-slide, half-dive, I landed on all fours and somehow got my body over the open fiddle case in time. I winced as the shower hit my back and head, each coin hard as a bullet. *No!* Even when I was sure it was over, I didn't move from my protective crouch—shaking as it all rushed in on me.

Money!

Value!

Price!

My brain reeled as I counted the risks I'd taken. What if I'd dropped the thing and smashed it to bits? What if another Pigez had come and grabbed it? What if the varnish— What if, what if, what if... I was all but sobbing with the mountain of fears I'd ignored.

And then the thunder came, a long, rolling clap that rent the sky, and the rain came down in straight, solid rods.

Punishment, I knew it! Punishment for leaving a quarter of a million pounds lying out on a pavement! For losing my own fiddle in the first place! For trying to make a sow out of a Stradivarius, for—

Sow.

"Where does the pig's voice come from, Mister?"

The English kid, with the West Country accent, in Rennes....

Nick.

As the rain teemed down my back, suddenly I knew, deep down in my weary bones, that he was part of it.

*

The coins went into the box.

"*Bonjour.* Berolet."

The voice was cold, pompous; the son, not the father.

"*Monsieur* Berolet, this is Alex Fraser."

The voice became even colder. "My father is not here," he said, brusquely. "It seems he has gone off to search the antique shops in the hope of finding your violin. Where are you calling from?"

"Vannes," I said, "but it's you I need to talk to, *Monsieur,* not your father. Your violin class that day. How many pupils did you have?"

"What is the purpose of this?"

"It may help me find my violin, *Monsieur.*"

There was a hesitation, and then he said, "I had five pupils, as always."

I knew it! I felt the excitement rise.

"There was a sixth child in the street, listening to me," I said, "carrying a Morocco leather violin case. An English child, a boy. Did you see him? I think—"

The line went dead. I dialled again, but all I got was a long tone. Engaged? Out of order?

I hung up. No matter—I'd established it now, the English boy had been separate, alone. Was it coincidence? If it had been him who made the exchange, how had he done it? And why?

With the water still dripping from me, I pushed out of the phone box, the sodden violin case in my hand. The car, I thought, looking down at it—dryness, for both of us, that was the priority. And then, tonight, back to Rennes, a room somewhere, and rest.

Enough rest to give me energy to search in the morning. As I picked my way down through the streaming gutters towards the quayside, I felt the first stirrings of something I hadn't known for long enough.

Hope.

*

But at nine o'clock the next morning, in Rennes, I wasn't as confident. I rang Georges Berolet's bell. No answer. I looked up at the first floor windows; still shuttered. I dug out pen and paper from my jacket, scribbled a quick note to say I'd call back either later in the day or first thing the next morning, and pushed it under the door.

And then I stood with the Stradivarius under my arm, gripped by sudden unease. Was what I was about to try feasible? No photograph, no more than a guess at age... All I had was my own description of this boy, and what I hoped was his Christian name, Nick. But I had no choice. I forced away doubt and headed for the first of the chic shop doors.

It wasn't easy, going through these particular doors. Few people are haughtier than the custodian of an expensive shop who sees the tone of their establishment being lowered—and the question itself didn't help, either; it smacked of the bizarre. On the 23rd of August, had anyone seen a small English boy carrying a Morocco leather violin case? The usual response was an impatient negative, followed by a steady shepherding back towards the street. I had to learn to stand my ground and insist—but not too much, for I didn't dare force it. A call to the authorities was the last thing I wanted.

So I crisscrossed the streets of Rennes, as exhaustively as I could—every store, every stall, every cafe, every boutique. And every rubbish bin as well. I rummaged in them without shame. The quarter of a million in the case under my arm had been exchanged for what was, effectively, a bundle of musical firewood. I was convinced that the motive could only have been to hide the Strad—and that meant that the remains of the other fiddle had to be disposed of somehow. A litter bin was a real possibility, and I wasn't proud. Every time I came to one I steeled myself, stuck my hand down through the greasy mess of cartons, the rotting fruit, the cigarette ends, but to no avail. There was no sharp sliver of neck, no abandoned peg or tailpiece, no St. Christopher. Around me, the well-dressed women made their little moues of distaste, the men gave me stony glares. And when the children pointed curious fingers, they were quickly moved on—shooed away, as though poverty and degradation were catching. I didn't care. Only once did my determination falter—when I heard a roar of protest from across the Rue D'Orléans. I looked up.

My nemesis, the beggar Pigez. The magpie...

Of course, I understood—once more I was in unwitting competition with him. The litter bins were his larder. I stared at him bitterly, the idiot sower of my harvest of troubles—and as we confronted each other across the crowded, moneyed street, his scowl changed to a drunken laugh. He let out a hoarse yell of triumph and launched into a lop-sided jig round the wine bottle at his feet. I felt the rage rise in me.

Nathalie, your Celtic Gods are cruel, I thought, to use him to taunt me in my defeat...

But then, as the passers-by put their heads down and hurried through between us, running the distasteful gauntlet between our twin madnesses, my anger vanished, and I wondered; had the cops worked him over as well? I moved away as quickly as I could, to the next street, the next dogged round of questions.

Luck came halfway along the Rue Duguesclin.

The shop was devoted to two luxuries. One *vitrine* contained a mountain of black and brown hide—gloves, desk diaries, shoulder bags—and the other was filled with bottles of perfume. Inside, the mixture of the two smells had a drug-like intensity. The middle-aged woman behind the glass counter wore a polished two-piece leather suit in an expensive shade of brown. Against the burnished copper of her tan, its padded shoulders looked like armour. Two younger assistants, less formidable in black skirts and white cotton blouses, eyed me from the back corner as they sorted Yves St. Laurent and Givenchy onto their respective shelves.

"And how can we help you, *M'sieu?"*

The tone made it obvious she was sure she couldn't, and even before I'd finished the question, the leather arm was showing me the door in exasperation—what could this shop possibly sell to a child with a violin, really *M'sieu*—

And then one of the assistants piped up. *"Mais oui!* He was sweet, the little English boy!"

Ignoring the snort of annoyance from beside me, I went over to the girl.

"And he had a violin case, one like that?"

I pointed to a Morocco handbag on the wall's display. She shook her head.

"Non, M'sieu, it wasn't him who was carrying the case, it was the man with him."

"Describe him, this man."

"He was tall."

She turned to her companion. Both of them giggled.

"And very handsome. And he looked very strong." Again the girlish giggles. "We called him the sailor."

"Why?"

"He had tattoos—" She pointed to her forearm. "—here."

Tattoos... I felt my adrenaline surge.

"One of the tattoos was a picture?" I couldn't remember the French word. "A girl? A girl who's a fish?"

She laughed. *"Oui, M'sieu'. Une sirène."*

"And letters? C-O-L?"

She nodded vigorously. *"Oui,"* she repeated. "Col-something, I forget exactly what." She turned to the other girl. *"Tu te souviens,* Chantal?"

Chantal shook her head and gave an apologetic shrug. I turned back to the first girl.

"And he was English, this man, like the boy?"

"No, not exactly, something like it, though. He couldn't speak French. *Madame* Claude said—"

And then the proprietress was between us, red-faced, flustered. *"M'sieu,* I really can't have you badgering my staff like this when they've got work to do, I'll have to ask you to leave."

Or I'll call the cops, was the unspoken threat. But why was she so agitated? Better to retreat, I decided. As I left the shop, I heard the beginnings of a furious scolding. I scanned the street to right and left until I found what I wanted—a doorway that would give me a view of the place. As I reached it, I heard a clock somewhere strike five; not long to wait, surely, till close of business.

I spent it in a strange mixture of elation and speculation. The conjunction of the English boy and the man who was so obviously my assailant from Concarneau put the matter beyond doubt—the Strad had come from the Morocco case. But how, if at all, did it bring me forward? I saw the boutique door open, the two assistants emerge and walk away from me. *Madame* Claude followed. Would she take the same route?

Thankfully she didn't. I waited till she'd levered herself into the parked Volkswagen at the kerb, then pursued my quarry. I found the girl I'd spoken to earlier at the bus stop. She eyed me doubtfully; the scolding's legacy, no doubt.

"I'm sorry if I got you into trouble," I said, "but it's important. What else can you tell me about this man, the sailor?"

She shrugged. "Not much. He'd come to collect perfume, it had been ordered on the phone. Chanel, the most expensive. More than eleven hundred francs," she said enviously, "just for a tiny bottle."

"Do you know who ordered it?"

She shook her head. "No, *M'sieu.* Not who—but I know where the call came from. Madame Claude had to check we had it and phone back. It was a hotel, the Hôtel Cabuchon." Again the note of envy came. "That's not cheap, either."

"When was this?"

"The Wednesday before last," she said happily. "I remember, because it was two days to my little brother's birthday, and the boy reminded me of him."

The same day, the twenty-third, the day it all happened... A bus appeared round the corner.

"M'sieu, I have to go now."

"Wait, please, one last question. Why was your boss so upset?"

She picked up her bag, ready to get on. "Oh, she's not so bad, *Madame* Claude—she was just embarrassed."

"Why?"

She giggled again, blushing now as well. "Because her sister was in the shop, and when he'd gone, I heard them talking. I wasn't going to tell you exactly what she said about him, not in the shop, but I suppose it's all right now. She said—" She leaned down from the bus's platform and whispered in my ear as it began to move. "—that the sailor man looked like a really good fuck."

7

CONFRONTATIONS

THE HÔTEL CABUCHON was on the city's outskirts, an ugly modern box hiding its drabness behind a pseudo-rustic facade, an accommodation factory masquerading as an *auberge*. As I passed through a trellised portal of trained vines, I wondered if I'd made the right decision, leaving the Strad behind in the car. The double glass doors read my presence and slid open.

A convention was in full swing—of insurance salesmen, I read it on a blackboard. The lobby was full of name-tagged delegates and cocktail hour chat about actuarial tables and endowments. At the front desk, the under-manager's smile—fixed, professionally obsequious—died as soon as he saw me.

"When will you people learn," he said, shaking his head, "not to use the main entrance? Coming in here, dressed like that—which job did you come about, anyway? Waiter or handyman?"

"Handyman," I said, accepting the luck of it—information would be easier to come by backstairs.

An imperious finger pointed me at a side door. Two corridors and a downward flight of steps brought me to a laundry room, full of industrial-sized washing machines. A fat teenage girl in filthy overalls was stuffing dirty bed linen into one of them, sweating, grunting with the effort. She looked round at my approach.

"Well, well, things are looking up. You the new fixer? Tool

box's in the cupboard, two doors down."

I decided on honesty—the handyman facade would be too easily punctured. As she stuffed the last of the soiled sheets into the machine I held up a fifty franc note.

"I'm looking for information."

The chubby face split into an earthy grin. Her ham-sized fist claimed the note and thumped the machine's start button in the same movement.

"Buy you a damn sight more than information, that, *chéri!"* she chuckled, winking at me, "If you were in the mood. But a girl can't have everything, can she? What d'you want?"

I only had to give her half the man's description before she broke in. "Oh, him! Mister Mafia with the shades and the car! Loverboy! At it night and day, everything from young 'uns to grannies, up there in droves, that's what my mate Clothilde told me. She does the sixth. Tried it on with her, he did, bold as brass! Stuck his hand up her skirt while she was doing the bed. Mind you, she'd've let him, she said, if it hadn't been for her Alphonse—kill her if he found out," she finished happily. "Still, I'm down here if he ever fancies something a bit meatier. Could do a girl a bit of good, all right, by the looks of him! Even hunkier than you!"

"Was there ever a child with him? A boy about ten years old?"

"Can't say I noticed, but I'd doubt it, not with all the goings-on up there."

She picked up another mound of bedding from the pile and looked up at me, a different kind of speculation in her eyes. "What is it, he owe you money? Get it off him now, before he has to pay the room service, 'cause that's going to give him a heart attack."

The implication took a moment to register. "You mean he's still here?"

"Sure! Six twenty-seven! The luxury suite, the sin-and-gin bin! Won't be around now, though—always out this time of the day, goes betting. The dogs, PMU bar in town, one of the waiters saw him."

Quickly, I left her to her laundry, my mind racing. What now? I stopped in the concrete corridor, forced myself to dissect the situation.

My quarry wanted the Strad, and he had some connection

with the boy who'd given me it. If I was right, that the boy had taken my own violin, then this man could very well have it. But he wouldn't take the thing to a betting shop with him...

The decision was obvious, and once it had been made, I moved quickly—the tool box was two doors down, she'd said. I found it, bristling with everything I'd need to get through a hotel door without a key. I lifted it and headed down the corridor. When the lift came, I got in, pressed the buttons, felt nerves come with the slow upward movement. What were the dangers? Caught committing burglary? I'd take that risk. The bell told me I'd arrived at the sixth floor.

The doors opened to reveal an overweight man with unkempt long hair, scratching irritably at one armpit of his hawaiian shirt. He pushed past me into the lift, giving the tool box a cursory glance in passing. I stepped out. The lift seemed to wait forever. *Close,* I thought. I rummaged in my pockets and tried to look like a man searching for a key. Had he pressed the button? *Close, damn you.* Finally, it happened. As I watched the numbers descend I felt the fatigue that rides on adrenaline's back; first hurdle. I went down the corridor, counting off the numbers. Room 627 was at the end. What would I need? A screwdriver? Or should I drill out the lock? When I reached the door I paused, heart thumping—and then I just knocked and waited. No answer. Again I knocked, harder—and this time it swung open from the force of my hand. It hadn't even been on the latch, never mind locked. Empty? I waited another minute. Silence. I walked in and surveyed it all.

So this was how he lived, this man who excited such frank admiration in boutique owners and laundresses...

The mess was centred on the sofa which faced the television. The surface of the coffee table before it was barely visible. A sticky collage—newspapers, magazines, chocolate wrappers—covered it, pinned down by a clutch of spirit glasses and a plate which still bore the remains of a fried egg. The papers were English, all open at the sports pages, the magazines were all about motorbikes, and the glasses bore different colours of lipstick, as did the cigarette butts in the overflowing ashtray. The floor around was a skittle alley of empty beer bottles in every direction, the carpet a greyish mess of ash and burns. I walked across to the sideboard—half-full bottles of vodka, rum, gin. A near-empty forty-ouncer of Glenlivet was holding down a pile of room service receipts, and the signatures indicated that I was in the room of a Mr. Smith. I did some quick arithmetic as I sifted through them. My friend the laundress hadn't been far wrong—over five hundred pounds in ten days. Ten days... He'd arrived in Rennes the same day I had. Was that significant? Thoughtfully, I put the receipts back under the bottle and looked round again—until the sight of the wall clock reminded me how easy it would be to get caught here. Quickly, I checked the cupboards and went through the connecting door.

The bedroom. More glasses, more beer bottles, but the dominant reek was of a different vice.

Sex.

A sickly mixture of perfume and sweat, the heavy odour of accumulated animal rut... He must have pulling power indeed, this Mr. Smith, I decided, to make his paramours perform for him on the cold musk of their predecessors. Again, mindful of time, I checked under the bed and in the cupboards. Still no fiddle.

The only other room was the bathroom, and in it I found the only bit of neatness, a polythene suit bag, hanging from the shower rail. I opened it; a uniform suit of militaristic dark grey, a peaked cap... You were wrong, girls, I thought—not a sailor, not a gangster—my assailant from Concarneau was a chauffeur.

I went through the pockets. Nothing. I repacked the suit in its bag and went back to the living room—and saw what I'd missed before. A note, on the coffee table, lying apart from the squalor. I went across, looked.

Call me. S. 6287298.

The handwriting was blunt, businesslike. A man's? Impossible to tell. Should I take it? No, I decided, better to copy it. On the sideboard I found a pen. I wrote the number on my wrist, then turned and surveyed the room.

A mess, disgusting, stale. No signs of occupancy by any small boy—and no violin anywhere. I bit back disappointment. What had I learned?

That Mr. Smith was English, that he was a motorbike fanatic. And that he had a nose-in-the-trough taste for the fleshier end of the good life. So who had been the recipient of the expensive perfume? Something as costly as that argued a female presence which was more than just transient... But what now?

First, it was time to go—he might return at any minute. Second, find a vantage point outside, wait, and on his return, somehow confront him without danger to myself. Carefully, I opened the door.

The corridor was still deserted. I hid the tool box behind an armchair by the lift, then pressed the button. It came immediately. Which way out? Past the front desk? No, until I'd settled this it would be better to stay as anonymous as possible. The lift panel told me there was a garage, right down below the kitchen, that would be the way. The descent continued undisturbed. At the bottom the doors opened—and as the cool air of the garage flowed in, I froze.

And he did as well.

The man who had chased me in Concarneau was standing about twenty yards in front of me, just behind the boot of a big car, a Rolls-Royce.

Standoff. Heart racing, I knew it—but the initiative was mine. I could close the lift doors faster than he could reach me.

"Stay where you are!" I shouted. "I want to talk!"

He nodded, slowly. I recognised the uniform he was wearing as the twin of the one upstairs. No dark glasses this time, though, just the black gloves.

"What have you done with my fiddle?" I shouted. "Have you still got it?"

"Sure," he answered, grinning.

One syllable was enough. The shopgirl's not-quite-English was explained—he was as Scottish as I was. He came forward, slowly.

"Upstairs, in my room."

I tried to keep my face immobile, but he saw the lie register—and broke into a run. As I flung myself to the side, stabbing at the lift buttons, I saw a flash of brightness. The knuckle duster? The hydraulic hiss of the doors came, and then a loud, reverberating clang that made the whole metal box flinch. A shot! He had a gun! Trapped in the rising metal box, the echo of it seemed endless. As the lift stopped, I realised I was shaking.

The ground floor doors opened to show me an army of smiling conventioneers. I roared some sort of warning, barged my way through to the main entrance, and ran.

*

Intelligence returned several streets away. Whatever else 'Mr. Smith' was, he was no professional. He had panicked, fired a gun in a public place. There would be evidence of the fact on the lift's doors—and almost certainly now, his logic would be to get out. How long would it take him to clear the room? Minutes, no more. Again I began to run—but this time with purpose.

It took five minutes to reach my car, but another fifteen of one way streets and curses before I came into sight of the hotel and the deep garage's entrance. When it was still fifty yards away, a red light stopped me, and as I waited, a big car emerged. The Rolls... Him? It had to be. As he came out into the main flow of traffic I made out the peaked cap, the dark features beneath. I rode the clutch gently, waiting for green, ready to go. The boot was on the other foot, now. I had a full tank, I'd follow him, wherever he ran.

The lights changed—and the Renault in front of me tried to change lanes without warning. A squeal of brakes, a refusal to give way from the Peugot in the next lane—and the Renault stalled. I was hemmed in. As the windows wound down and the shouting began, I flung open my door and got out. The number plate, I had to get that at least!

But the Rolls was gone, round the next bend. I stared after it—until a blare of horn from behind informed me that the road was free, and that I was now the obstacle. I got back in and let out the clutch, cursing.

Just in time to see another car come out of the Hôtel Cabuchon's underground car park.

A red sports car, the top down. Behind its wheel were the unlovely and unmistakable features of Philippe Berolet.

*

An hour later, as I looked round, I couldn't help but think of Nathalie and the *fest-noz.*

The discotheque was a tin barn that wouldn't have been out of place on an industrial estate, its interior a factory that produced nothing except heat and vibration.

Its only cool was on the dance floor. The beer was warm, the walls ran with condensation, the lights flashed, and the music was chain-saw loud—screaming melody lines that barely distinguished between song, synthesiser and saxophone, underpinned by a sledgehammer bass and the moronic tin-tray bash of an electronic snare drum. There must have been nigh on five hundred people dancing, ninety per cent of them teenage and female, smacked together into one sweating, amorphous mass by the unforgiving beat. The idea of one-to-one intimacy only existed in dark recesses away from the dance floor, and even then, the music's tyranny was all—the verbal was impossible, so the tactile ruled. Secreted in my balcony corner, surrounded by a gallery of steamy fumblings, I watched Georges Berolet's son.

And there was no secret to what I was watching. A deeply solitary man was staring at sex, examining the disembodied mass of femaleness, its carefully designer-dishevelled clothes and hair, its sugar-coated sensuousness, its leggy, look-don't-touch perfection...

He was totally alone, as were each of his companions, a whole row of them, perched on a Bermuda Triangle of bar stools, lonely men sunk in personal seas of hopelessness. Not all of them were as middle-aged or as flabby as he was, but they all had that same furtive intensity of watching, as though the batteries of their fantasies could only be recharged by their own absolute stillness, by fanatical absorption of the female energy before them. Occasionally a pair of eyes would break ranks, follow some mini-skirted icon as she walked past, or fix on some narcissistic display of litheness on the dance floor, but the only woman any of them actually spoke to was the barmaid.

Sad? As I watched Philippe's Pernod-sipping, slack-jowled watching, I wondered how much this meant to him. The drive here had been twenty kilometres of urgency, of boy racer impatience. For this? How long would he stay? And was there some deeper purpose to this, something to do with the chauffeur? Without warning the thought came.

He'd give anything to be the chauffeur, the stud...

But was there a connection between them? Or had Philippe's presence at the Hôtel Cabuchon been innocent, a coincidence? Had I pursued him here for nothing? As if in answer he finished his drink and stood up.

I waited till I was sure he had left, then followed. Out in the car park, he sat in the red sports car with the door open, dialling on a mobile phone. A contact? With the mysterious Mister Smith? After a brief exchange, he started the engine. Again, I followed.

We stuck with the main road for a while, then moved off it into lanes that wound gently up through the surrounding hills, until we reached a lay-by on a bend. He stopped so abruptly that I had no choice but to pass him. Luckily there was a farm entrance not far beyond. I turned into it, switched off the ignition, then walked up to the main road and crossed it. I went on, up into the long grass of the field opposite, unworried about disturbing him, for his stereo was playing full blast, a muted version of the disco music we'd left behind; so much for the classics... There was an outcrop of rock above where he'd parked, and that was what I was aiming for. I reached it without hindrance and lay down on my stomach on the cool grass.

I was almost on top of him. The car's hood was down, and he was lying back on the reclined driver's seat, smoking, his free hand tapping out the rhythm of the music on the steering wheel. What was this?

The sound of another car came, up the road we'd just travelled—fast, the driver gunning it round the corners. Philippe's head turned at the noise, but he didn't move. The second car came round the last bend and pulled in behind him with a screech of tyres. A different stereo's disco sounds merged with his into an unholy confusion. What was going on here? I heard doors slam, and footsteps, and then the lights were doused, and all the music died. I could see and hear. A short bald man was standing beside Philippe's car.

They argued. About money. I couldn't hear the mutter of details, but finally agreement was reached. The short man made a come-hither movement with his hand. The passenger door of the second car opened.

The fact of what I was watching was obvious the minute I saw her. Fur coat, high heels. As she got into the car beside Philippe and opened the coat, displaying her nakedness, the bald man leaned against the car's rear bumper, counting banknotes. I saw the greedy grab of Philippe's hand for her thigh, heard her cry of protest at his manners as I rolled over on to my back. The thought came too fast to suppress.

In the morning I would meet his father.

As if moved by modesty, the moon disappeared behind the clouds. I lay, staring up at the sky, hearing it all—his grunts of exhortation, the sucking sounds, the tortured bleat of his orgasm, the faint noise of her fastidious spit. Then heels, slamming doors, the bland passionless thump of the disco music, and the sound of engines. Within seconds, both cars were gone.

And I thought I'd been following my fiddle.

The moon came out again. I lay on my back and stared up at it, wondering why it had ever brought me to Brittany.

8

PROVEN

"IT IS A PROVEN Stradivarius! And it even has a name—The Singer! Built in seventeen twenty-three, between the Rode and the Sarasate!"

The words came tumbling out of Georges Berolet as soon as he'd opened his shop door. Sighing with a detective's satisfaction, he turned and led the way into the violin room. I put the Strad down on a shelf beneath the banked rows of her sisters. He walked across and opened its case, contemplated the Sunday morning sun's shine on the rich brown wood.

"*Oui,* The Singer," he repeated. "Why it should be so called, *mon ami,* I do not know."

But I did—I remembered the voice, child-like and pure, that I'd pulled from her on the street in Vannes. Before I could tell him about it, however, he'd gone to the pile of open reference books on his desk. He smacked the top one with the back of his hand.

"One of the last examples in private hands. No individual or institution has had access to it, and thus it has not featured in any of the more lavish catalogues, but there is speculation in the standard works that it may be one of his finest."

"So how did you trace it?"

"Ah," he said. His brows furrowed. "Simple, and yet not so simple..."

He launched into the explanation. Friends of his in England had tracked down the violin's records. In 1948 a Sir Peter Holcroft had taken the instrument to W. E. Hill's, the London Stradivarius experts, for valuation, but although it had been priced at twelve thousand pounds, there was no record of any subsequent sale. The next area of research had been the insurance companies, and sure enough, that had resulted in an address and telephone number. As soon as it had been relayed back to him, Georges had phoned.

"And that, *mon ami,*" he said, "is where the confusion begins." He settled back in his chair. "I dialled the number, the phone was picked up, I stated my business to an English lady. She seemed a little agitated by what I had to say, but finally an elderly gentleman came on the line. He was Sir Peter Holcroft, he said, and yes, the violin was his—but there had been no theft! He was adamant! When I ventured to suggest that I had seen the instrument, here, in Rennes, he asked if I would be kind enough to mind my own damn French business. I think those were the exact words," he finished, dryly. The look he gave me was amused. "Bizarre, *n'est-ce-pas?* Neither Philippe nor I could make anything of it."

"But why—"

His hand came up to ward off the interruption. "Then, as though all of this was not curious enough, an hour later I received a phone call in my turn—from a woman. Very English, very well-spoken. She was Lady Holcroft, she said, and there had been a misunderstanding. She wished to apologise for her husband's rudeness, but he had not known the facts of the matter. She was not phoning from England, she was here, in Brittany—and the violin had been lost here. Her son, a boy of ten, who is not entirely sound of mind, had given it—*Pardon,* Alexander, the phrase is hers, not mine—to a vagrant, and she had been trying to trace this 'vagrant' ever since."

Finally I had to ask. "And there was no mention of my own violin being found in the boy's case?"

"None, I am afraid," he said gravely, "and I regret to say that my own researches have been equally fruitless. Your luck has been better?"

I kept my face immobile. What to tell him...? Not about Philippe, or the night before's excesses, that was certain—but about the chauffeur, the business in the garage? I almost did—and then I saw the newspaper on the edge of the desk, one of the side columns was titled *Hotel Shooting, Police Investigate.* No, I thought, it would be unfair to involve him—he was a businessman with a name to protect.

"No," I said simply. My eyes came back to the violin in the case by the wall. "And why was the Stradivarius here in Brittany?"

"Exactly the question I put to her," Georges replied. "She is here for a family holiday, it seems. The child has been allowed to play this violin for some years, she told me, he is emotionally attached to it. And therefore, despite its worth, he was allowed to bring it with him. *Fantastique,* eh?"

A Stradivarius violin, brought on holiday like a beach toy...

"But fantastic or not, it fits the facts, does it not?" he finished, quietly.

With omissions, I thought. Again I looked at the paper on the desk—no mention of tattooed chauffeurs, or brass knuckles, or guns. And why did the violin's certification have to travel with it? Surely that was a double bonus to any thief...

"How much of this do you believe?" I asked him.

He grunted, went across to the case, and lifted the fiddle. "A nick in the tailpiece, a longish scratch across the left shoulder, a discolouration of the purfling just beside the fingerboard. She has described all of this to me—she knows the violin, and not merely from its description in the certificate, that much is clear; some of this damage is more recent. So that much I believe, that she is familiar with The Singer. But the rest of this rather strange song..."

His hand came up flat, palm down, and shook gently from side to side in the classic gesture of equivocation.

"The first thing I did, Alexander, was to ascertain with the house in England that there really is a *Milady* Holcroft, and that she really is here in Brittany. After some difficulty—for it really seems a most confused household—both points were confirmed by the lady I spoke to first. And then I checked—discreetly, I assure you—with the police of both France and England. No Stradivarius violin has been reported stolen. So it may all be true, stranger things have happened. But that is not the end of the story." He sat down again behind the desk. "When Lady Holcroft rang again I felt obliged to tell her that the violin was not in my hands, but in yours, and that you were her so-called 'vagrant'. Her response was an offer. To you. She is still here in Brittany, on the island of Belle-île, and she wants the violin returned. If you will deliver it to her there, today, then she will show you identification and take the Stradivarius violin known as The Singer back from you. For this service, she is willing to pay you the sum of ten thousand francs." He paused. "If you will not co-operate with her, however, she will inform the police. The violin was not the boy's to give away, and technically, its non-return could be made into a charge of theft."

I stared at him. Finally I said, "What would you do?"

He went across to the open case. As he looked down at the violin, he spoke.

"Never before have I had a Stradivarius in this shop," he mused.

He gazed down at the instrument. It was the first time I had seen longing in his eyes. And then it died. He turned, abruptly.

"What did you think of her, The Singer? Did you like her?"

I gave a regretful smile. "No," I said, "but I learned from her."

"Then your time together was not wasted, that is good."

He ran a light finger across the strings. The open fifths made a winsome sound, inconclusive—but it seemed to bring him to a decision.

"You have discharged your obligation of conscience to this instrument, Alexander. I would not like to see you once more involved with the police."

The genuine affection in his voice touched me. With the strings still ringing, he shut the case and drew the watch from his waistcoat pocket.

"If you leave now," he said, "you can be on Belle-île by mid-afternoon," he said. "I will phone this woman, arrange for her to meet each of the afternoon boats until you arrive. And if she seems to be—what do you say in English—'above board', then I suggest you take her money."

"You've done more to earn this money than I have," I said, quietly.

"Non." It was said with simple force, but then he laughed. "Look around you, Alexander. My business thrives, I have all the money I need. Allow an old man the vanity of thinking himself, in a small way, your patron. The violin is the instrument I love above all others, and you are a fine player of it."

The sincerity of the compliment silenced me. He went back to the case and fastened the locks. When I rose, he handed it to me.

"Ten thousand francs is small enough recompense for your trouble," he said, as we walked out into the hallway. "And as for your own violin, when we find it—"

Before we reached the main door, it opened.

Philippe—red-eyed and unshaven, too hung-over for even the pretence of pomposity. Briefly, his shaking hands struggled to disengage the key from the lock, and then he saw us—and the sight of his father and me together startled him into an unguarded look. I saw fear, then jealousy—and then the eyebrows came down like vultures over the tired battlefield of his face, picking it clean of all emotion but resentment.

How must it be, I thought, to love a father you know you can never live up to… The anxiety it must bring...

For there was no doubt that he saw me as a rival for Georges' affections—the brief look of anguish had told me. But what did his father think of him? Did he know what kind of man his son was? Georges' voice broke in, soothing, pacifying.

"When we find your own violin, Alexander, Philippe will restore it. Philippe is a fine restorer."

A father calming an infant's fears; look, I love you, I know your worth, really, I do... As Philippe's face twisted into a smile of childish triumph, I realised that Georges Berolet knew exactly what his son was.

"A fine restorer," he repeated, gently. He turned to me. "Goodbye, Alexander, and good luck."

I mumbled a farewell, then pushed my way past the sour breath, wondering if Philippe would ever begin the most important restoration job of all.

On himself.

*

The phone box at the *autoroute* services was like a furnace. I decided to give the number I'd found in the chauffeur's room one last try. I dialled.

A brief silence, then—unobtainable.

Sweating, I put down the receiver and pushed my way out. Ten times I'd tried now, ten different regions—on balance, I decided, that made it unlikely that the number was French. But I knew now that he was Scottish, Mr. Smith. A British number?

Worth a try, I decided. I went back into the sweltering heat. Big cities first. I dialled the British Isles code, then 171 for Inner London.

Once again, number unobtainable—and I got the same for Outer London, Birmingham, Manchester, Newcastle and Glasgow. But Edinburgh's 131 prefix brought success, the familiar double tone of an old-fashioned British telephone. After half a dozen rings it was picked up. A female voice answered.

"Hello?"

Breathless, slightly cross. In the background I could hear piano music. I went into the spiel I'd prepared.

"Good afternoon. Sorry to disturb you, my name's Scott, George Scott. I'm telephoning from France. I was in a café this morning, and the gentleman at the next table dropped his wallet. Big chap, good-looking, tattoo on his arm, Col-something-or-other and a mermaid. This number was in it, and rather a lot of money, but I'm afraid there was no other information. If you could give me his name and address I'd be happy to send it on."

No answer came. The piano music was slow, measured, accompanied by a low rumbling sound.

"Hello," I said, "are you still—"

The receiver at the other end went down.

Puzzled, the fiddle case handle sweaty in my hand, I came back out into the sun's full glare, trying to concentrate—that music, I knew it... My only answer was the rumble of the passing lorries. Only when I reached the car again did it come to me.

Orange And Blue. A strathspey, one of the first I'd ever learned...

What did it signify?

9

RICH

LE PALAIS, PRINCIPAL town of the island of Belle-île, shimmered in the early afternoon heat. As I surveyed it, a yellow beach ball bounced off the violin case. Involuntarily, I flinched. The little girl who was the culprit stopped, gave me a cheery *"Pardon, M'sieu"*, then ran off in pursuit of her ball. As she caught it, I saw the legend inscribed on the sphere's hot plastic.

Belle-île, Paradis des Vacances.

I forced my mind away from the problem of the phone call and settled back in my seat on the terrace of the Hôtel de la Frégate.

A holiday, Elly's original plan...

Under the circumstances it was ironic. I had the requisite access to sun and sea, and the massive fort across the harbour mouth, beached on the water's edge like a giant stone starfish, gave the tourist vista the necessary qualification of quaintness. I watched the barefoot black photographer who was working the quayside stop a young couple and persuade them they needed a souvenir. A grave ceremony; he arranged the girl's prettiness into a deferential pose that was calculated to flatter her boyfriend, stood back, and—click! A smiling memento of one of nineteenth-century France's most feared prisons.

The brutal as backdrop to the beautiful, the dungeon tamed by the tourist... Was it better that way? As the three of them clustered round the camera, waiting for the Polaroid to develop, I turned back to the scene before me.

A holiday...

The Acadie, the ferry which had brought me here, was about to leave again for its mainland destination, the town of Quiberon on the Breton peninsula's south coast, where I'd left the car. The deck was bright with its human cargo, chattering about seasick pills, clean beaches, where to get the cheapest *steack frites*—the quick, inconsequential friendliness of casual acquaintance. As I listened to it I wondered—could I ever see myself doing that? Could my days be arranged as neatly as those of the people before me, these supplicants at the altar of summer, dressed in its ritual robes of pale pastel and polished tan? I examined them—the cool, the sweaty, the complacent, the disgruntled... Video-cameraed and sun-lotioned, their babies over-tired, their teenage daughters underdressed and their purses empty, they seemed to have claimed no special happiness as compensation. As the boat pulled away, they cast their watchful eyes over the quayside's doubtful elements. The barefoot negro with the cheap camera was the first—but when one coal-black arm came up in a cheery wave, he became acceptable.

That left only me. They turned, examined me frankly, openly curious, doubtful, waiting for an explanation of my part in their landscape.

No, I knew it; no holiday, not ever. I would always be a traveller, yes—but I'd never pass for a tourist. On this quayside I was as conspicuous as a fish in a tree.

A loudspeaker van came round the corner, noisily announcing a *fest-noz* that night, up in the ramparts above the town wall. At ten pm, three bands would play Breton music, entry forty francs. As I listened to the loudspeaker's crackle, the waiter brought my bill. And as if to place the subject even more firmly on my mental agenda, an old woman passed, carefully counting the bundle of notes in her hand.

Money...

I watched the boat's white wake dissipate into the harbour's blue waters and thought about it—or rather, I thought about ten thousand francs.

About a thousand pounds... It was a fortune to me—but it was also a sum of money that meant something, a sum that was within my understanding as well as my reach. A quarter of a million, what was that? I found myself smiling—a quarter of a million was just a weight that made you uneasy when coins were flung at it, or when a beach ball came too near. I felt the violin case with my foot—even though the thought of The Singer's value had only been with me sporadically, I knew I'd be relieved to be rid of the responsibility.

But where was she, this Lady Holcroft? Georges had said he'd telephone, that she would meet my boat, that she'd know me by the fiddle case. I looked at my watch—half-past three now, how much longer?

"Mister Fraser?"

I looked up. A girl was standing at the terrace's edge. She wore a dark green blouse and a long white skirt, and her red hair was tied back in a thick pony tail. She was holding the upright handlebars of an old-fashioned black ladies' bicycle.

"You're from Lady Holcroft?" I asked.

She parked the bicycle against the terrace's edge, a cool smile playing about the edges of her mouth.

"I am Sylvia Holcroft," she said.

Not possible, that was my first reaction. Georges had talked of the husband as an elderly man... But as she came forward through the tables, I saw that she was older than I'd first thought—much older. As she folded the crisp cotton skirt beneath her legs, I guessed; late thirties—the crows' feet at the corners of the eyes gave it away. But she was a woman who had preserved her looks with startling efficiency, there was no doubt of that. She sat, put her handbag on the table, then pulled at the ribbon which held back the hair. A mass of curls came tumbling down. The blouse had been chosen to match her green eyes, I realised. I watched them quarter me efficiently, taking in my worn jeans and denim shirt.

"You'll forgive me if we get straight down to business," she said, gesturing at the case between my feet. "This is my son's violin?"

The accent was upper-crust English. I nodded. She opened the bag's flap and handed me a passport. I flipped through the pages. Unless it was a very good forgery, she was who she claimed to be—Lady Sylvia Holcroft, born 6.9.60, married. Thirty-seven, the same age as Elly... The picture fitted. Her occupation was given as 'housewife', and the document had been issued less than a month ago. Without being asked, the waiter came with two coffees. As soon as he was gone, she launched into what was obviously a rehearsed speech.

"Well, Mister Fraser, first of all, let me apologise for the trouble to which you've been put. And for my own stupidity. If my son Nicholas hadn't been allowed to walk around without so much as a by-your-leave with that horrendously expensive piece of wood under his arm, then none of this would have happened. You're probably wondering how a twelve-year-old comes to have a Stradivarius violin in the first place."

"The question had occurred to me," I said.

She settled back in her chair. "It's been in my husband's family for years, and when Nick showed an interest..." She looked at me. "Frankly, Mister Fraser, there's not much fun in my son's life. He's a little, well, 'simple', I believe that's the best term—learning-impaired if you want to euphemise." It was said in a carefully inflectionless voice. "When he wanted to learn to play, my husband gave him the Strad and told him it was his. It was a way of saying, well..." She shrugged. "...that Nick's happiness is more important than money. Can you understand that?"

My husband, not *Nick's father...* Still, I didn't want to pry—and the impulse was only to be applauded. I nodded. I believed it—but there were still a lot of unanswered questions.

"Is your son here on the island?" I asked. "Can I talk to him? About my own violin?"

The red curls shook. "I'm afraid not. The emotional upset of all this..." She shrugged, unhappily. "I simply had to send Nick home. I'm sorry. And anyway, I already told your *Monsieur* Berolet that there was no other violin."

"I must speak to your son—it's vital."

I tried to keep the sharpness from my voice and failed. It irritated her. When she spoke again, the quality accent had retreated into haughtiness.

"I really don't think this is getting us anywhere. I repeat—when my son Nicholas was brought back to the hotel in Rennes, there was no violin at all in his case. Is that clear enough for you?"

"Which hotel would that be? The Hôtel Cabuchon?"

"I don't remember the name," she said, too quickly.

There was silence.

"Lady Holcroft," I said, quietly. 'Let me make one thing clear in my turn. This violin of your son's—I have not the slightest interest in keeping it from him. But, whatever your threats, I won't return it to you without information about my own violin in exchange. And lies," I added, "will not help. Now did you stay at the Hôtel Cabuchon in Rennes or not?"

She said nothing.

"And do you know a certain man, a Scot with tattooed arms who signs himself on hotel registers as Mr. Smith?"

The mouth pursed. I could see the go-to-hell outburst rise in the green eyes—and then it was deflected from me. She was looking over my shoulder.

"No!" she shouted.

I turned. The black photographer was grinning, apologetically. He spoke in Caribbean-accented English.

"But Missy, you so pretty, you make a lovely couple! Only forty francs, lovely—"

"Don't you dare!"

The icy authority stopped him in mid-pitch. He raised a placatory hand as he shuffled away, backwards.

"Okay, okay, no problem, keep your cool, Missy."

She stared down at the untouched coffee, brows furrowed as though concentration alone could restore her calm. When her eyes met mine again, the anger was gone.

"I'm sorry, I'm not at my most approachable." She paused. "Perhaps it's best if you know all of it," she went on. "You're looking at a very stupid woman, Mister Fraser. A middle-aged woman who's done just about the most predictable and boring thing any middle-aged woman can do."

She looked away, across the blue expanse of the sea, gathering herself. When she spoke again her voice was abrupt, factual.

"My husband is in his seventies. Anything physical between us stopped years ago. The man you are referring to, the Scot with the tattoos, is—or rather was, oh, yes, very definitely *was*—" Her self-control broke with a bitter laugh. "—our chauffeur. He is twenty-five years old, his name is John McPhie." She stopped, forced herself to go on. "And he is very attractive to women."

The last of the patrician facade crumbled. She began to twist at the wedding ring on her finger.

"I'm sure I don't have to spell the rest out for you," she said, miserably.

So. The chauffeur, the man with the unfailing sexual magnetism... I was looking at another one of his...

His what, I wondered—what could you call this woman? A partner? A conquest? A victim?

"Good, isn't it," she went on. The approaching tears pushed her into a vicious parody of herself. "Screwing the chauffeur. Typical bit of Sloane Ranger slumming. Top peoples' double-think; one doesn't, but of course, one does—everyone does. And one deserves everything one damn well gets as a result, doesn't one?" She delved into the bag again, brought out a handkerchief. "Anyway, that's why we came here to Brittany. Nicholas, I'm ashamed to say, was mostly camouflage to convince my husband that it was a genuine holiday."

The misery in her voice deepened. The tears were open, now. She wiped them away, roughly.

"But you see, Mister Fraser, I've been doubly stupid. Doubly screwed, you might say. Because the minute Nick, poor simple Nick, gave away his violin, Mister McPhie was off like a shot from a bloody gun." She turned to me. "The sex was just camouflage, all of it, I see that now—keep the silly bitch with her legs in the air and she'll never notice what's really going on, will she? And I didn't. It was the violin he was after—he just used me to get it away from the house. When the right time came, Mister oh-so-bloody-handsome McPhie would have ditched me and taken the Strad. So Nick, my poor daft Nick, was really the only one who did anything sensible."

Again she wiped away the tears, then gave me a wan smile. "Thank you for looking after my son's violin, Mister Fraser. He said you were a nice man. That's why he gave it to you. He's very kind-hearted, you see. If he likes someone he gives them the thing he loves most—only usually they're around to give it back to him when he misses it."

I felt embarrassed for her. Her age showed now, openly. When she saw my scrutiny, she began to recover herself, camouflage it all with business. Again, the accent recovered its haughtiness, but this time it was friendly.

"Look, I thought we'd better do all this formally, so I've got hold of an English lawyer here, a chap who lives on the other side of the island. He's drawing up a proper deed for us both to sign—a receipt, just to keep the whole thing absolutely legal—but he can't make it till late this evening. My house is on the main street, at the top of the hill just before the Porte Vauban, number 42. If you were to come there at, shall we say, eleven-thirty? We can do all of the business there." There was a rush of words as her nerves broke again. "I'm so sorry that all this has happened—and for threatening you as well, the police and all that, but I couldn't really know what kind of man you were, no matter what Nick said. Anyway, I've got the money in cash for you—is that all right? I mean, cash would be better, I thought, perhaps you wouldn't have chequebooks and things, accounts..."

The breathless recital died under the weight of its own confusion.

"There's no problem, Lady Holcroft," I said. "Cash will be fine."

She stood up, obviously relieved that it was all over. A fifty franc note came from the handbag.

"For the coffees."

"That's not necessary—" I began.

"Oh, I insist," she said. She reached out a hand to me. "Goodbye then. Until this evening."

We parted on a formal handshake, and then she hurried back to the bike. She tied the hair back in its ribbon, then perched herself on the saddle, smiled at me, and pedalled away. As she moved off down the quayside, I saw male heads turn. No wonder, I thought, a beauty. I watched until she was out of sight, then lifted the violin case onto the table and opened it. The Singer's fine top shone in the sunlight. Time to part, I thought. Was I sorry? Was I—

A polaroid photograph came down beside my coffee cup. The images were still forming; the two of us, talking. Her red hair seemed to take up most of the picture. I turned to find the black face grinning a gap-toothed conspirator's grin.

"I figure, what the hell, man, I take it anyway!" He winked at me. "An' now you wan', yes? Girl like that leave a man, he gonna wan' a souvenir, sometin' to help keep him warm at night, no?"

When I didn't speak, his face became aggrieved. The Caribbean accent deepened.

"Hey, man, whassa matter with you? You loaded, you got to be—thassa rich man's woman!" His finger stabbed at the print. "Only forty francs, a lousy forty! You a rich man!"

Before I could react, he'd snatched the fifty franc note she'd left on the table. He waved it at me.

"You rich!" he repeated, accusingly.

He loped off down the quayside, still brandishing the note, scowling over his shoulder at me, fearful of pursuit.

But I made no attempt to stop him. After all, he was right. I tucked the photo away in the case's ripped lining.

About a thousand pounds...

10

CHAMELEON

I ATE IN A CAFE that was too shabby to charge tourist prices, then spent hours trying to find a room. Everywhere the answer was the same—high season, *M'sieu,* try two doors down—and by the time I succeeded, in the maze of streets behind the harbour, it was already late evening. I showered and laid myself down on the lumpy bed, determined to catch at least an hour's sleep, but it was impossible—too much had happened. I simply lay there, smelling the garlic cooking smells of the household below, too restless to rest and too tired to think.

It was the faint sound of rhythmic music, coming in through the open window beside me, which brought me back to life. I listened; Breton music, but with an electric backing this time—as well as bombarde and biniou I could hear bass and drums. A tape, a record? A single instrument, an accordion, began a melody line that quickly drowned in a distinctive high whine. Feedback—that meant amplification, live music. I remembered the loudspeaker van, the *fest-noz*—yes, that would be it, up in the ramparts beyond the old town wall. Electric Breton music... I found myself smiling in the room's warm darkness.

Nathalie...

No doubt she would use that fact to try and convince me that Breton culture wasn't at all at odds with the twentieth century. I stared at the PSB lapel badge she had given me, still on the shirt that hung over the chair. The sight sombred my mood.

Her father... Had she forgiven me yet for knowing? It came to me that I had thought about her a lot in the last few days...

And then the sister to that thought came, very quickly—I'd almost never thought of Elly. Had something changed in the twelve days since Rennes? Was it just because of all the other business, the fiddles? Briefly, I resisted, until the music's never-ending question-and-answer line forced me into a response. No, it wasn't just because of the fiddles. Now was the wrong time to think about it, though...

But it was the right time to think about something else. I looked at my watch, then began to dress. The Stradivarius case felt cool as I lifted it. It was time to earn a thousand pounds.

*

Number 42 didn't prove easy to find, for the street's doors were unnumbered. I guessed. My first knock went unanswered, the second brought me an old woman with a dripping wooden spoon. I asked. She shared a suspicious scowl between my face and the fiddle case, then grunted a grudging reply. Last house, *M'sieu*, other side. As the door slammed I heard the beginnings of a grumble about *les Anglais.*

My destination proved to be a substantial-looking villa only a few steps from the Porte Vauban, the tunnel that pierced the sixty-foot thick town wall. As I knocked, I realised that the fest-noz was very near, just on the other side of the ramparts. Footsteps came. The door opened to reveal a tall man in evening dress, with an undone black bow tie.

"Fraser, right?" he said, in English.

He waved me in. The noise of the music followed us down a dark corridor.

The room we came into was large. Once, its spacious airiness must have been attractive, solid and bourgeois, but now it had been forever compromised by neglect. Blooms of damp flowered on the plaster of the walls, the paintwork was peeling, and much of the ceiling's fine cornicing had fallen away. Its furniture consisted of a dresser, two armchairs, a threadbare sofa, and a chipped coffee table. A decanter and glasses stood on it, their cut-glass opulence the only thing I could see which would have fitted the room's original character. An archway off to one side led to an equally bleak kitchen, and through the dilapidated French windows I could see a large garden run to seed. I tried to conceal my surprise—she lived here, in this? Even temporarily? I turned my attention to my companion.

He was painfully thin, with an unruly shock of wavy brown hair that was in sharp contrast to the lined and drawn face beneath it. It had been a healthy face, once, an outdoor face—a cragsman's or a hill-walker's—but now the impression it gave was of sadness, of vitality which had somehow ebbed away. The clothes were brand new, and he didn't look comfortable in them—they seemed too confident for his faintly invalid air. As I listened to the sounds of the *fest-noz* coming through the open windows, the idea came to me that I knew him, but I couldn't think why.

"Drink," he said.

It wasn't a question, and as he walked to the coffee table I saw that he'd already left sobriety well behind. Without waiting for a reply he poured two glasses from the decanter.

"I'm Michael Knight, by the way," he said. The voice was carefully unslurred. "I live here. On the island." he added quickly, as though the added phrase was important.

"You're the lawyer, Mister Knight?" I asked.

He nodded and handed me a tumbler half-full of neat whisky. His own glass held the same, but not for long. I watched him down most of it in one gulp—and saw that he was nervous as well as drunk. His fragility made me feel uncomfortable, as though I was the host here, the person who should be putting him at his ease. He gave me the opening.

"So, you're from Scotland, eh?"

"Yes," I said, "and yourself?"

"English," he barked nervously. "Cornish, actually. Haven't been back for years, though... Got a job over here, too good to pass up."

Once again, the second half of the statement was an addition, a forgotten part of something learned by rote.

"What part of Cornwall?" I asked, more to keep the conversation going than anything else—my curiosity was hovering on the line of wariness, now.

"A village..." he faltered, refilling his glass. "A village called Ottery St. Thomas. You wouldn't know it. Lovely place, specially this time of year. Ottery St. Thomas," he repeated. Without warning, his voice filled with emotion. "Some day I'll go back, I'll damn well go back."

Odder than ever... He pointed at the violin case.

"What kind of music do you play?"

"Scottish traditional music."

"Ah..." The word was a long sigh. His face became calm, with sadness, regret. "I never tried that."

"You play the violin?" I asked, surprised.

His nervousness returned in full measure. "Used to," he said, brusquely.

Curiouser and curiouser... I drank to hide my confusion. Lawyers as a breed were pretty foreign to me, but he seemed an unlikely one. Where was the deed I was supposed to sign? And where was the woman? Before I could speak, he said,

"First things first. Before Sylvia gets here, we might as well take care of all this business."

He pulled a pile of notes from the dinner jacket's inside pocket and handed it to me—thousand franc notes, old ones. I made to put them away in my shirt pocket, but he quickly intervened.

"Oh, count it, please."

"There's no need," I said, "I'll take it on trust."

"Lady Holcroft was most insistent—" He had trouble with the word. "—that you should count it. And if I could see the violin?"

I hesitated. He was drunk, I didn't trust the thing in his hands. I settled for a compromise, walked over to the sofa, put the case down, and lifted it out of its velvet bag. He stared at it, then turned away and took another pull at his whisky.

"Count the money, please," he said.

It was as though he feared the consequences if I refused. I riffed through the sheaf, trying to conceal my puzzlement. Ten one thousand franc notes... As I tucked the wad away in my shirt pocket I heard the front door close. The noise made him almost physically jump. His drink spilled.

"Hello, Mister Fraser."

I turned. Sylvia Holcroft? It couldn't be...

The red hair which had been so appealingly unruly in the afternoon was now sculpted across one bare shoulder in a shining wave so lustrous it could have been ceramic. The earrings were diamond, the dress was the classic little black one, satin and strapless, with a tight bodice that pushed the swell of her breasts into a deep vale of cleavage. Its hemline barely reached the pale curve of bare thigh. The heels were high, the evening gloves elbow-length, and the pose, one arm leaning on the door jamb, unmistakably brazen. She paused long enough to make sure the effect wasn't lost on me, then turned to Knight.

"You've done it, then?"

I caught the expression of hurt before he nodded and turned away. His back to me, he gestured at the open case and reached again for the whisky. She walked across to the violin—and smiled. The silence became heavy with the intensity of her pleasure. It was Knight who dared to break it.

"Sylvia, perhaps it's better if I go now—" he began.

It sounded like a plea.

"No," she said brusquely.

His nervousness burst into peevish revolt. "Look, I've done everything you told me to. Why can't I just go?"

She ignored him. As she walked through the archway to the kitchen, she said, "Pour me a drink."

An order. His rebellion died at it—and as he turned his back on her for the decanter, something odd registered. Her accent, it had changed...

Suddenly, everything jarred—she wasn't right, neither was he. I moved towards the case, speaking as I went.

"Look, I'm not satisfied—"

The room seemed to explode. Knight's body jumped forward in a disjointed jerk, sprawling across the coffee table, his hands scrabbling for support. There wasn't even time for surprise. I gaped at the small ragged hole just below his shoulder blades. As the smell of the spilled whisky from the smashed decanter reached me, her voice came from the archway.

"Don't move."

The gun in the gloved hand was rock-steady. She came forward, the cordite reek joining the whisky smell. I stared at Knight, at the wet darkness spreading across the dinner jacket's back. He was hanging on the table's edge, still breathing, I could hear it—a harsh, tortured sound that made nonsense of the music from outside.

She walked quickly across and looked down at him, at his right hand, twitching through the mess of broken glass and whisky. And then, almost casually, she emptied another two shots into the centre of his back. Again his body jerked—and the hand's twitching stopped.

She straightened up, came across the room slowly, and planted herself in front of me, legs apart, the gun pointing at my stomach. I didn't dare move. A muscle on the inside of her thigh was trembling. She saw me look down at it. The silence roared, endlessly. And then I heard my own voice, fear-laden, repelled.

"What do you want from me?"

She stood there, rock-still—and then my words seemed to register. The glazed eyes came back into focus. She took a step back from me, gave a nervous snort of laughter. She turned to the corpse—and then, as though seeing its horror for the first time, her expression changed. Eyes open in fright, she took another step back. Her free hand came up to her mouth in a balled fist. She dropped the gun and ran again to the kitchen in a nervous skittering of heels.

My paralysis died. Two steps took me to the gun. I lifted it. She was crazy! She'd—

Once again, her voice came from the archway. "Fine, Mister Fraser, fine. How nice to have, for once, a leading man who knows how to take his cue."

I could still feel the heat of her hand on the butt of the gun I was holding—but I was staring at the blued steel barrel of another.

"I'm afraid to say the one you're holding is now empty," she said. The red mouth was wide open now, in a frank laugh, the green eyes sparkling with amusement. "But mine is very definitely loaded."

I pulled the trigger, heard the click—and understood the trick. I was holding a gun which had just killed a man. My prints were on it, hers were not; the gloves...

"The money, please. Take it out. Slowly."

I did it.

"Throw it down. Beside him."

Again, I complied. The notes fluttered down into the spilled whisky; a gun and money, both with my prints... I found my voice.

"Who are you?" I said.

"Who do you want me to be?" she replied. The voice changed, startlingly—to a broad Scottish accent. "A wee Saturday night scrubber, is that what ye'd like? Three Carlsbergs an' a quick one in the back seat?" She laughed, gestured at the corpse. "Or Mister Barrington's choice?"

The voice was London, now, Cockney. Her free hand indicated her own outfit.

"A nice, obvious tart? Mature gentleman like Mister Barrington always prefers a professional."

Barrington? The corpse's change of name registered with me as I watched the gloved hand come up to her chin in a gesture of mock regret. The accent moved itself up several social notches, to the Sylvia Holcroft I'd met that afternoon.

"Or a nice bit of too-too-feckless aristocratic tail, Mister Fraser? A lady who's made a terrible, terrible mistake. A lady—" She paused, gave a stage fluttering of the eyelashes. "—no nice boy could possibly refuse to help."

Again she laughed. The accent returned, savage now with contempt, to Scotland.

"My, my, though—the home-grown ones are always the best. You love it, don't you? Doffin' the cap. To your English betters."

The last two words were said with slow venom. The gun came up.

The dead man saved me—by finally sliding off the coffee table's corner. As the sound jerked the red helmet of hair round, I barged forward, flailing at her with the empty gun. *Out! Now!* I heard her fall as I stumbled through the french windows. Glass shattered behind me as she fired.

I ran—a stone path, slippery with moss. A trellis fence, a wall—I didn't even pause. As my hands caught the top I heard her voice, Scottish and shrill, shouting. I heaved myself up and over—and into a back lane. Where to? I heard running steps from the garden behind me. Not hers, too heavy... *Who?* No time to waste. Before me the town wall loomed. I sprinted up the lane towards it. Off to my left I could see the main road—and the black mouth of the Porte Vauban. Yes, out into the fields! As I reached the tunnel I saw that I'd almost completed a square. I could see the house's front door—and if there'd been the slightest question of who was following me, it was gone now. The black mass of the Rolls gleamed in the street lights.

The chauffeur... I plunged into the Porte Vauban, stumbling through the darkness. How far behind was he? A car, horn screeching, only just missed me.

I came out into artificial light. The *fest-noz* ground was on my right, fenced off, but the gate was unmanned. I ran through, made straight for the crowd surrounding the dancers. Only when

I was safely hidden among them did I turn and search the darkness from which I'd just come. Would he work out my logic? If he did—

A chill ran through me. He was already there, at the unmanned gate, his dark glasses scanning the ground. I kept my head low and walked away, along the line of food stalls, keeping the crowds between us as much as possible, searching my surroundings as I went. To my left, the stage. To my right, the town wall. In front of me, a wire mesh fence. I stopped.

I had trapped myself, bottled myself into a corner. With no exit.

I forced myself to act. In the darkness beside the stage I found a pile of clothing, no doubt discarded by the dancers. I stuck a nautical cap on my head, pulled a sweater round my shoulders. Where was he? My eyes found him, following my path, exactly. One hand was in his jacket's bulging pocket. He was armed, no doubt about that… A shot here...? I looked up at the stage—seven musicians, a huge sound system. If he fired, it would never be heard. What could I do? I looked over to the other side of the stage. Was there a back way out? Into the open countryside? I had to try.

I pushed through the crowd, parted two hands, and inserted myself into the chain of dancers. Had my pursuer noticed? The people on either side, a boy and a girl, laughed at my efforts and tried to show me the steps, but gave up when they saw I wasn't concentrating. *Where was he?* I faltered along, hoping for anonymity, searching—and found the glint of the glasses down in the corner where I'd stolen the hat and sweater. He was still on my tail. I'd reached the other side of the stage now. I let go of the hands and ran into the darkness. More mesh fence! It stretched as far as I could see in both directions. As I ran along it I felt the rise of panic.

I'd reached the area where the bands had parked their vans. The nearest was a large white Mercedes, its back doors lined with a neat row of anti-nuclear stickers. I turned, found the glint of the glasses, coming round the crowd's edge. No choice! I opened the van's back door. As I jumped up inside, an angry shout of protest came.

"Oy! What the hell d'you think you're playing at?"

In the dim light I made out a man and a girl on a mattress. His fist was bunching even as he rose. Fear lent me inspiration.

"Help me, please—the cops!"

The fist stopped in mid-swing. He examined me, then came to an instant decision.

"Quick!"

He thrust me over the half-naked, giggling girl, pushing empty drum cases out of the way, then pressed me down against the metal bulkhead that separated the back from the driver's compartment. A bundle of plastic guitar covers landed on my head. I burrowed down. The girl's laughter grew, and the man started to laugh as well, a deep throaty chuckle.

The van door flew open. Him, the chauffeur, it had to be! I heard my protector's roar.

"Bugger off, you bastard!"

After what seemed an age, the door slammed shut again. I lay, buried in the cases, heart thumping, listening to the girl's now uncontrollable laughter.

"Thank you," I said.

"It's nothing," my protector replied. "Any friend of Patrik Riou's..."

My brain flooded with confusion—and then I worked it out; the badge, the PSB badge Nathalie had pinned on my shirt, a week ago... He'd seen it, it had saved me. His voice came again through the girl's mirth.

"You need to be away from here, *mon ami?* Off the island?"

"Yes."

"Then stay where you are, we'll take care of it."

As I slumped back against the bulkhead, I heard the girl's laughter falter, become a desire-laden murmur. Almost immediately it was reciprocated by gruff male endearments. The van began to shake with the rhythm of their coupling—and I felt myself shiver in disgust.

I could still smell Sylvia Holcroft's perfume.

*

My protector was as good as his word. When the dancers had all gone I was brought out into the darkness. As I scanned the deserted field, there was a whispered conference between the musicians, and when the van was packed, they made me a bed inside, with their mattress on top of the speakers—disguised so that I couldn't be seen even if the back doors were open. There was enough air to breathe and enough comfort to sleep, if I'd had a mind to. I lay in the darkness, staring at the metal roof's condensation, trying to work it all out.

I had been set up, expertly—a gun covered with my fingerprints, a wad of money. The questions burned. Who was the man who had given me it, the man I was supposed to have murdered? This Mister Knight who became Mister Barrington in death...?

And who—God, who—was this monstrous chameleon of a woman?

I tried to follow the chain through—the boy to the chauffeur, the chauffeur to the woman, the woman to the man she had shot. It was like the dragon of the Breton dance—the faces kept moving, in rhythm, round each other. In this strange, tight, sense-deprivation tank the musicians had built for me, I reached a state that was neither sleep nor waking—fear and bewilderment had blurred the line between speculation and hallucination. How long I lay there, trying to think it through, I don't know.

But then I was aware of the vehicle shaking. Voices came, laughter and good-natured sleepy cursing—the band were in the van's cab. Was it morning? A voice I recognised as my friend's whispered to me.

"*Eh bien, mon ami,* you are all right?"

"Yes," I said.

"Good, make no sound for a while. There will be *flics* around the harbour"

We began to move. Our progress was easy to measure from the extent to which I was thrown about—the bumpy field, the road. And then downhill. When we stopped, I could hear water—the harbour? Were they after me, the cops? I heard a window wind down, a bad-tempered voice ask for a ticket. Again we moved, slowly—and I worked out what was happening; the van was being loaded onto the ferry. It seemed to last forever. But then I felt the vibration of a different engine, and knew the boat was moving. I was off Belle-île...

Safe?

Safer, anyway. I felt the tide of tension leave me. When real sleep came, I offered no resistance.

*

And when I woke, I was sure I was in hell. I was sweating, there was light filtering through the top of the van.

And noise, near. Noise that grew louder, rhythmic noise, its beat one-two-three, one-two-three, like some drunken version of the Breton dance. It got louder. I yelled out in fright.

"Where am I?"

Somewhere near I heard laughter. The rhythm intensified—and then it wasn't far away, it was all round me, being banged out on the sides of my metal prison. The van stopped. The back doors flew open. As hands pulled away the huge flight cases, I blinked against the unaccustomed light, and found the face of my bearded friend, grinning savagely.

"Well, my friend," he said, "there's a time to play music, and there's a time to fight."

The banging rhythm took on meaning. A chant—roared out by thousands of voices.

"No nu-clear, dum-ping here! No nu..."

I staggered out into the sunlight. I was on the brow of a high hill, overlooking the nuclear waste facility of Kergorff.

11

STRUGGLE

A RAT, A GIANT squat rat... A rat that could not be killed by poisons, only fattened by them. From my giddy vantage point up on the hill, the graphics I remembered from the handbill and the poster now made perfect sense.

I could see the site in its entirety. It was huge—a vast central brown body, rounded and rodent-like, gripping its territory with long claws of brightly-coloured chemical piping, its glazed sides gleaming like armour. It didn't seem connected to the clumps of metal chimneys behind it. Arrow-straight and arrogant, they pointed their lazy plumes of smoke high into the sky, unconcerned with the earth below. But why should they be, I wondered; what rat ever cared about its droppings?

But its food was a different matter—that, it had taken great pains to guarantee. The waste could come by road, winding down from the hill where I was now, or by sea—I could see the business end of a jetty, jutting out from the rocky shoreline beside the chimneys. And the site itself, the lair where the rat would hoard and feast—that had been chosen with cunning, with the foreknowledge that on some fine summer's day, balmy and calm like today, it would be hunted.

A headland, made impregnable on three sides by sea and cliff, and on the fourth, facing me, by a wall.

And such a wall—a modern Roman wall. On it I could see the ranks of the rat's legions, black-clad and impassive, a long, unmoving line of them. One man, no more than a tiny stick-figure to me on the hill, walked along them. Inspecting? Exhorting? I saw him turn, face the black legion's foes.

The rat's hunters, the tribe...

Bannered, flagged and placarded, a seething mass of humanity convinced of its cause, come to cleanse. How many thousands were there? Ten? Twenty, as Riou had said? They were still streaming past me down the slope.

I stood on the hillside, hearing their chanting, watching the helicopters hovering over them like dragonflies in the heat, listening to the voice in my brain.

Leave here, it said, *this is not your fight.*

But I ignored it. I stumbled down the hill towards the demonstrators.

I had nowhere else to go.

*

The crowd was a perpetual roar, a white-noise choir of conflicting chants that made hearing redundant.

But not seeing. Numb, detached, I watched it all as I moved.

At the rear they seemed a normal cross-section; more young than and old, certainly, and more hippy than housewife—but not so far removed from the holidaymakers I'd watched the day before on Belle-île. The placid, the perturbed, the petulant, they were all here, dealing with one another in the different ways that humanity does. There were kisses, laughter over a shared swig of wine, annoyance at the heat, even boredom. But the further into the press I got, the less diverse everything became. Individual emotion began to hide itself, as though it knew how badly fitted it was for what was to come—and by the time I neared the front ranks, beneath the towering shadow of the wall itself, every face in the spectrum had merged into a frightening solidarity, an intensity that was anger, stubbornness and conviction rolled into one. A final push took me through into open space and clear sight of what they had come to challenge.

The legions, the riot police, up on their wall... I looked up at them.

Each man had two faces. One, pale and void of expression, was all but hidden beneath the plastic helmet visors—but it was at least still human, this face, still recognisably kin to those of the tribe it looked down upon. It was the second face which struck a chord of fear.

For it was the real face of brutality, the faceless face. Rubber-skinned, black-goggled and snout-nosed, it hung heavily from every shiny black belt, a flaccid personality waiting snugly behind baton and riot shield to be donned at the first sign of trouble, the first high arc of molotov or tear-gas canister. Sombre and saddened, I walked along the wall beneath the grim rows of gas masks. There could be no question of what was to come.

The nearest thing I had to a purpose was to find Nathalie. Instead, I found Prosper.

He was standing on the road, at the site's main entrance, so still he might have been cast from the same thick steel as the massive gates. Despite the heat he wore his leather jacket and black beret. When he saw me, nothing at all showed in his eyes, not the slightest hint of surprise, neither pleasure nor its opposite. He simply gestured at the concrete wall.

"Look at it," he said. "Five metres high, ergonomic design. Everything rounded—no protrusions, not a single place you could get a hand or a rope to grip. Slopes inward from the bottom so that you're never hidden from the top's field of fire, then juts out so you can't keep your balance to climb it. Rampart along the top to walk along or disappear behind when things get rough."

The tone was respectful—a general saluting the good staff work of his enemy, a professional assessing and admiring the work of his peers. It could have been a sales pitch for the company which had erected it—until he went on.

"No point in attacking it, none whatsoever. So we wait, don't we. For them to attack us. All we need is the spark."

He sounded easy, happy. Confrontation as release, I could see it—the learned response of a life whose everyday currency was conspiracy, rolled away and secreted like the cigarettes in his tin. As though in confirmation, one of them appeared in his hand.

"Just the spark," he repeated.

And as if he had willed it, a sound came, the sound of heavy engines. Around us, the crowd's roar swelled to meet it, drown it. Prosper lit the cigarette, grinning, but he didn't turn. He didn't need to, I could see it—he knew what was happening, he'd been waiting for it. I looked up towards the hill that had been my vantage point.

Trucks, heavy ones, loaded with barrels. The first of the

waste trucks... I remembered Patrik's voice, back in the van outside Concarneau.

Every ship that dares to dock, every truck that tries to deliver, we shall fight it.

Prosper's grin—peaceful, free from tension—widened. He had his spark, he knew it—and as suddenly as it had begun, the roar around us died, leaving absolute silence. A waiting silence. I looked from Prosper's face to the crowd's.

Everything I had seen before, all the anger, the rightness, had been swept to a new intensity by the common thrill of fear. At one and the same time I heard Prosper's gentle laugh, his final satisfaction, and the sound of the heavy gates behind me opening.

I spun round, saw the uniforms, the shields, the batons.

And the gas masks. The faceless rubber faces had been donned. The battle for the road had begun.

*

Chaos.

Screams, whistles—the sudden gleam of sun on helmet, the raised club—

And then, like everyone else, I was running. *Away! Back! From the gas!*

But cohesion reasserted itself as soon as we stopped, for though we fled as a hundred separate units of fear, what we saw when we turned again made us once more into a single animal.

An orgy of brutality, clubbing and kicking—a vengeance wreaked upon the slow, the stumbled, and the sainted few who had been brave enough to stand their ground. Even through the sound of the screams and the helicopters above, the sickening thud of the batons could be heard. The anger surged round me in an electric wave. Prosper knew how to direct it.

"Stones!" he shouted.

They rained down on the riot shields. A ragged cheer went up as the captives were abandoned—but it was premature. There was no real retreat. The clubbing had been incidental. The real object of the riot troops—to establish a bridgehead in front of the metal gates—had been achieved. The shields settled into a solid line, separated from us by a stone-littered no-man's-land.

Immediately, it was challenged. Youths broke ranks to recover the fallen, to scoop up the tear-gas canisters and throw them back, or simply to taunt, running up to the line with that nervous sideways dancing skip that is the hallmark of every riot from Belfast to Beirut—until the bridgehead's usefulness was made clear.

The line of shields parted, the metal gates opened again. The water cannon's science-fiction snout came out—fast. It went up the road towards the waiting trucks, its powered jet skittling people off to either side like ninepins—and then it left the tarmac, zig-zagging at random across the ground before the wall. Its brief was obvious—to make panic. As it went about its business, the trucks began to move down the hill.

A whistle sounded. It triggered another charge, more determined, even more brutal; the dogs were off the leash. This time the faceless faces had been given liberty to identify individuals, to pursue, and to beat bloody. Again I ran, but more gas came from the top of the walls, and this time I wasn't fast enough. I went down, choking, gasping and crying all at once, surrounded by a light yellow-grey fog. When I could see again I found myself in a hellish son-et-lumière, a dumb-show of swinging club and soundless scream.

And then the gas cleared, and I saw him

The warrior chief himself, Patrik Riou.

He was standing with his back to the gates, directly in the first truck's path, the centre of a line of people whose arms were linked across the width of the roadway. Their space was being protected with desperate courage by a bunch of boys who had improvised their own armour and arms—motorcycle helmets, long staves and bars.

Unflinching, Riou's line waited—and when the huge vehicle was almost on them, all of them raised their arms. I saw the glint at Patrik's wrists and understood—they were showing the truck's crew that they were chained together. I heard the squeal of brakes, saw the driver's ashen face through the armoured mesh of his window. Patrik stayed alive by a hair's breadth.

As soon as the truck had been stopped, its immobilisation began. I saw Prosper, standing calmly beside it, one hand up in a gesture of command. A boy in a Palestinian-style headscarf came from nowhere, ran from wheel to wheel. I heard the shots, saw the vehicle's lurch—the tyres! The truck behind pulled out, trying to go round the trouble and reach the gates. Could it? If—

A yell of warning came from behind me, but too late. A gigantic blow caught me across the shoulders—the water cannon! I went forward, down, bowled over in a welter of limbs and spray. As I hit the ground I could hear nothing, but I knew I was shouting. I tasted grass, earth. Dazed and dripping, I struggled up again. I was at the road's edge, now. I saw the cannon's jet catch the Palestinian-scarved boy across the tarmac—and with the horror that came, everything stopped. I saw with the sharpness of a photograph.

The boy with the chequered scarf, stranded on his back like a crab on the tarmac.

The wheels of the still-moving second truck, heading inexorably towards him.

And across the road, within easy arms' reach, Prosper.

Standing.

Watching.

I yelled. "Pull him! Pull him clear!"

If he heard me, he gave no sign. The boy on the tarmac tried to roll over onto all fours and rise. Prosper reached out, grabbed his shoulder—and yanked him back down again, squarely into the truck's path. I heard the boy's scream and closed my eyes.

"Alex!"

I turned—Nathalie! By her face, I knew she'd seen exactly what I had. She was rooted to the spot in horror—so much so that she was oblivious to her own danger. I saw the gas mask of the policeman behind her, the baton's swing. I shouted something unintelligible as I dived for the black uniformed figure. The two of us went down, clawing, kicking, gouging. Somehow I wrenched the baton from him. With one hand I raised it, with the other I reached for the black mask, tearing at the rubber until it came away. Nathalie screamed.

"No, Alex! *NO!*"

And then I saw his face.

I scrambled away from him and stood up. I couldn't hit him, not again—I couldn't hit anyone. The shame of what I had momentarily become brought me nearer to tears than the gas had done. He stood up as well—and as the madness went on round us, we stared at each other.

He was the policeman I had hit in Rennes.

I dropped the baton. He didn't pick it up. The only sound I could hear was Nathalie's sobbing—and then the cannon's jet came again, slamming me once more to the earth.

*

The inside of the paddy-wagon stank—of blood, vomit and the acrid remains of the tear gas. There were fresh air smells enough, ozone-laden from the sea, coming from the high ventilation grilles, but they were not enough to remove the accumulated stink that the Kergorff prisoners had left behind them. As we bumped along the road, I wondered for the hundredth time why I was alone.

Why they had separated me out from the others after the arrests? Was there something special to come? Another beating, like the one in Rennes? The thought of it didn't appal—nothing did, not any more—not the murderous chauffeur, not Belle-île, not even the memory of Prosper, deliberately creating another martyr for the cause by pushing a boy under a truck's wheels. My anger had run its course against my paranoia in an eight-by-ten cell for twenty-four hours. I was drained.

Without warning we stopped. I shifted on the cracked plastic of the seat, as much as I could with both hands chained to the rail below it. The back doors opened. What time was it? Late afternoon? All I could see was drizzle and the tarmac of a big car park.

"Free him."

No mistaking that voice, even if I couldn't see the speaker—I'd heard it disembodied more often than not. The van's uniformed driver unlocked my hands. Rubbing my chafed wrists, I came out into the light to find Christian Gwernig, holding a newspaper in one hand. I heard the deep blast of a ship's horn—and felt the dread finger of certainty touch my spine. So that was it. They'd found out about Belle-île. I was to be taken back, charged. With murder? Gwernig turned to the driver.

"Leave us a minute."

His voice changed as he turned to me, took on a coldness that I recognised as emotion suppressed. "I pay my debts, Mister Fiddler. I was on the wall at the end. I saw you save her—and I saw you turn the other damn cheek as well, so I know you're no thug. But this changes everything."

He held up the paper. The collage of pictures told the story—the crowds, the batons, the legs stuck at their obscene angle beneath the truck's wheels, the PSB banner. His voice became even colder.

"You've got trouble written all over you, and I don't want any part of it."

He gestured at the big building, thrust an envelope into my hand. A ticket envelope.

"You're at Roscoff, the ferry for Plymouth leaves in twenty-five minutes." You walk over there to the terminal, you get on it—and you don't come back." The fury in his voice redoubled. "You don't come back to my country. Ever. You don't come back to *France."*

So, not arrested, deported... I looked down, trying to keep the relief from my face.

From somewhere behind me an engine came gunning towards us, fast. As Gwernig's expression become stone, I turned—an ancient green Volkswagen van. It squealed to a halt beside us. The door opened, the driver got out.

Nathalie.

Brother and sister stared at each other in a silence of pure hatred. I turned and walked away from both of them.

*

The rain-lashed deck was big enough for each of us to be alone and together at the same time. From the stern rail I watched Brittany's coastline recede. When the footsteps on the metal warned me of her approach, I didn't turn.

"What will you do now?"

I closed my eyes, let the rain's freshness hit me. "Find my fiddle, or at least what's happened to it."

"But if it's all as bad as you say," she said, "how can you possibly begin to find things out? Let me help! Let me—"

"I've already told you," I said. "You owe me nothing. You don't know what you're getting mixed up in."

"I want to help you prove your innocence."

The word broke my anger. "Clearing myself is my problem—when this boat gets to England, you stay on it! You turn around and go home!"

I heard a cry, small, half-stifled. I turned. Not tears, not now, I couldn't cope with tears.

"Look," I began, "all—"

But it wasn't tears. The fists came at me in a furious pummelling, a frenzy of anger.

"Don't say that," she shouted, "don't tell me that!"

I caught her by the forearms. Her head collapsed on my chest, sobbing.

"There is no home, Alex!" she wailed. "How can I go home after what they did! You don't understand—the boy, the one Prosper killed! It was René!"

12

AFTERMATH

THE LAST FEW MILES of the journey to the village of Ottery St. Thomas were all but subterranean. The trees on either side of the roadway had grown unchecked for so long that their branches had intertwined above it, making a thick canopy over the pot-holed tarmac, a bizarre bower which the dawn light only penetrated in isolated, misty patches. It was eerie—I felt as though I was driving down the barrel of some long, winding organic telescope, some backwards-looking cylinder full of Celtic twilight. What would the final lens show me? Some strange atavistic vision, some rare manifestation of Cornwall, land of Arthurian legend? On the front seat beside me, Nathalie, as though called by the thought of things Celtic, stirred and muttered. I watched her stretch, then shift sinuously into a different bundle of grace without waking.

But when we came out into the light of day there was nothing of Celtic Cornwall to be seen. Whatever it had once been, this was England now—and picture-postcard England at that, thatched, half-timbered and placid. The centre of the village was overlaid with a deep layer of stillness, a quiet that seemed designed to accentuate its rural quaintness. I pulled up the green van in a sloping, cobbled market square, pegged down at its four corners by pub, church, Victorian fountain and village shop-cum-post-office. It felt pleasing, unspoiled. There were a few signs for bed and breakfast and clotted cream teas, but the place didn't seem to have succumbed to the tourism that was so often Cornwall's only economic lifeline. Why, I wondered. Simply too far off the beaten track? And why did I have the nagging feeling I knew the name? Ottery St. Thomas... Somewhere in the trees behind the steeple, a lark sang.

I looked down at the sleeping girl. There was a big double bunk in the van's back. Wouldn't that be more comfortable? Should I wake her? She'd stayed doggedly awake for most of the overnight drive from Plymouth, only succumbing for the last two hours. No, best leave her, I decided, we'd rest properly later. The dashboard clock told me it was five-thirty. Again I surveyed the village. How long before the quilt of dawn quiet was ruffled?

As if in answer, activity began. A stocky girl in a pink nylon overall appeared from the shop's interior, yawning as she put an ice cream sign out on the pavement, and a middle-aged woman wearing an old-fashioned headscarf came out of one of the side streets and began to cross the square towards her. As they exchanged greetings and disappeared inside, I prised myself out of the driving seat.

The quaint Englishness stopped dead at the shop door. The interior had been kitted out with plastic efficiency as a small supermarket, and the headscarved woman was already halfway round it, filling a wire basket with fruit and vegetables, talking over her shoulder as she did so. Behind the post office counter, the pink-overalled girl was stamping counterfoils with machine-gun efficiency and keeping up her end of the conversation in grunted monosyllables. An enamelled badge at her breast told me she was the postmistress. The exchange between the two women died at my entry, and the face above the pink nylon collar broke into a generous smile.

"Well," she said, "you've got the best of a fine mornin' an' no mistake, sir. What can I get you?"

"Only information, I'm afraid. An old friend of mine used to live here, but we've lost touch."

I hesitated. Which name to choose? The murdered man had been more honest in death, I decided.

"Barrington. Michael Barrington."

The bucolic content of her face crumpled. But disappointment only lasted an instant. Defiance quickly replaced it.

"If you're another journalist we've nothing more to say. It was five years ago."

Before she could finish or I could reply there was a crash from behind me. I turned, saw oranges and apples roll from the headscarved woman's dropped basket. Suddenly the narrow aisle seemed too small for her. She staggered forward, careering into a stacked display of tins in her desperation to escape. Through the clatter of their falling I heard a thin cry that could only mean hysteria. I reached the open door in time to see her stumble and fall to her knees halfway across the square. I ran to help, but the postmistress was quicker. She shouldered me out of the way without ceremony.

"Leave her be! You've done enough harm, bloody reporters!"

"I'm not a reporter—"

"I don't give a bugger what you are. Maud lost three kids 'cause of that man. She don't need remindin' of it."

As she reached down to help the stricken woman, footsteps came. I looked up to see a middle-aged man in a grey suit hurrying across to us. A large brown dog loped along in his wake.

"Good heavens! Maud! Are you all right?"

Between the two of them they got the weeping woman to her feet. The dog circled all of us, tail wagging.

"What happened?" the man asked.

The woman called Maud stood between them, head bowed. As her weeping petered out, the postmistress launched into fierce denunciation.

"It was this fellow here, Mister Caldicott," she said, putting her arm round her charge. "Started on about the old business. About Barrington."

The contempt in her voice was withering. What was all this about? I felt a hand touch my sleeve—Nathalie, dishevelled, roused by the commotion.

"*Qu' est-ce que c'est,* Alex?" she muttered.

The face beneath the headscarf whipped up. It was tear-streaked and still pale, but there was more than grief to it now. It had been a fine face once, I could see—a handsome countrywoman's face, perhaps even beautiful, but the emotions which ruled it now had nothing to do with beauty. I felt Nathalie's grip tighten on my arm; there was no mistaking the anger or the hate—or the fact that both were directed at her. Why? The postmistress's voice broke in.

"French! Barrington and the bloody French! None of it would've happened—"

This time it was her turn to be cut off. The grey haired man's voice fell into some no-man's land between nervousness and authority as he addressed me.

"If you're as innocent of this as you seem, then perhaps you'd better come with me."

In the silence which followed, I noticed the clerical collar at his neck—and then Maud's grief came again.

And as we all stood, listening to the utterly lost sound of the weeping, I remembered why the name Ottery St. Thomas was familiar.

*

AT ETERNAL PLAY
IN LOVING MEMORY OF THOSE WHO DIED
ON THE MORBIHAN
6.5.1992

The Morbihan disaster...

I read the inscription, trying to muster what I knew of it. There had been a storm, a big storm off the French coast. The Morbihan had been a car ferry on its way from St. Malo to Portsmouth, aging and badly maintained, with several drunk crew members and unlaunchable lifeboats. When she had capsized, hundreds had died.

And among those hundreds had been the children of an English village, Ottery St. Thomas. Almost all of its children... Why had they been on the ship? I struggled to remember until the vicar's nervous voice gave me my answer.

"They were coming home. They'd been to France for their annual school trip. The papers were all over us for weeks afterwards. There was an enquiry. Surely you must have heard about it?"

I stared at the gravestone. It was plain, tasteful, but the mason's attempt at quiet dignity had been undercut by the sheer size necessary to accommodate so much lettering. Twenty-two names... The vicar pointed at three near the top of the list.

JOHN BATES, AGED EIGHT.
GEOFFREY BATES, AGED NINE.
WILLIAM BATES, AGED ELEVEN.

"Maud's children," he said, quietly. "She's never recovered, I'm afraid. Only a few of the families have."

He shrugged. His embarrassment deepened as he turned to Nathalie.

"I'm sorry, the enquiry blamed the crew, and they were French..."

The nervous voice's embarrassment petered out. Her only reaction was a slow nod. My gaze went down the cold stone list. The inscription I was looking for was right at the bottom.

MICHAEL BARRINGTON. TEACHER. FRIEND.

My eyes went back to the gold-embossed date at the stone's top.

The man I had seen die three days before on Belle-île had already been dead for five years.

*

The vicarage's damp living room was lined with paperbacks—cheap editions of the classics, tattered philosophy, the orange spines of twentieth century conscience; Kant, Orwell, Greene, Huxley... In their shadow my equilibrium returned, and it seemed to me that the Reverend's nerves had also been conquered—until I noticed his spoon, stirring, stirring, long past any notion of the tea's sweetness. A calming ritual? Mr. Caldicott saw it himself a second later. The movement stopped. Briefly, both of us watched Nathalie, seated on the garden bench outside the window, the dog's head in blissful repose on her lap. Her stroking of its ear had the same rhythm, the same absent-minded preoccupation as his stirring. Instinctively I knew she was deep in thought about her own troubles. When the vicar spoke, his voice was at once sad and irritated.

"Forgive me," he said, gesturing at the spoon. "Trauma, no doubt, or dysfunction, or whatever fancy name the psychiatrists use these days for an accumulation of hurt. I don't suppose we'll ever be able to bury it, really, no matter how much normality we try to pour over it." He turned to me. "How good a friend of yours was Michael?"

I was calm enough now to slip into the lie. "We were at college together," I said. "Teacher training."

It was all the cue he needed. Animation came to him, vitality.

"And what a teacher, he was, don't you agree? Much more than just gifted—the word brilliant doesn't seem an exaggeration. And exactly what this village needed—outgoing, optimistic about the world. He challenged the conservatism of this place, but without alienating people. That's a gift, you know, a real gift. He taught by example, showed the children how to help each other, how to learn from each other. A practical socialist, the best kind."

Could this be the same person as the sad shell of a man I'd seen on Belle-île? The Reverend's voice rose in sudden vehemence.

"It's not right that they blame him—if you only knew how I had to fight for the inscription on that stone!" He shook his head. "No, it's wrong. Wrong, wrong, wrong," he repeated, "and unchristian."

The last word was almost an afterthought, one that somehow embarrassed him even more. The pipe came out again, and tobacco. The tamping began immediately, a new physical mantra to replace the teaspoon.

"It was his decision, you see, to take the children to France. A week, camping. Most of the parents opposed it at first. They wanted the school trip to do one of the normal things, go to Wales or something, Worcestershire. Michael would have none of it. He'd been teaching them French and he saw it as an opportunity. And because of his reputation, because of the trust they had in him, they let him. The rest you know."

"There were no survivors from the village?"

Again he shook his head. "Only those who didn't go. That's what made it worse, of course—the fact that Michael's own children hadn't been on the trip, the fact that they were the only ones left alive in the village. Nick was still too young, and..."

Whatever he said next was lost to me. I forced myself to concentrate.

"I didn't even know Michael had married," I said, carefully.

"Oh, yes." His eyes found Nathalie again, in the garden. "Lovely girl. Beautiful hair. Red hair."

It was said with a gruff wistfulness. He seemed to hear the tone himself, for he hurried on, as though it was shameful to remember beauty in such circumstances. When he spoke again his voice was businesslike, determinedly vicar-and-flock.

"Always ready to help. Like Michael, got involved with things. Causes—Nicaraguan orphans, unmarried mothers, whatever it was, Sylvia always had time."

Sylvia... I felt my mouth go dry at the name as he went on.

"The star of our amateur dramatic society."

An actress... Yes, I could testify to her skills in that direction. I tried to keep my voice unconcerned.

"Is she still here? In the village?"

He shook his head, slowly. "Terrible loss when she decided to go. Understandable, of course..."

The sentence dwindled to uncomfortable silence. The tamping stopped.

"She was one of the first to leave."

There was a definite difference to his voice, now, a different note. Disapproval?

"She married again." He punctuated the statement by knocking out the unlit pipe on the tablecloth. "She married the judge, the one who presided over the accident enquiry. Sir Peter Holcroft. Up in Bristol. They live in the midlands somewhere. Old family home, Shropshire, I think." Again he paused. "Some people were surprised that it all happened so quickly."

No, not disapproval, I realised—what I was hearing was disappointment. The woman I had met on Belle-île would never be short of admirers; the Reverend John Caldicott was one of them.

I looked away from his reddening face, round the room. The shabby sofa, the worn leather armchairs, the dog's basket. It reeked of bachelordom, loneliness. What easier prey could there be for a hearty, socialist-tinted, country beauty? Her real personality, I wondered, or just another shrewd bit of theatre, taken on to facilitate victory? My eyes found the last paperback on the top shelf. *She Stoops To Conquer.* But why conquer a lonely country vicar? Was there purpose to it, or was it just the scratching of some dominant female itch? Unwittingly, the Reverend came to her defence.

"Lovely girl," he repeated.

The tamping of the pipe began anew. Outside, Nathalie's hand went on with its quiet stroking.

*

We didn't reach Bristol until late afternoon, so to save time we split forces. Nathalie's English was good enough to handle the Registry Office, so while she did that, I went to the local newspaper, then on to the library. A dingy, anonymous cafe by the bus station was the rendezvous point. As I reached it, just after five, half a dozen blank-faced teenagers came running out.

I pushed open the door and found myself in an electronic armageddon of sound—bullets, explosions, sirens. The games machines were lined in two long rows, facing each other, jammed so close together that there could hardly have been room for the players, but thankfully the narrow corridor between them was all but empty. I ran the gauntlet of the dubious skills they offered, reading the names—Strike Force. Street Fighter. Line of Fire. Punch Out... At the end of the screaming corridor my progress was impeded by a bespectacled child, perhaps twelve years old.

Marketing had already made a teenager of him. He wore spotless white trainers, black lycra cycling shorts and a t-shirt many sizes too large for his scrawny frame. A baseball cap was jammed down backwards on his head, and in his hands he held a black plastic imitation of a sub-machine gun. It was connected to its mother machine by a luminous yellow umbilical cord. I waited, watching his imaginary bullets travel along their electronic beam to decimate the figures on the screen before him—cartoon robots, metal-bodied and helmeted, faceless, futuristic versions of the troops who had charged me down two days ago. On the scoreboard above, his tally mounted, and as I watched I wondered—what was he learning here? That killing scored better than wounding? That death didn't hurt? There were no dead students in this game... As I tried to banish the thought of René, the plastic muzzle rounded on me. My eyes rose to the face above it. One corner of his spectacle frame was held together by sticking plaster, instantly redefining him as vulnerable child rather than designer pre-teen. He frowned as his finger pressed the trigger. Over the electronic rat-tat-tat he shouted at me.

"You're terminated! You're dead, you're fucking dead!"

He dropped the toy gun. As it clattered off the machine's side he squirmed past me and ran out through the door. A mirthless laugh came from the other side of the room. I turned to find a fat man in a dirty white shirt, drying cups behind the plastic counter, his leaden eyes expressionless. He shrugged his shoulders.

"Kids," he said.

I ordered coffee, paid for it, and found a seat. The place was all but deserted, its only other customer a heavily pregnant woman, morosely watching the smoke of her cigarette rising from the tinfoil ashtray before her. I took out the photocopies I'd made in the library and the newspaper office. The sheet from *Who's Who* was on the top.

Holcroft, Sir Peter, DSO, DFC 1952, Kt 1964; Rt. Hon. Lord Justice Holcroft; a Lord Justice of Appeal 1983-90. b 2 Aug 1930; s of late Sir Thomas Holcroft and Lady Jane (née Douglas). m 1st 1953 Lady Anne Graham, (d. 1958) 2nd 1964 Elizabeth Anderson (marr. diss. 1970) 3rd 1972 Alice Jean Burnley (marr. diss. 1978) 4th 1992 Sylvia Barrington. Educ: Charterhouse, Corpus Christi Coll. Oxford. Coldstream Guards 1949-53 (Capt) MA Oxford. Called to the Bar, Inner Temple, 1962...

The rest of the entry—committees sat upon, commissions chaired—deviated not one whit from the picture already established; the man who didn't care about losing a Stradivarius was a pillar of the establishment. I turned to the entries I had culled from the newspaper files.

He had been a dull judge. Tired hero of the right, aunt sally to the left, he'd been predictable in his extremism and controversial only because his decisions had been almost uniformly reactionary. He had never made a secret of his opinions or tried to justify their obvious contradictions. Under his judicial guidance rape had been a male peccadillo, retaliation by battered wife a heinous crime, alternative lifestyle of any kind a sign of obvious criminality. His own words, in the profile *The Times* had published on his retirement, expressed it best.

His appointment to the bench had missed the era of capital punishment, he said, and he regretted the fact. Britain would have been a far better place if hanging had been kept as a deterrent, along with flogging, birching, etc., etc. His homily finished with the statement that modern Britain was in crisis—the country had lost its commitment to excellence, its youth had been ruined by excess, the only way out was a return to conscription and family values. As I read, the sound of coins in a slot came. I turned; the electronic marksman was back, a willing recruit to military service. What would Sir Peter make of him? As I wondered, Nathalie's graceful figure appeared from the row of machines.

"Success?" I asked, as she picked her way through the tables.

Her face blank, she pulled a photocopy from her bag—the marriage certificate, good. I ran my eyes over it. Mr. Caldicott had been right, the groom's home parish was given as Shrewsbury. A family home, he'd said—and now we had a name, Holcroft House... Congratulations on my lips, I looked up again—and saw that her face's blankness was no accident.

"What's wrong?"

She pulled a rolled-up newspaper from the bag, spread it out in front of me; *Le Monde,* yesterday's edition. It was already open at the relevant page. The headline covered three columns

TOURIST ISLAND SLAYING

I read, quickly. A brutal murder. An English resident of Belle-île, Michael Knight, had been found dead twenty-four hours ago. Shot, probable motive theft, a large sum of money was missing. The island was in uproar, hoteliers were worried about the effect on trade. Police were searching for a man of medium height, probably English, carrying a violin case...

I pushed the paper away. How did they get the description? The neighbour, I realised, the old woman I'd asked for directions... My eyes rose, met Nathalie's.

"Christian will know," she said, quietly.

I nodded, slowly. Yes, her brother would know—everything. And everything meant that I was identified, that the British police would already be alerted. And Gwernig knew that Nathalie was with me, which meant—

She read my thoughts. *"Oui,* Alex, he knows my vehicle."

So they would have the green van's registration. Had they traced us to Cornwall? I looked round the room. And beyond? Here? How long before the registration was noticed? Nathalie's voice broke in.

"This Holcroft House, Alex—is it far? Can we reach it tonight?"

I forced myself to concentrate—an easy enough drive, only a few hours... But then rational thought returned; we still had no exact address, and by the time we reached it, sources of information—libraries, newspaper offices and so on, would be shut. I shook my head.

"Better if we wait," I said. "Spend the night somewhere, rest.

Avoid a hotel, if we can."

She nodded. "The van's comfortable," she said, "the bed's big enough..."

The sentence died as she realised what she was saying. Both of us spoke at once.

"Je ne veux pas dire—"

"I'm not suggesting—"

The silence was tense, an avoiding of each others' eyes. Through it I stared at the French paper. On top of its news this confusion seemed insurmountable. Awkwardly, I tried to end it.

"Nathalie, do you remember what you said at Carnac? That neither of us needs—"

She cut me off. *"Oui,* Alex. It's still true, I think."

Again the silence engulfed us. I scanned the room's bleakness; the pregnant woman's cigarette, the fat man's dirty shirt, the kid's mindless aggression.

The words clung to me.

Neither of us needs a lover at the moment.

As she folded up the paper, our eyes met again across the table. Yes, it was still true—but not as true as it had been ten days ago.

13

MANSIONS

WHEN THE MANSION called Holcroft House had been built, first impressions had been everything. The facade was an object lesson in eighteenth-century symmetry, a square box, Georgian and solid, decorated with just enough pillar and portico to suggest classical Greece, surrounded by just enough manicured parkland to be classically English. Even the late afternoon sun, luminous against the clear sky, seemed to have been hung in harmony with the Palladian proportions. I felt myself smile as I surveyed the place from the locked iron gate—God might be in his heaven above Holcroft House, but like any other self-respecting aristocrat, he knew better than to tinker with a landscape laid out by Capability Brown.

But how meticulous it all was... Nothing had been left to chance—from where Nathalie and I now stood, the watcher's eye was concentrated on the house itself by the avenue of poplars on either side of the short metalled central driveway, and to left and right of the gate, gravelled paths led to twin lodge cottages which were perfect miniatures of the main building. As psychology it couldn't have been bettered—no aristocratic stranger could have remained unimpressed, no servant unintimidated; order, pattern and proportion, at once commanding and benevolent, the powerful set firmly in the pastoral, its elegance underlined by the peacock wandering over the drive, its ethic brought firmly up to date by the sleek snout of the Jaguar car poking out from behind the ivy at the far side.

But for all the obvious wealth, was it a fitting home for a Stradivarius? The thought came unbidden, with the image of George Berolet's fingers on the open strings of The Singer. Who had first brought that unfortunate instrument here? Had it been stolen from this house or not? As I speculated, Nathalie turned to me.

Reluctantly, I took the cue. I had mixed feelings about hiding myself, but it made sense. I was a murder suspect; the fewer people who could identify me, the better—especially the woman who called herself Sylvia Holcroft. Had she returned here after the events of Belle-île? I retreated on the thought, to the safety of a thicket of bushes across the road. When Nathalie rang the bell, I heard it sound in the lodge cottage to the left. Almost immediately, footsteps crunched on gravel.

I was on the cusp of earshot. I heard a heavy male voice query her business, and Nathalie give the name Holcroft. The answer she got was low and blunt. I heard her insist, the gravel footsteps retreat.

After a long silence, new steps came, down the tarmac drive from the house—heels, a woman, unhurried. Her? Sylvia? No. I heard a lowish voice which might have been pleasant had it been less charged with upper class overtones. It demanded Nathalie's business, and when Nathalie replied, it issued an immediate and firm rebuttal. I caught the words *not at home.* When Nathalie insisted, the answering haughtiness became icy. Frustration rose in me. Were we to be so simply rebuffed?

And then there were other steps, light ones, hesitant and uneven, on the gravel. They also stopped at the gate, and a new voice asked a question.

A child's voice, well-bred, with just a hint of West Country accent...

I stepped out from the bushes and walked up to Nathalie's side. The woman behind the iron gate could have been anywhere from forty to sixty. She was already dressed and made up for evening, her silver hair up in a tight, formal chignon, the blue silk of her dress set off by a single string of pearls. The small boy holding her hand made an almost comic contrast; jeans and dirty white t-shirt, his free hand curled protectively round a large white angora rabbit.

"Hello, Nick," I said.

I got a shy grin for an answer. The woman spoke.

"Who are you?"

It was Nick who replied, his voice excited. "He's my friend, Aunt Angela! The one I told you about, the man who makes the pig noises with his violin! The one—"

He stopped in confusion—and as his face began to lose its sunny confidence, one more piece of the puzzle fell into place.

On the island of Belle-île, the features of the man I had seen killed, the man called Michael Barrington, had seemed familiar, but I hadn't been able to work out why. Now, watching Nick, I could. Unhappiness was a sorry key to resemblance—the expression on the boy's face now made it a mirror of Barrington's, just before he was shot. Father and son?

As I speculated, his face fled further into unease. His grip on the rabbit tightened. He turned, and with the shuffling gait of a very old man, walked awkwardly away from the gates. But why? I had done him no harm. And he hadn't walked like that in Rennes, I'd have noticed... I searched the silver-haired woman's face for enlightenment, but all it gave away was the knowledge that she had noted what I had seen—and then, as it retreated into its patrician hauteur, the silence was broken.

The peacock's cry was plaintive, raucous, a disconsolate punctuation mark to our confrontation. For some reason it disturbed the silver-haired woman, but she suppressed the frown as quickly as it came. As she turned, an answering cry came from further away. Inside the house? Animal? Human? Whatever the source, it was pain-filled, somewhere between despair and rage, at once more elegaic and more desperate than the peacock's.

She ignored it. Why, I wondered—the peacock's cry was startling enough, but the response... As I tried to work it out, she sang out a terse sentence of command.

"Let them in, Mallory."

She turned and walked away from us, back towards the house, considerably faster than she had come.

*

"I see."

She was Angela Holcroft, the judge's sister.

That was as much as she had told us, and the two clipped syllables which were her response to my story gave nothing more away. She tucked back an imaginary stray lock of the silver hair, swirled the whisky round in her glass, then drained it and rose. As she turned to the decanter by her side, I wondered; had she believed me or not?

For I had told her the truth—as much of it as I dared, omitting only the story of how I'd met Nathalie, and all mention of Barrington. She seemed to know nothing of the murder on Belle-île—and if that was the case, I was happy not to enlighten her.

But all the rest of it, from my first meeting with Nick, fifteen days ago on the pavement in Rennes, to the fact that the Stradivarius had been tricked out of my hands on Belle-île, she now knew. And I had missed out none of the criminal acts in between. The judge's sister knew that I had been shot at and deceived—and, more importantly, she knew that I was well aware that all the illegalities which surrounded The Singer had begun here, in this house. There was an implied threat in that—it wasn't the way I would have chosen to deal with her, but it seemed the surest way of bringing pressure to bear. But as I watched the barest splash of soda reach the generous measure in her glass, I wondered if I was right—we'd been here half an hour now, and the flow of information had been entirely one-way.

Whisky in hand, she crossed the expanse of the drawing-room. The walk was full of poise, hardly rippling the blue dress's folds, and I recognised the studied ease of performance. The catwalk? Ex-model? Again, I tried to work out her age. Late forties? Early fifties? Not so long ago she had been a beauty, that much was obvious. I turned, saw Nathalie making the same appraisal, but from a different standpoint—they had disliked each other on sight, these two. I watched the graceful progress stop beside a Minton vase full of roses, the whiskyless hand reach out to rearrange the ferns round the blooms. The action was at once deft and languid—and the unhurried ease of it stirred my impatience. It was time to exert more pressure. What I needed first was confirmation of the Cornish vicar's story.

"Your brother, the judge, is he here?"

"No."

"But the woman I met on Belle-île, the woman who called herself Lady Holcroft, she really is his wife?"

"Yes."

"And she is Nick's mother?"

The last of the ferns seemed suddenly much more difficult to place, but the reply came firmly enough.

"Yes."

"Is she here now?"

"No."

"When did she bring Nick back here?"

This time it couldn't be answered with a monosyllable. "She didn't. The boy was sent. He's old enough to travel on his own."

"And the dark-haired man, the one called McPhie? He was her chauffeur?"

Again, a terse nod.

"Just hers, or did he serve the whole household here?"

For some reason, that penetrated the patrician armour. She became every inch the judge's sister.

"What exactly do you want, Mister Fraser?"

I felt the coldness of my own voice match hers. "My own violin back, if it's in this house. If it isn't, then I want any information you have about it. The other violin, the Stradivarius, that's not my business. If you're not concerned about the theft of a quarter of a million pounds, that's your affair."

Theft. It was the first time the word had been used. The result was a deafening silence. I had no compunction in using it to press home my advantage.

"What did Nick tell you when he got back here?"

She faltered, visibly. "The story was so fantastic I gave none of it credence."

"But you believe it now," I said, quietly, "because Nick told you about me, didn't he? About a man who could make his violin sound like a pig, on the street in Rennes. What else did he tell you?"

"Nothing."

It came far too quickly, and both of us knew it. Her anger rose, brought back her command.

"Your violin is not in this house, Mister Fraser, I assure you. And no one here has any knowledge of its whereabouts."

"I want to talk to Nick," I said.

"No."

There was nothing for it but direct threat. "If you let me speak to him," I said, "you have my silence. If you don't, I go to the police with everything I know."

She wasn't to know it was bluff. Her face reddened, this time with open anger, but she knew she was beaten. She turned to Nathalie.

"On the table behind you there's a bell. If you would be kind enough."

I watched Nathalie's mouth tighten at the command's condescension, but she did as she was asked. After several uncomfortable seconds, the man who had let us in appeared.

"Would you fetch Master Nicholas, Mallory?"

The door closed. Beside me, Nathalie's voice came, stubborn.

"The boy, Nick, *le petit,*" she said. "What is wrong with his legs?"

I expected reprimand, a none-of-your-damn-business reply, but there was only silence. Again the whisky glass was drained, but as Angela Holcroft turned away, back to the Minton vase, she couldn't bear to put it down. When she replied, the haughty voice was iron in its lightness.

"He fell. From one of the apple trees in the orchard."

As the room lapsed once more into jagged quiet, Nathalie's eyes met mine.

A lie, an open lie, both of us had heard it. Why?

I looked away, round the walls, for the first time aware of the grandeur which surrounded me; silk, damask, brocade, all the well-worn opulence of old money. The fireplace was Adam, the table in the bay window was Sheraton, the portraits could hardly have been more venerable...

My eyes came back to that elegant hand, so poised above the blooms, so determined not to shake.

...And the judge's sister could hardly have been more frightened.

*

"...but I'll have to go and pick some more dandelions because Fluffy ate all the leaves. And the guinea pigs have chewed through their cage again, and Mister Mallory said if I asked you perhaps he could have an hour to build a new one for me. Would that be all right, Aunt Angela?"

The news about Fluffy and the guinea pigs had been delivered to the room at large, but the last question was directed firmly at Angela Holcroft. Being Aunt Angela rather than the judge's sister seemed to calm her—for the moment at least, the fear I'd glimpsed in her was gone. She reached across the sofa and ruffled the boy's hair. For the first time, I heard her voice soften.

"Yes, of course, darling." She turned to me. "Nick takes very good care of his animals, Mister Fraser. He has quite a menagerie out in the kitchen garden."

"Three rabbits, a guinea pig, five gerbils and two puppies. And hamsters with new babies," the boy said proudly.

How old was he? Beside his aunt on the couch, he looked a tousle-headed ten or eleven, but the voice and delivery were those of a much younger child. I remembered the description his mother had given me on Belle-île, and realised how clever she had been. Like all good liars, Sylvia Holcroft had stuck as close to the truth as possible—Nick was exactly what she had said he was, what older generations would have deemed 'simple'. As I watched the boy's shy sizing-up of Nathalie, I wondered; how much else of Sylvia Holcroft's tale had been based in fact?

"Nick," I said, "the day you first met me, on the street in Rennes, do you remember it?"

Still smiling, the boy nodded.

"You swapped the two fiddles, didn't you?"

Again he nodded.

"When did you do it?" I asked. "When I was on the ground and the policeman was holding me?"

Once more, my only answer was a shy nod.

"You did it behind the flower pots, didn't you? So that no one could see you."

A last nod, final confirmation. I leaned back in the chair. It was all as I had suspected. The confusion which followed my fight with the police must have covered it—that, and the boy's absolute innocence, his guileless way of doing things. Somehow I knew that his actions would have been exactly like he was, open and undisguised. If anyone had noticed him, his straightforwardness would have made them presume that he had permission to do what he was doing, or that there was some other exterior logic at play.

But the only logic had been Nick's... I had to ask the question.

"Why, Nick? Why did you do it?"

The word *why* was an obstacle, knitting the boy's brows—and then the face's clear look returned.

"Because you needed it," he said, simply. "Because your fiddle was all busted up and you wouldn't be able to make the pig noises any more."

I looked at Nathalie, then at Angela Holcroft. Both faces held the same expression; adults, humbled by a child. The germ of everything which had happened was this one act of kindness. A simple boy's kindness... But again, the grim thought came.

Simple and generous... Once more, in the service of her lies, Sylvia Holcroft had described her son correctly.

"And what did you do with the other fiddle, Nick, the bust-ed-up one?"

Confusion came to him—and then the slow descent into distress began, just as it had at the gate; some memory was reaching him, something very bad.

But this time, he seemed determined to fight it. Slowly, he levered himself off the sofa and came across the room towards us. Or rather, towards Nathalie.

"Would you like to see my new hamsters?"

Behind him I saw Angela Holcroft's face crumple back into concern, but Nathalie beat the coming protest. She rose, took the boy's hand.

"Ça me ferait grand plaisir, Nick. That means I would like that very much."

He grinned, began to tug her gently towards the door. I felt obliged to speak.

"Thank you for giving me your violin, Nick."

The boy turned, puzzled. "It's not my violin. I don't play the violin."

The matter-of-fact rebuttal was the last thing I expected. "Then who does it belong to?" I asked.

"Nick, run along now, I'll—"

But this time it was Nick himself who silenced his aunt. "It's Ewen's. My big brother, Ewen, it's his violin."

From outside, the peacock cry came again—and across the room, the head of silver hair bowed in utter defeat. This time the answering cry was much louder. Natalie's hand gripped mine.

Human, definitely, and awful in its pain.

14

GENIUS

THE LONG STRAIGHT corridor down which I followed Angela Holcroft's angry lope was a determined progress from the Palladian to the Victorian. Halfway along its length the painted portrait gave way to the sepia photograph, and towards the end its width was narrowed by bell jars of stuffed owl and eagle, glass display cases filled with the sterile brightness of dead butterflies. I paused beside a mahogany cabinet. Three violin cases were stacked on top of it. The blue dress had rounded the turn at the corridor's end. I stopped and quickly opened each of them in turn.

I hadn't really expected to see my own instrument, but what I found disturbed me. Violins, yes... Badly smashed up, every one—but each instrument was old and yet the damage was obviously new. Why? I closed the cases again, repelled, my heart beating faster—it was as though a parody of my own situation had lain here in wait for me. I walked on, but I had let myself fall too far behind. I turned the corner to find myself alone.

Alone, and at the heart of the nineteenth century aristocracy's ethic.

The space I had reached was something between hall and passageway. One solitary, stiff-backed chaise longue catered for those who wanted to linger, but the long, straight runner of carpet which headed for the door ahead acknowledged that they would be few and far between. The only other escape route was a metal spiral staircase which corkscrewed up into the panelled ceiling. I stared at the walls.

To my right hung the most lethal collection of weaponry I had ever seen—sabre, pike, dagger and axe, their points and cutting edges gleaming with burnished care. Rifle, pistol and musket were poised above them, their barrels oiled and rust-free, and at the far end stood a glass-fronted cabinet of businesslike shotguns. There was no lock on it, I noticed—in fact, there was nothing to stop anyone removing anything from the wall. Wasn't that illegal…? My eyes were drawn to a blank space beside a wartime Webley officer's pistol; two empty retaining hooks...

The gun McPhie had fired at me? In Rennes, at the hotel? Why not? I could see nothing to make me doubt that every one of these weapons was usable.

I took a step back, surveying it all—an arsenal, efficient, soulless. There wasn't a single sign of any personal memory, of any nostalgic reason, however misplaced, for the amassing of it all—no photos, no regimental insignia, nothing remotely connected with any one person's life. The wall's remit was the mechanics of killing, not the circumstances of death. I turned to the facing display.

Lion, rhinoceros, zebra, antelope, ibex... And stag after stag after stag, their heads lined up in dreadful measured symmetry, the points of their antlers reduced to barbarous pointlessness. The image of the stag Nathalie and I had seen across the Breton glade came to me. Regal, commanding, mysterious...

Did the perpetrator of this gallery imagine that he had captured any of that? I stood, fixed—to be trapped between these two walls, between bullet and victim, was to be caught in the very instant of death. I closed my eyes—and heard the peacock's cry once again. I knew what would follow—and when the answering cry came, very near now, one long, inarticulate vowel of pain, guilt gripped me. Listening to the trapped echo of it reverberate round the walls, I wanted such raw emotion to be my own. It would have been a more apt response to this place than any measured silence of disapproval.

"In here, Mister Fraser."

Angela Holcroft was standing beneath the stags' heads, at an open doorway in the panelling, a bulky, fair-haired man in a nurse's smock by her side.

The room into which I walked was no less Victorian than the

hallway, but here the era's legacy was functional, positive. A classroom—some past lord of Holcroft House had taken education seriously here. Solely for his own offspring, I wondered, or had the servants and their children been lettered here as well? I looked round; blackboard and desks, abacus, sets of brass weights and scales, several long benches which bore indentations. Vices? For woodworking?

But now the room had been given over entirely to one subject. An upright piano stood against the far wall. A pair of music stands braced it, and the walls upon which maps had no doubt once shown the pink of empire were now the domain of Beethoven, Mozart, Bach and Verdi. From their glossy posters they all looked down with benign authority on the little classroom. Only the dignity of Haydn and Tchaikovsky was compromised—by a brown stain which glistened down from their shoulders across the white plaster. Food, still wet. The last drops of the meal were still dripping from the plastic plate which had held it. It lay on the ledge below the posters, beside a shiny cassette recorder. Who had thrown it? I turned—and saw a boy, older than Nick, but dressed in similar jeans and t-shirt. He was hunched down in the corner, his red head down on his knees. Angela Holcroft's voice came from behind me.

"This is Ewen, Mister Fraser."

He looked up.

I had never imagined that a face could so disturb me. If Nick was his father's child, then the boy staring sullenly up at me now was most definitely his mother's—the same red hair, the same elfin features. But in her the beauty was merely physical. The features of this child were illuminated by an inner intensity which somehow doubled and redoubled their physical perfection. Mentally, I struggled for a word to describe him; handsome was the only male adjective my mind could come up with, but it seemed hopelessly inadequate. I was looking at an angel's face, caught in the most terrible moment of his fall from grace, frozen between heaven and hell... Again, Angela Holcroft's voice came.

"Quite something, isn't he? Twelve years old and already the ultimate ladies' man, but I doubt he'll ever know it."

"How long has he been like this?" I asked.

"As disturbed as this, only since his violin went. But it began about four years ago, not long after he first came here. The doctors say the root of it's in his real father's death. He died in the big ferry disaster off the coast of Brittany."

Barrington... My hidden knowledge turned my stomach as I looked into the boy's eyes, fixed on me in their unblinking stare. Her voice went on.

"A steady withdrawal from the world. Not that I'd blame him," she said bitterly, "not after some of the things which have gone on in this house. But he doesn't speak at all, now. And sometimes he has to be fed, and sometimes he messes himself." I could hear the hopelessness in her voice, and the love. "The violin was his only link to the rest of us—his own violin. He's smashed every other instrument we've tried to give him."

The violins in the hallway...

"His own instrument was the Stradivarius?" I asked.

She nodded.

"How did that come about?"

"It's been in the family for years. His real father had begun to teach him. When he was brought here, my brother—" I heard her voice harden. "—gave him the Strad to play while he was being taught. Since then it's simply been Ewen's violin. Until it was stolen, of course."

Stolen... I noted the admission.

"Does he play well?" I asked.

In answer she walked across to the back wall. I heard the metallic click of the cassette recorder's button—and then the room filled with the unmistakable tones of The Singer. Bach, a partita, brilliantly executed. I stared at the boy's immobile face as I listened; a prodigy, a retarded prodigy... Over and over again, the playing found the instrument's strength, the child-voiced sweetness of tone which I had stumbled across on the street in Vannes—and as I watched the boy's immobile face, I had sudden insight.

I knew why Ewen answered the peacock.

The cadence of the bird's call was sister to The Singer's distinctive falling note. Ewen was calling out to his violin.

Were there others around him, I wondered, who might hear that, understand it? Still the boy's eyes never left me. When Angela Holcroft's voice came again, it was bitter.

"Do you understand now, Mister Fraser? A quarter of a million pounds, stolen by an unscrupulous woman from this house—yes, that's a blow, a shameful one. But look at it a different way. Look at it as Ewen's violin, stolen by his own mother.

That's a tragedy."

The burly nurse's voice came from the doorway. "It's his bath time, Miss Angela. Will I see to Master Nick's—"

She cut him off very quickly. "Yes, Jenkins, take care of that, would you. I'll tidy up here." She turned back to me. "If you'd be kind enough to help me, Mister Fraser."

Between us we coaxed the boy to his feet. He acquiesced readily enough, but his movements were so clumsy that I was convinced he was unaware of their purpose. He walked like a sleepwalker. I helped as far as the door, then watched the two of them begin their ascent of the spiral staircase. When they turned the first bend, both her eyes and Ewen's met mine. As the boy's gaze looked straight through me, I asked the question.

"Why did his mother need to steal his violin?"

Whatever rapport there had been between Angela Holcroft and myself died. When the voice came it had retreated again into glacial hauteur.

"Because she's a dirty little gold-digging slut." The final noun was pure venom. "An adventuress who miscalculated. Is that candid enough for you, Mister Fraser? Have we satisfied every vestige of your curiosity now? About our bizarre family?"

"How much more is there to be curious about?" I asked, quietly.

The only answer I got was a lightning reprise of the drawing room's look of fear, and then the boy was shepherded up out of my sight. The echoes of the footsteps subsided. I heard a heavy door slam above me, and then I was alone again, in the deathlike gloom between weapon and victim. I took one last look round, then made for the door at the corridor's end.

Escape. Air, summer, sanity...

I found myself in the tended perfection of a small rose garden, its colours somehow intensified by the last light of the dying day, its air a scented coolness sprinkled with birdsong. It looked down a long green slope to a small river, plump and placid, its banks willow-lined, its curving progress in no hurry to traverse the dozen or so meadows that led to the spires and smoke of the next village. I watched a tractor cross it a few miles away, towing a load of hay across a hump-backed stone bridge. Nothing could have seemed more ordered, more English.

Or, I reflected, more ironic, given what I had just witnessed. What kind of life lay ahead for Ewen? And what about my own quest? I sat down on a rough bench, contemplating my failure. What had I learned of Barrington, or my own violin? I hadn't the slightest idea how to take my search further—indeed, I was no longer sure what my search was, and I had alienated the only person in this household who was capable of giving me reasoned information. So what next? Question the male nurse, or the man Mallory? I had a feeling I wouldn't get far.

But Nick...

Why had his elegant aunt been so frightened of me talking to him? It could only mean that he knew something which was being concealed. If I could get him on his own...

Nathalie was with him now… No better time, I reasoned. There was a path round the house's side. I took it, my brain beginning once more to function. The kitchen garden had been mentioned.

But it was Nathalie who found me, coming in the opposite direction. When I made to speak, she put a finger to her lips. Taking my arm, she led me back the way she had come, till we came to a window. She motioned that I should look.

A small room, spartan, barely furnished. Nick was lying in the middle of it, face down on a leather couch. I saw the male nurse's blond head, the tubes of salve, the dressings.

And then, as the boy's jeans came down, I saw the backs of his legs.

The bruising covered both of them, a dozen shades of yellow and purple. At the top of the thighs, there were thin red stripes as well, the marks of some kind of whipping. But it was the darker spots, clustered at the back of the knees, which made my skin crawl. I felt the scarred circle of cigarette-burned flesh on my left hand become livid, alive; someone, with methodical cruelty, had done exactly the same to Nick. This was the source of his confusion, of his aunt's fear—this was what we had not been meant to see. I turned to Nathalie, and saw all of her dislike of this place, crystallised into open anger—the same anger I had seen in the Breton farmhouse kitchen, when she had confronted her brother. Now it was there, white-hot and ungovernable, on Nick's behalf. Before either of us could address it, the noise came.

The sports car, starting.

Nathalie was up like a hare from cover. I yelled, but I was nowhere near fast enough. Inside the room, I saw the blond nurse's head jerk round as I went after her.

I reached the house's corner in time to see the red Jaguar, picking up speed as it went down the drive—and Nathalie, sprinting across the grass to cut it off. The man Mallory was already opening the gate in a wide arc. He saw the danger and reached for the running girl, but she sidestepped him easily. She grabbed the gate's heavy iron with both hands and heaved. As it clanged shut, she fell. The Jaguar screeched to a halt, its bumper almost on her.

I ran. Mallory, red-faced, was shouting. The nurse, Jenkins, was stumbling down the drive. I saw Nathalie rise. Would it come to blows? If either of them touched her…

The sight of Angela Holcroft, emerging from the car, white-faced and shaking, stopped everything. We all halted. In the following silence, I saw both men take in the car's back seat.

The suitcase, the hurriedly thrown-in raincoat... Their faces hardened as the realisation dawned.

She was deserting Holcroft House, deserting the two children.

She lifted her shoulder bag from the car, then walked round the bonnet. She shot Nathalie a look of pure poison, then spun round and headed straight into the nearest of the lodge cottages. When she reached the door she turned back to me.

"Just you," she said.

15

TRUTH

THE BEDROOM SMELLED of damp, and one quick look round it told me who had lived here—bottles, cans, glasses, an unmade double bed with greying sheets, one glutinous, ash-covered plate...

The only decoration was a tattered calendar showing a pouting nude on a motorbike. It was high on the wall opposite, positioned for optimum visibility from the pillow, the girl's buxom torso given diseased reflection by the pitted mirror propped on the dresser. How many of McPhie's conquests had measured themselves against those silicon charms? My eyes came to the figure at the window, taut with anger, her back to me. She had been one of them, of course, stupid of me not to have guessed. I turned back to the room's disorder; a fine layer of dust on the bottles and glasses, mould at the plate's edge, every sleazy manifestation of his presence left lovingly untouched...

An altar, a foetid shrine.

She let the big bag slide off her shoulder onto the dresser's battered wood. The soft leather folded in on itself, the polished Gucci logo at once taunt and offering to its surroundings. When she turned to me she looked old.

"How much do you want? All of it—" She gestured at the bed. "—or just the porn?"

"Just the truth," I said.

She pushed past me, back out of the room. I heard a cupboard open, then the chink of glass. She returned with a half-full whisky bottle and two chipped tumblers.

"Here, drink something, show me you're bloody human at least."

I took the proffered glass. Before I'd taken my first sip she was pouring her second measure.

"Right, the *truth*. Let's see if we can find some *truth* for you. How do you want it? Unvarnished? Nice and brutal?"

Still I didn't reply. She pulled off the trench coat and flung it in the corner, then lifted the bottle again. She spoke as she poured.

"Family truth first, Fraser. You've never met my brother, have you? The judge, the great Sir Peter." Her voice invested the name with casual loathing. "Huntin', shootin', fishin' and the law, hang 'em an' flog 'em. Someone once called him the class system in aspic, but they don't know the half of it. *Sex.*"

The bottle slammed down on the dresser's top like a battle's opening drumbeat.

"A brace of maids pregnant by the time he was eighteen. Wore out one wife, tried the same with the next two but they saw the light in time. After them, any number of brainless ones—debs, waitresses, whores, take your pick, if it could be bought or bribed it ended up on its back for him. Money's the finest aphrodisiac money can buy, Fraser, the lecher's one really essential accessory. He was born with it and he used it. Not that I'm any different, you understand," she added, turning to the mirror. "We both philander well. We share the ability to *rut.*"

The word was a barb of self-contempt. She stared at the glass, impaled on her own reflection, then went on.

"And it was that endearing family trait which landed us with her. Five years ago. Mrs. husband-lost-at-sea, Mrs. black-becomes-me. The widow Barrington."

"That was the first time your brother met her?" I asked. "At the accident enquiry for the ferry, the Morbihan?"

"Met!" She snorted her amusement. "Oh, yes they met—a real meeting of minds, that was. The learned judge and the grieving widow. She took one look at him and knew he was money that could be led by its cock—and he saw what he'd always wanted; sex on a stick, with all the trimmings. She pitched it exactly right—fired up the hormones first, then showed him she knew how to gild all the heat, wear the clothes, be gracious to the peasants, act the lady."

The bitchiness faltered. She took a long swig of courage from the chipped glass before going on.

"And she was beautiful," she said quietly. "Stunning."

The pain of the admission was palpable. Again, the whisky was her refuge.

"So what happened?" I asked. "They began an affair?"

The question refuelled her malice. "My, aren't you old-fashioned, Fraser—they did no such thing. For once the old goat had met his match. Lady of the Manor first, not a smell of it did he get till the prenuptial agreement was signed. And she was fast, the fastest I've ever seen, I'll give her that. Wed and installed in a month, widow's weeds to confetti in thirty days."

Once more the mirror drew her. Still clutching the glass, she turned and leaned over it. As she spoke, the middle finger of her right hand played along her right cheekbone

"For more than four years," she went on, "it was okay. Parties, polo, charity balls, Ascot, Cowes, the demure wife. I knew it was all a lie, but she went out of her way to be charming to me, and we kept out of each other's hair. I kept waiting for her to stray, pick up a bit on the side, but if she did—" She tugged gently at the skin beside her eye, but the wrinkles stayed. "—she was bloody clever about it. As far as I could see she was just screwing Peter silly and waiting for him to die."

"So she could inherit?"

"That seemed to be the plan, all right."

The caress had moved to the left side of her face, now. The tugging made its expression impossible to read.

"Did your brother know?"

"Oh, yes, Peter knew. Couldn't have cared less as long as his hand was in the honeypot."

"So what happened to change it?"

The hand dropped, her eyes found mine in the pockmarked glass. The prim mouth relaxed into a long sensual line.

"*He* happened, Fraser. John McPhie happened."

"When?"

"About eight months ago."

She gave a self-deprecating little laugh, but by the time she had turned to the bed it was a sigh of satisfaction. She sat. The long legs swung up, the fine ankles came round in an elegant sweep to rest in a taut—and taught—pose; the model girl relaxes.

She nodded at the window.

"You like sex, Fraser? Give her one, do you—Joan of Arc out there? Like it nice and wild, does she?"

The contempt was casual—other emotions had her in their grip, now. She reached up to the back of her head with both hands. The pins came out. The silver hair's fall to her shoulders was overt, sensual, the unfurling of a sexual flag.

"Well if she does, she'd've sat up and begged for him, just like the rest of us. John McPhie, the maiden's prayer, the hunk. The chauffeur. That didn't matter—he could've been a brain surgeon and that wouldn't have mattered either, as long as he was Big John. Big, hard John," she repeated, mocking herself. "What was it you said, up there in the drawing room? Did he *serve* the whole household?" She laughed with genuine amusement. "Could've *served* me the first day he got here, if he'd wanted. I was at the tennis club and she sent him to collect me with the car. Toby Humphries had thrown me over, I hadn't had any for months—and she knew it, the bitch. I came off the court and he was just standing there, by the Rolls, holding the door, all gorgeous, all muscle and chin. She mimicked a stern face and a Scottish accent. *I'm the new man, Miss, where shall I take ye?* Up against the nearest tree, on the back seat, any damn where you want, I swear to God I nearly said it, if there'd been no one else around I'd've had him there and then. But I couldn't, so I just flirted with him all the way back." Her smile flitted between guile and fondness. "Where was he from? Some Godforsaken island. How did he get the job? Agency in London. All grudge, all dumb insolence, all Scotch resentment—and at the same time he couldn't keep his eyes off my legs in the mirror. I liked that, Fraser, from the start I liked it. A challenge." The mouth's sensual line twisted in amusement as the glass rose to it. "So I kept my cool, made him wait. Months. Distinct advantages—after all, we can't have the servants getting out of hand, can we? And it's always better with a bit of game, a bit of chase. So it was stick and carrot—plenty of stick, oh, yes, plenty of that. Plenty of *Take me shopping, John,* plenty of *Fetch the bags, John.* I'd go out to dinner with someone in the car, flirt outrageously, make sure he could see." The laughter came again, at once brittle and sensuous. "It was all timing, all knowing when to ease off, show him the carrot." She shrugged off one shoulder of the blue dress, exposing a tanned curve of breast almost to the nipple. "A bit of this, a bit of *Oh, John, you surprised me, I'm not quite ready yet,* and lots of this—" The blue hem twitched up to the top of the thigh. "—in and out of the Rolls. Never hurts, does it? What do you think, Fraser—should've worked, shouldn't it? Should've kept the peasants interested."

When I still said nothing she turned back to the whisky glass. "Fuck you," she said, equably. One gulp brought her back to the story. "So I kept it up for nearly two months—stoking it up, getting myself randier and randier, fantasising like mad. What would be the best way? A hotel somewhere, a weekend? Or up against a wall, or just the back of the car? Then I saw him in the village, being chatted up by the girls in the shop, and I panicked." She shook her head, ruefully. "I just broke, didn't I? Came down here with a bottle of whisky, knocked on the door and just did it. Oh, it was easy enough. Neither of us said a word." She paused. "And believe me, it was the fuck of the century."

The tumbler's whisky spilled over, made an oily rivulet down the inside of her left thigh. By the time it reached the bed the smile was gone.

"And I thought it was for him too—I can perform, Fraser."

Her anger swelled round the word, then collapsed. She picked up the glass again and reached for the bottle.

"Except there was someone else who was performing even better than me."

"Sylvia?" I asked.

She nodded, forcing detachment on herself as she poured. "Lady Holcroft herself. They knew each other," she said. "Long before either of them got here, they knew each other. It was all planned. I'd been had, set up."

"You're sure of that?"

"Certain. There were pictures of the two of them together, taken years ago." She anticipated the next question with a grim laugh. "Oh, yes, Fraser, I did it all—went through his pockets, his wallet, his luggage—no fool like an old fool, especially when she's jealous."

"What kind of pictures?" I asked.

She rose, went to the dresser's top drawer. The elegant hand reached out with a handful of battered prints.

McPhie and Sylvia, much younger, toasting each other across a polished bar... McPhie and Sylvia in leathers, rider and passenger on a big bike... McPhie and Sylvia in denim, posing beside the open back of a van, littered with musicians' gear...

I looked across the bed, at the expressionless face beneath the silver hair. She had the glass in her hand again, and she was staring at its emptiness. I put the pictures down beside her. She lifted the bundle, then spread them out on the sheet in a fan, the loser's hand in a card game—and then she looked up at me, defiant again.

"And then I decided I just didn't care. I'd have done anything to keep him, you see, even the bit of him I had. You don't give it up, not when it's like that. You beg, you capitulate, you do anything you have to, anything at all. He wanted me dressed like a cheap whore, he got it. He wanted leather, he got that too." She gestured at the calendar on the wall. "All the props—I even bought him a motorbike. And of course, he wanted three in a bed—Christ!"

Her anger exploded again. She stared up at the ceiling, jaw taut with the memory.

"I hated her guts, but if that's what it took to keep him..."

Again the rage subsided. She shrugged.

"I'd've fucked regiments for that," she finished, quietly. "And all the time, of course, she was scheming her head off."

"What do you mean?"

"You really are naive, aren't you? Like all the rest of the plebs—one look at his lordship's house on the hill and you're mesmerised by money. Most of the place is mortgaged, Fraser. Oh, not up to the hilt, there's enough to keep us in bread and circuses for now, but when my shit of a brother finally dies the death duties'll take anything that's left. Do you understand?"

When I didn't reply she waved the whisky glass at me as though it was the only thing capable of making the right emphasis. "She worked it out! She saw that to get her hands on any real money, she had to take it *now.* Why wait to inherit nothing when a divorce'll put you in clover? If the grounds were right, the prenuptial deal was worth more than a million to her."

"So why steal the Stradivarius?"

"Ready cash, Fraser. Lawyers could take years to sort it all out. She wants the good life now. The violin was just the down payment."

"How did they do it?"

She leaned back on the bed. "Two weeks ago she said she needed a holiday, a break, she said, to get away—to France, she was always in bloody France. She took Nick for camouflage—and of course, John had to drive her. They hammed that up to the hilt, couldn't keep their hands off each other, made sure I was so seething that I wouldn't think straight, wouldn't see it coming." She looked up at me, all artifice gone now. "They simply took Ewen's violin with them. It took us a day to discover it, but there was nothing we could do."

"Why?"

She laughed her brittle laugh as she delved into the Gucci bag. A brown envelope, ten by eight... I knew what it was even before it landed on the bed. I opened it, leafed through the photographs—every possible combination of three bodies was there, coiled round each other. In most of them, Angela Holcroft's face was clearly visible. The accompanying note was neatly typed on good paper. I read, quickly; no police, no private detectives, no action to be taken to recover the violin, a divorce to be set in motion immediately on the grounds of irretrievable breakdown of marriage. Otherwise, the Sunday papers. Sir Peter Holcroft could keep the children, custody would not be contested. I laid the paper on the bed.

"And you agreed to this? Your brother as well?"

The scorn of her reply was frightening. "What do you think? The News of the Screws—High Court judge's wife and sister in love triangle with chauffeur? Bondage on the bench? Lesbianism? Christ, don't be so bloody stupid!"

I checked my anger. "Do you know where they've gone?" I asked.

She paused. Again she fingered the photographs on the bed. "Scotland."

"How do you know?"

Again the elegant hand went into the Gucci bag. This time the envelope it came out with was smaller. I pulled out the contents.

A very different kind of blackmail note, crudely written on a torn-off page of lined paper, addressed only to her. Ten thousand pounds, otherwise the photos, etc. Instructions where to send it would follow. I went back to the envelope—Edinburgh, postmarked the 4th of August. Two days ago.

"It arrived this morning," she said, brusquely.

"And the first demand, the typed one, when did that come?"

She laughed, cynically. "It was left on the drawing room

table, the day they took the violin, two and a half weeks ago."

Two demands inside such a short space of time... It didn't make sense. I gave her back the Scottish letter.

"You'll pay this?"

"Ten thousand in cash won't be easy," she said, quietly.

"What about your brother? Does he know about this one?"

She shook her head.

"Where is he?"

The contempt returned to her. "Out whoring, chasing barmaids."

"Where?"

"How the hell should I know!"

I turned away from the desperation of her anger. To the window, to the imposing facade of Holcroft House.

Contentment. Wealth. Nobility. And power... The car was once more beside the roses, the upstairs lights shone, the Union Jack hung from the flagpole. Everything normal, everything back in its appointed place, wrapped in plush moonlight.

England, their England...

"And Nick?" I asked, softly.

Behind me, I heard her brittle anger break. When the voice came, it was fighting for control.

"They dumped him. In a lay-by near St. Malo. Tourists found him, English girls. There was a name and address on his bag and they phoned. I went immediately."

"The burns, on his legs, the welts. That was McPhie?"

She said nothing. I waited. Still nothing. The rage rising in me, I turned. She would answer me! She would accept her part in the boy's suffering!

Her face, bleak with pain, killed my anger. All I could find was the one syllable.

"Why?"

My only reply was a single tear. I watched it etch its way down her powdered cheek, then went across to the dresser and poured myself another measure, the question burning in my brain.

Why...

The whisky tasted like a wound. I was beyond reproach or rage, now—but as I put down the glass and turned back to her, I knew I had to ask the question.

"Did you love him? McPhie?"

She exploded at me through the tears. "Love! What the hell's love got to do with anything!" She rose, advanced on me. "Who ever gave me love?"

As we faced each other, the dress slipped further from her shoulder. The blue-veined breast was exposed, completely. She saw my eyes move down to it. Both hands came up to the dress's bodice. The silk came apart in one long rip of frustration that exposed the body from neck to crotch.

"That's right—look! Stare! What use is love to that, Fraser? It's fifty years old and it's hungry. Love doesn't feed it—*heat* feeds it! *Hardness* feeds it! I don't need love, I don't *want* love!"

The nipples quivered at me in accusation, daring me to challenge the desperation of the lie.

And then the challenge came, from a different direction.

The cry, the peacock's cry.

The effect of it was terrible to see—her soul was rent apart as completely as her dress, her grief exposed as surely as her body. Our eyes met in a moment of total candour. However much she might deny it, even betray it, she loved both children; Ewen's pain was unbearable to her.

She put her hands to her ears to shut out the inevitable reply and collapsed on to the bed. When the boy's tortured voice came it was barely audible over her sobbing.

16

ANCIENT

THE PUB CALLED The Cock, less than twenty miles away from Holcroft House up the plump river's valley, was testament to a different England.

It was a building which had endured by camouflage—a structure at once fluid and squat, without a straight line in it, its weathered sandstone moulded by the contours of the hillside behind, so tightly pressed into its lee that the honey-coloured roof seemed like an extension of the slope. The barn which stood further down the hill had been built on the same principle, but not as solidly—it was more open to the valley's wind, and the weather had claimed one end, baring the roof's skeleton of joists. The grey electrical junction box fixed to its side was a wart of technological incongruity, the cable which brought current from the main building, an impossibly frail connection to the twentieth century.

But were we in the right place? As we got out of the van, I wondered. The man Mallory had directed us here, but it seemed unlikely...

"Regarde, Alex."

I followed Nathalie's pointed arm. Amid the car park's collection of the rusty and ill-repaired, sitting like a prim duchess fallen upon hard times, was a sleek 1950's Bentley. The number plate matched the one Holcroft House's gatekeeper had so grudgingly given us. Our quarry was here. We picked our way in silence through a clutter of oil drums to the scuffed front door.

The space we came into was more passageway than room, thickening out as it wound away to our left, filled with men and smoke. Our entry brought silence, questioning faces—hard faces, bleak, unwelcoming. Why? Because we were strangers, or because of Nathalie? As we moved towards the polished wooden bar, the plaintive sough of an empty beer tap came. It seemed to sanction our presence. Slowly, the talk resumed, a low mutter, more animal than human. The landlord eyed us warily.

"What can I get you?"

"'s all right, George, they're expected."

I turned to the female voice which had broken in—and found a woman who would never see forty again, black-haired and dramatic, glamorous rather than beautiful. Angela Holcroft's voice came back to me.

Out whoring, chasing barmaids...

But who had phoned ahead? Mallory, of course, the faithful servant, it had to be... Did the forewarning matter? The dark-haired woman's face stayed carefully neutral as she perused us, and then she looked away, to her left. I followed her gaze.

Falstaff.

That was my first impression—a luxuriant shock of white hair above a florid face, no neck, a squat barrel of a body perched on a bench behind a slim walking stick. The features were immediately recognisable, an overtly masculine, jowl-flanked version of his sister's beauty. Slowly, I took in the clothes; blue shirt with white collar, spotted silk bow tie, elegant patent leather shoes. On the table beside him lay a cream linen jacket with a rose at the buttonhole. I looked back at the florid face. Falstaff trying for Beau Brummel? Falstaff come courting? What had I expected, that he'd be wigged and gowned, dressed in sober judicial black?

And then I noticed the stains on the jacket's lapel, the tie's slack knot, the three-day stubble. No, Falstaff might have been Beau Brummel for a while, but now the dandy was gone; elegance no longer mattered to this man, somehow I knew it. I waited for him to speak, but instead, one long hand left the stick's top to gesture at the two empty chairs before him. As we approached, the grey eyes left me to peruse Nathalie, but once we were seated, he turned back to me.

"Fraser, isn't it? My man Mallory tells me you're trouble. What do you want?"

"Information," I said. "As soon as we have it, we'll be gone."

One eyebrow came up. The florid face turned again to Nathalie.

"Ah, the Scots—so refreshing, so direct. Especially in the matter of threats, don't you agree, my dear?" He leaned forward. "A threat," he said, "is nothing more than an order with conditions—you will do this, or I will do that, and so on. Great takers of orders, the Scots, great channelers of command, the best of N.C.O's. The Jocks I had in Malaya—you pointed the finger at a communist and said kill, and they killed. No questions asked, no tiresome conscience." He smiled benignly. "It was as simple as that. And higher up the ladder they were good as well—great passers-on of directives, good, solid adjutants." He turned back to me. "But givers of orders, sources of that initial command—" The stick rapped the floor for emphasis. "—No sir! Too much self-doubt for that, not enough thrust, not enough certainty." He eased the thick body back on the bench. "If you want to give orders, Fraser, learn how to formulate them. You'll never make effective threats until you do."

An academic attempt to goad, spleen whetting its appetite by patronising... The only reaction I could find was impatience. There had been enough games, now.

"Do you know where your wife is?" I asked.

He surveyed me with obvious satisfaction, grand master to novice, spider to fly.

"Ah, wives. Inconvenient things, aren't they? Especially active ones—they lead to all sorts of complications. And marriage itself..." The smile widened. "I know men who would compare marriage to prison. As someone who has knowledge of both institutions, would you agree?"

There was no mistaking what he was telling me—he knew I'd been in prison, and he knew why. But how? I realised I was staring at Nathalie's hands; I had never told her about it. He would tell her, now... As the confusion rose in me, his voice went on.

"You mustn't imagine, Fraser, that my retired status is any bar to the acquisition of information. I have contacts enough, and the computer is a wonderful invention, a watchdog which never sleeps, no matter how late the hour." He turned again to Nathalie. "Manslaughter—such a neutral term in one sense, and yet, by today's pseudo-liberal standards, it might even be considered, shall we say, sexist? What about *womanslaughter?"*

The reply was not what he expected.

"Why did you give the boy Ewen a Stradivarius violin to play, *Monsieur?"*

It would have been hard to tell who was more surprised, myself or Holcroft—a challenge, a firm rebuttal of his assumption of power. The Falstaff face surveyed her with new interest now, with respect. A different note came to his voice.

"Excellence!" he said. "Do you believe in excellence? I do. I spent my working life in wig and gown, sitting in judgment, lending dignity to sordid crimes committed—" The grey eyes found mine. "—by second-rate human beings. Long ago, I became convinced that only excellence could save this nation. Save this race."

It smacked of manifesto, of a speech learned and often repeated. When she didn't answer him, he rapped his stick twice on the floor—not for effect this time, it was a signal of some sort. Then he turned back to her.

"Excellence!" he barked again. "When the boy was first brought into my house, it was obvious he had it. I saw it, his teachers confirmed it. Music is not an excellence I understand, or care for—but I was in a position to encourage it and I did so. The encouragement of excellence is a moral duty."

Again, the ring of manifesto—but a slightly hollow ring. What was he hiding? My confidence had recovered, now. I broke in before his rhetoric could begin again.

"So why isn't it your moral duty to get the boy's violin back? We know your wife has it. Where is she?"

He didn't even consider it. "As to your first assertion," he said, "I gave the boy the violin as a tool, not as a crutch. He can learn to live without it—the talent in him will be maximised in some other way. As for his mother..."

He shrugged. Behind me, I heard the barmaid's approach. The grin became wolfish.

"I gather," he said dryly, "that you are under no illusions as to the exact field of her excellence. Due to my fool of a sister, the price of recovering that now is simply too high."

A glass of some dark spirit came down on the table before him. He stared up with frank lechery at the woman's blank face.

"Especially," he went on, "when it can be acquired elsewhere."

He reached out as she turned. The bony hand openly palmed one of her buttocks, fondled. It was repellent, a gesture of ownership; a man was assessing a piece of livestock.

"And at such commercial rates, too."

As I watched the careful neutrality of her face, his voice came again.

"A useful bargain, Fraser, don't you agree? This house and its activities are under my protection. In exchange I exercise certain rights. What might be described as a modern *Droit de Seigneur.*"

Activities...? What did he mean? My eyes found Nathalie's face, caught between amazement and disgust. Behind the bar, the bell rang again, as though confirming the Pavlovian responses we'd just witnessed—lust and flesh, sex and power... The landlord's voice came, a troubled midland burr.

"Time, now. Let's have your glasses."

Gradually, I became aware of the changes around me. The room's conversation had once again become a whisper—but expectant, now. Before me, the wolfish grin widened. I turned away from it—and found the landlord's gaunt face, frowning at our table. The implication was clear—we were to go. Behind us, Falstaff's voice boomed out.

"My guests, Mister Miles. They stay."

The landlord gave a slow nod—he wasn't happy, but he accepted the order. What hold did Falstaff have here? As I wondered, men began to rise from their tables. Again Holcroft spoke.

"Such children, such craven children, all of them. When I discovered this diversion of theirs, they imagined immediate retribution. How surprised they were that I should insist on its continuance."

Two men appeared from the back room. Each held a wire cage.

"After all, Fraser, even the lower classes should never be denied it, don't you agree? The pursuit of excellence."

Revulsion and understanding came together. Cockerels. Their staring eyes were a match for the mad voice. It was seductive now, purring with the pleasure of a trap well sprung.

"Stay. Both of you, stay and watch. Watch it and I'll tell you where my wife is."

*

The blood lust was palpable, the faces tense, sinewed with excitement. Somewhere behind, the rainwater leaked from the barn's pierced roof in a steady, rhythmic drip, ancient time being kept to ancient cruelty.

At the centre of it, in a pit of floodlit brightness, the cocks were a nightmare. Elizabethan-ruffed, steel-spurred, rakish to the point of emaciation, they craned forward at each other across the sand, round eyes fixed in obsessive stare as they circled. Behind them, recording it all from a high tripod, was a different eye. New technology was serving old obscenity; the video camera followed every jerking move. Around us, the voices muttered their fevered incantations.

"Six to four, six to four, c'mon the brindled!"

"Flank him! Rip 'is heart out!"

"Go for the wing, my lovely! Spur in the wing!"

My eyes found the figure of the judge, presiding over the proceedings from a high-backed chair directly opposite me. His face was cold, dispassionate, all excitement gone now, all relish. It might have been some dry-as-dust civil court in front of him instead of this debased gladitorial contest. Was the man mad? Would he take the carcass of the loser back to Holcroft House and mount it on his wall of death outside Ewen's classroom? Would he add the winner's spurs to the blades and barrels opposite?

Was he mad?

As I watched, I considered it as dispassionately as I could. A High Court Judge, protector and patron of cockfights, blackmailer of barmaids for sexual favours. He couldn't hope to keep any of that secret for long—and yet he was prepared to let himself be deprived of more than a million for the sake of his family's good name. It didn't add up—it was a paradox which only madness could explain. As I tried to work it out, the man at my side grabbed my sleeve. His words came tumbling out in a sour-breathed whisper of excitement.

"Great, aren't they—I'd buy 'em both, if I could! Match 'em at home in my own back yard, just for myself!"

I stared at him—and then my eyes whipped round again to Holcroft.

Buy them both...

Just for himself...

The lawgiver, above the law.

The arrogant aristocrat, never denied.

Yes, that was it... He would do that, he would—

In the sawdust pit, one spurred leg quivered up.

A collective sigh of release echoed round the bare walls—and then a chorus of yells erupted. As if blown by the breath of aggression, the birds locked, tearing at each other, screeching, fluttering. My gorge rose. I couldn't watch this!

Nathalie's hand landed on my arm in a tight grip. "*Non*, Alex," she whispered. "They'd kill you."

A terrible squawk of pain came, only to be drowned in a roar of approbation. I turned and pushed my way out of the building.

The rain's freshness was blessed. I walked over to the crumbling hillside, waiting for the tightness in my chest to subside. Behind me I heard footsteps. I turned to find her face torn between misery and concern.

"What could you do, Alex? One man against thirty? And even if you succeeded, stopped it, they would just take their horrible birds somewhere else."

The rage burst out of me. "We can't just walk away from that, do nothing! If we do, we're as bad as they are—as bad as if we'd stayed and watched!"

I closed my eyes, waiting for the anger to subside, the disgust. When I opened them again, she was looking above my head.

"What if no one could watch?" she said softly.

I turned and followed her eyes.

The power line.

Without light, it had to stop, there would be no point. I scanned the length of it—a flimsy affair... I turned, found her face full of that familiar fierce joy. She ran to the van. I heard the door open, metallic noises—and then she was sprinting past me, across the car park towards the metal junction box. I saw the gleam in her hands. An axe! I reached her just in time to kill the swing. She stared at me, puzzled.

"Not yet," I said. "Get in the van, drive. Make them think we're gone. Once you're clear, I'll do it."

Her anger was immediate. "You don't have to protect me!"

"I'm not protecting you." I nodded back at the barn. "I want one last crack. At him."

Again the protest rose in her, but I cut it off. I reached out, grabbed the axe's shaft.

"Trust me. Go, come back in half an hour."

She stood her ground, ready to fight me—until another roar of approval came from the barn. She swore softly, then let the tool fall into my hands and strode off.

As soon as I heard the engine start, I went back to the rock face. Cut it? No, too chancy... Carefully, I eased the axe head in, over the cable and behind it, and then I tightened my grip on the shaft, put one foot against the wet rock—and pulled.

It gave. As I fell backwards the flash seemed to surround me. The lights died. I staggered, but I kept my footing. Axe in hand, I ran.

The lights of the pub had gone too, now—it had worked, shorted everything. Dizzy, I scrambled across to the oil drums by the main door. As I dropped down out of sight behind them, I heard the hubbub of voices spill out of the barn. One of them was yelling about 'that Scotch bastard, him with the girl!', another was cursing that it was too late, they were gone. A third voice, more threatening, was insisting that all bets were off.

From my hiding place I listened. Would they search? No footsteps came near. I heard their anger metamorphose—suddenly they were more preoccupied with reclaiming their wagers than with anything else. I heard notes being counted out, mutters of grudging acceptance—and then, within seconds, cars starting. Inside ten minutes, the silence was total. Crouched behind the drums, I felt relief. So far so good, the ruse of sending Nathalie away had worked. But the next part...

I gave it another few minutes, then stood up. The car park was empty except for one vehicle. The Bentley.

I'd been right, he had waited. He knew what I had done, he knew I wouldn't let it end there. There was enough light to let me see that the barn's door was open. Still holding the axe, I walked towards it. Was I right about this man? Was the insight which had come to me across the cockfight correct?

Inside the barn, my footsteps seemed thunderous. The smell was still there—bodies, excitement, birds, smoke, all bound together in an arid tang that was the embodiment of cruelty. Where was he? The voice boomed out from across the dark space.

"Clever, Fraser. I am as much impressed by your decisiveness as I am amused at your squeamishness. Or was your shapely companion the instigator? If so, then I congratulate you on your choice of bedmate—physical perfection *and* intelligence." He laughed. "Although it isn't my experience that clever women couple well. Is she an exception?"

I didn't let my anger reply. "You know, don't you. Where your wife is. You've even talked to her since she left. How else could she have known that a Breton violin dealer knew the Singer's whereabouts? That means you've condoned it, sanctioned the deal."

The disembodied voice laughed, then found a chilling composure. "Any arrangements my wife and I have made are none of your damn business. Your meddling in my affairs is now at an end. Do you fully comprehend that?"

Cocksure... The word came to me, a bitter irony in the darkness. Never had I heard a voice so certain it would never be contradicted.

"Oh, yes, I *fully comprehend,* all right," I said. "I comprehend a lot of things, now. You don't care about reputation, do you? Yours or your sister's. You've conned her into believing you do, but if it was really true you wouldn't have been here tonight, taking part in this obscenity. So what's worth a million pounds and a Stradivarius to a man like you?"

I took a step forward in the darkness. I could just make out the shape of him, the squat mass occupying the chair.

"It's the children, isn't it? The two boys—you're making sure you avoid any kind of custody battle. You're purchasing two children for a million pounds. You're trying to buy yourself some love, before it's too late."

His sister's reaction to the accusation of love had been despair. His was a sneer.

"Ah, the moral murderer, the perceptive thug, axe in hand. The question is, though, will your perception make any difference? Do you think what you've seen here tonight is some kind of lever? Do you think the police will believe you? A High Court Judge against a convicted felon—a felon once again on the run, wanted for murder in France. How did you do it this time, Fraser? The axe? Have you regressed so far?"

The barn's clammy darkness closed round me. Not only did he know about the past, he knew about the present, about Belle-île! I saw movement, then something silver-edged in his hand, gleaming. Fear touched me—a mobile phone. Could it be bluff? Even as the thought came, a distant siren mocked it. I began to back away; Nathalie—how long before she returned? His voice followed me out of the barn, a triumphant shout.

"Fifteen minutes, Fraser! Since I spoke to them. At the very most you have ten more."

Outside, the rain had stopped and the moon was up. Across the car park, I saw her, standing hesitantly by the green van's open door. I didn't shout, there was no need—the urgency of my run spoke for itself. By the time I reached the vehicle, it was already moving.

17

MORALITY

Without her, they'd have had us, for I was numb with the shock of it. If I'd been driving, our ten minute lead wouldn't have lasted seconds.

But Nathalie... She was ice-cool under pressure, completely in charge. In less than a mile she was off the main road, tackling the back lanes like a rally driver, scything lightless between the hedgerows, taking the curves at hair-raising speed. My fear gave way to wonder—at her confidence, her fierce concentration. Where had she learned to run like this? At first it was merely puzzling, but then, in the tense darkness, it came to me. Of course… This was the PSB, this was the implacable practicality of the guerrilla. This was Riou. I gave him silent thanks—and then stopped myself.

No, not Riou—the man who trained the PSB's elite in evading authority, that would be Prosper... I felt a sharp, confused pang of loss. I didn't know what she meant to me, this girl, but the thought of that cold little man instructing her in the arts of war, that disturbed.

Only once was her single-minded silence broken, by a terse flurry of questions. Did I know this area? Which way would she find open country, broken by farm roads? I told her that to the West was Wales, foothills which gave way to real mountains. She shook her head; no hills, hill roads had fewer side turnings, hill roads were easy to block off, if we wanted to evade them—

She stopped in mid-sentence, suddenly thoughtful. A decision had been made, I could see. She didn't share it with me, but the way she looked up at the moon told me she was now navigating as well as driving.

After half an hour the rain returned, briefly, and she had to risk lights. She slowed down, letting the beams search, inspecting each opening we came to. Finally, she pulled off down a rutted dirt road. It descended gently past a clutch of deserted farm buildings to peter out in a tiny clearing. When the sound of water came, I worked it out.

The plump river. We were back beside it, at the valley's centre. On the far bank ahead of us, the ground rose, a black mass, unidentifiable in the dark. To the left was an overgrown path along the water's edge, to the right, tall thickets of hawthorn bushes with a willow's hanging branches just visible behind. She examined both directions, then switched off the engine and got out. I followed.

"The tracks," she said. She pointed at the bushes. "Branches, big ones."

I lifted the axe and did as she bade me, attacking the hawthorn. As soon as I'd cut a few, she took the biggest from me and began running back the way we had come.

"Viens, Alex!"

I grabbed a branch and followed. At the junction where we'd turned off she stopped, listened. Nothing. She began obliterating the tyre tracks, walking backwards, raking the the green fan of foliage over the damp earth. I worked beside her. Inside ten minutes there was effectively no trace of our descent. Back at the van she motioned at the thicket to the right.

"We need a tunnel, a way through. Every time you take a branch, rub dirt on the cut."

I understood; by daylight or torch light, new wood was easy to spot. Again I advanced on the hawthorn, cutting methodically. It took ten minutes to hack through to the willow behind. The space beneath the hanging branches was muddy and uneven, but it would do. She ran back to the van and started it, steered it stubbornly across the cut stumps. Metal and wood screamed their intolerance of each other, but finally the Volkswagen was entirely beneath the hanging foliage. She switched off, got out and took the axe from me. Methodically, she began chopping at the ground, using the tool to dig. I understood. I gathered the hawthorn branches, handed them to her one by one, watched her thrust the ends as deep into the earth as she could, stamp them firmly in. Within minutes the thicket looked as though it had never been disturbed. We were closed in. She stood back, inspected her handiwork, then turned to me.

"The van goes no further. In daylight, with the number circulated, we wouldn't get ten kilometres. Here, we might be lucky, it might be a day or so before she's found. If not..." She shrugged. "Either way, we go from here on foot. That way."

She pointed to the path along the river. I could make out lights, now—a faint glimmer a few miles away, street lights. A village? A small town?

"We crossed a railway line further back, heading down the valley towards it," she said. "There must be trains, buses." She looked at her watch. "Three hours till dawn. In the last of the darkness we'll go."

There was an oddness to her words. I couldn't place it at first. What it was only became obvious as she moved back to the van.

Nervousness…

An undercurrent of it had crept in through all the fierce competence. Why? I was about to ask when the moon came out from behind the clouds, silvering the river. The black mass of the hillside took on a clear silhouette now, its apex sculpted, classical.

Holcroft House.

We were directly across the water from it. As the shock subsided, appreciation came—she had doubled back, clever... They'd not think to look for us here; clever guerrilla... For a long time, I stared at it. Finally I spoke.

"And now?"

My answer was a familiar sound, domestic. I turned, saw the side door of the van, open. She had taken off her jeans. She was sitting cross-legged on the bed, her head cocked to one side. With one hand she was brushing her hair, with the other she was unbuttoning her blouse.

Desire welled in me, confusion rode its back—guerrillas didn't do that! Brush their hair... But the ridiculous drowned in the desperate. I looked away—at anything, at the curtain of willow, the water, the thickets of hawthorn that hid us. What had we built? For the green van, a perfect hide... And for a guerrilla with a hairbrush and a fugitive from a cockfight, what? A lovers' hideaway? A sudden fear, clear and precise, cut through the panic, saving me and damning me at once. I knew I had to ask.

"In the pub," I said, "with Holcroft, when he started to talk about my past, about prison... You knew already, didn't you?"

The hairbrush fell to her lap. She stared away, through the willow branches.

"Prosper checked you out," she said, finally. "He wanted evidence, something that would make me stay away from you."

"So why didn't you?"

She didn't answer. My mouth was dry as I spoke again.

"You know all of it?"

She lifted the hairbrush, began again the tough tugging at her curls. The terseness was back in her voice, now.

"You killed your wife for sleeping with another man. You struck her in anger. She hit her head, the fall killed her. If you had appealed, you wouldn't even have gone to prison."

"I struck her in rage. It's not wrong that rage should be punished."

"And the punishment should not last forever. Debts can be paid."

The brushing stopped. Finally, she faced me.

"Years ago, when I learned what my father had done, it nearly destroyed me. Don't let that happen to you, Alex. Sometimes rage rules, we all know that. When it rules right, it can be used, when it rules wrong, it can be forgiven. In time."

I stared across the water at Holcroft House. A cold stone box full of love, desperation, betrayal and violence. Had rage ruled there? I closed my eyes. Her voice came again, neither harsh nor gentle now, simply determined, a hollow refuge carved out of stubbornness.

"And when its rule is in the past, it should be left there."

I turned. She put down the hairbrush. Her eyes dropped again as her hands went slowly back to the buttons.

*

After we made love, I lay awake. I couldn't have slept. The urgency of what had passed between us, the honesty of unashamed physical need, was too fresh, too alive. The van's side door was open, the coolness of the night air fanned me from one side, the coolness of her steady breathing from the other. In the moonlit water I could see my situation reflected with diamond-hard clarity.

And hers. I heard her breathing change. As gently as I could, I turned, found her lying on her side, her face pressed to the pillow, lips singing in silence, eyebrows and lids twitching in the depths of dream. I smiled. The innocence of it seemed so far from the cold efficiency that had saved us, only a few hours before.

Innocence...

I pondered it. She could still walk away from this. She had committed no crime, technical or provable, she had seen me commit none. If she had to face the police, there wasn't a thing they could pin on her. But from here on in it could be very different. What would that mean, to her? I slid off the mattress and out of the van. The grass was wet with dew.

And as I looked across at Holcroft House, I knew that for me, nothing had really changed. I hadn't found what I needed there. I still had to go after Sylvia Holcroft.

Either she or McPhie knew what had become of my fiddle. More than anything, I wanted it back—and I wanted my innocence back as well. I had murdered no one on Belle-île, and the mad judge's wife had the only evidence in my favour, slim though it was.

The picture.

The one the black photographer had taken of the two of us together on the terrace—I had thrust it deep into the fiddle case's lining. Unless she had discarded that case for a better one, there was no reason to suppose that the polaroid wasn't still there, right beside The Singer. It had me, Sylvia, the fiddle case, and it had a newspaper headline from which a date could be traced. With George Berolet's testimony, it might just be enough to convince the cops that I was telling the truth, that I had been lured to the island and set up. Without it...

Again I looked across at the forbidding house. Dawn wasn't far off. I turned back to the van, ready to wake Nathalie—and just before my hand reached her shoulder, a faint noise came over the water.

A falling musical cadence, perfect, elegaic...

I turned, slowly, waiting for the inevitable human response. When it came, ragged with pain, I felt the small, nagging truth which had snapped at the heels of my reason since the first time I'd heard the bird and the boy.

I could name it, now, that truth. I stood, watching the lightening silhouette of the building across the water, acknowledging it to myself.

My fiddle was my soul, my freedom was my sanity. For the sake of both, I had to find Sylvia, but that wasn't all.

Soul and sanity had been added to.

The boy Ewen had become my conscience.

Someone had to help him answer the peacock.

If I could, I would bring his Singer back to him.

18

GUERRILLAS

THE MINUTE WE stepped out of the thicket that hid the green van, our relationship changed.

There was no tenderness now. The physical closeness we'd shared was granted one soft kiss—and then she was once more the leader, so cool, so confident of her mastery of the mechanics of evasion. She checked the cover of the bushes, pulled a few branches better into place—and then simply turned and walked away from the green van. I followed her along the water's edge, but as soon as we came into open ground where we might be seen, she let me catch up, took my arm, and began to smile.

It disturbed me, that smile. It was a false thing, a mask. It reminded me of someone else, someone disturbing. It took a moment, but then I had it.

Philippe Berolet. Of all people, Philippe… Withdrawn, armoured against the world...

Was that how she needed to be to command? To survive? As we walked along, the picture of the happy couple in the morning dew, I felt troubled. I'd been on the run before, but this was so different—was it because I wasn't alone, because I wasn't in charge? Some kind of loner's curse? By the time we'd reached the village further up the river my confusion had whittled itself down to a small but chilling truth—that a subterfuge shared was in no way a subterfuge halved.

But there was no denying her expertise. We reached the village by five in the morning—too early for public transport. I wanted to take the first bus that came, but she vetoed it. A later one, she insisted. People were the best cover, she said, if there were road blocks a near-empty morning bus would be stopped. So we spent two hours in a ditch behind a pile of paving slabs. The bus we finally took was full of local shoppers headed for the nearest market town, and the police cars stationed at every roundabout never gave it a second glance.

From the town it was easier, a succession of local trains, then more buses, a steady spiralling away from the hinterland of Holcroft House. Tourists, she decreed. We went to local markets, fetes, we sipped flat beer in crowded pubs where we could watch the door, arguing in whispers about what to do next. We became fake sightseers, attenders of events—places with a fast turnover of people, places which wouldn't have a heavy police presence.

Places like the one we'd arrived at now. As we followed the crowds out of the tunnel that led from the car park to the site, the air was heavy with sighs that mixed satisfaction and incredulity.

Stonehenge.

The monument of circles; inner stones, outer stones—and then the floating ring of worshippers, hundreds of them, the impressed, the bored, the indifferent. The sight of it held me. I looked beyond the people at the weathered solidity of the huge stones. Reality swam; they seemed so much more real than what was happening to us now... I heard a voice I hardly recognised as my own.

"Does it feel the same as Carnac? A church?"

Nathalie stopped, abruptly and I felt immediate guilt; the question belonged to her quiet kitchen garden, to the time before our messy and complicated ejection from it. She stared at the long shadows of the stones, then looked down at the ground.

"Non," she said, softly but vehemently. "Don't ask me that now, it isn't fair. Ask me if we ever come back here in peace, with time to think. Everything's different now."

We walked on, two tourists, come like thousands of others to see the big stones—and then as soon as we were out of earshot of anyone else, she stopped again. When she turned I saw that she'd recovered, forced herself back onto the even keel of the clandestine. I knew what was coming.

"Alex, whatever you say, it's at least a plan. There has to be one—if there isn't, then the pursuit becomes everything. In the end that means the pursuer controls. That means you get caught."

My temper flared—we'd argued this all day. "Another line from the PSB handbook? Who are you quoting, Patrik or Prosper?"

"C'est stupide, ça," she said quietly.

The glances of the passers-by measured our discomfort as they strolled round on their circular pilgrimage. Suddenly her face was no longer dark; the smile, the infuriating false smile.

"The attendants are watching," she said, brightly.

This time, I just couldn't summon it up. She saw my frustration and turned away.

"Alex, leave your anger behind and think it through," she whispered. "Our money is nearly gone. You have next to none, I left France with hardly any. If I use a credit card it's like leaving a footprint. We have no choice."

"I've already told you, I know someone in Scotland who can help us."

She stopped and faced me. "You've phoned twice now. No answer. And I'm not sorry, Alex—this is a known contact, isn't it? Someone the police can connect you with? It's stupid and it's amateur and it's asking for trouble. And we don't need it."

The mismatch of the light smile and the determined voice silenced me. She took my arm, began to guide me back towards the underpass; two lovers, strolling...

"What we need is a car," she said, "a car and money. Now, today. Patrik has access to both, and he has contacts here in Britain, contacts who are prepared for just this kind of emergency. We could be on the road again in just a few hours. On the road and secure. Everything you said earlier—yes, you're right, for me it will be difficult. But whatever Patrik is to me now, he was always a friend as well as a lover. Always, he has given me respect. And support. I don't think he'll let me down now."

I turned, looked at her—my guerrilla, smiling, implacable. Now that she'd chosen her course I'd never deflect her from it, I knew. She took both my hands in hers.

"I'll phone, now—there's no risk. There's a number we use for emergencies, a number that won't be tapped."

She didn't wait for an answer. As she walked away from me, down through the underpass, I turned and looked back at the immense stone circle.

Certainty, massive certainty, had built this. I would have given anything for just a few grains of it now. I'd come to a decision, I knew. But was it the right one?

*

The tube train was hell, its cargo of late workers and early revellers crammed in like battery chickens, its recycled air reeking of decay. Nathalie was crushed in behind me, her hand touching mine on the overhead rail.

"The tickets," she whispered, "the other ones, *pour l'Écosse?"*

Her nerves were plain, now. How much longer could she keep this up? I remembered her other voice, the confident one, only ten minutes ago.

There has to be a backup, always. If something goes wrong tonight, there has to be another way out of London...

She had sent me to get them, at King's Cross, with the last of our money. She fell against me as the tube train lurched and swayed through a station at breakneck speed. The posters flashed past, charges of hallucinatory colour verging on the subliminal. She let her body hang close to me. For comfort, for strength, I knew it. I looked up at the wall map—two more stations to go, twenty minutes to the rendezvous... She put her hand over mine on the rail and whispered again.

"Where are they, in your jacket? Are they safe?"

I nodded.

And then, without warning, I felt her lips on the back of my neck

The kiss was fierce, chaste, loyal, her tension seeking its lightning rod. The only person to see it was a middle-aged woman, hemmed in by shopping bags. She smiled, turned to her neighbour. I caught the whispered word *love* and looked away.

If she'd known exactly what I'd done at the King's Cross ticket counter, she wouldn't have whispered *love,* she'd have whispered *betrayal.*

*

"...now exactly five minutes to go. Someone will meet us here at exactly eleven minutes past eight. Should there be even a minute's difference in the time, we walk away. Do you understand,

Alex?"

She spoke without looking at me, her hands deep in the pockets of her jeans, her eyes scanning the drizzle at the grimy mouth of Finsbury Park tube station.

"If anything stupid happens, Alex, I want you to know—"

"Bonjour, Mademoiselle."

We both turned at the same time.

The beret, the leather jacket...

Prosper.

This wasn't what she'd agreed on the phone. He ignored me.

"Left out of here," he said, "along to the end of the road. Turn right. There's a line of parked cars. Patrik's in the seventh one. He wants to talk to you."

I stirred, uneasily. This wasn't in the plan either.

"All I asked for was help. It could have been delivered." Nathalie said, tightly. "I think I've served the movement well enough to deserve better than this."

The face beneath the beret was expressionless. "You serve, you don't exploit. But you'll get what you asked for if you do as you're told."

She looked at him, then at me. "It seems we have no choice. I'm sorry, Alex."

We both made to move. Prosper's hand came across my chest.

"Not you. She goes alone, we stay here together."

She began to protest. *"Mais non!"*

His voice cut in again, undeflected. "Everything you asked for is here. If you want it, you talk to him. Alone." He was looking at me now, but his words were still addressed to her. "You owe him an explanation. At least that, I think."

Her eyes met mine. She was unsure, now, all the command gone. The choice was mine, I knew it.

"He deserves a hearing," I said, quietly.

There was a long silence—and then the rain came down, heavily. It seemed to force a decision.

"Lend me your jacket," she said.

It wasn't just because it was waterproof, I knew. It was a talisman, a piece of me to wrap around herself while she talked to him... I took it off and handed it to her. She put it on, then, without another word, she turned and marched out into the rain. As soon as she was out of earshot, I heard the measured voice by my side.

"If I had my way, I'd just get rid of you now."

"Like you got rid of René, you mean?"

He didn't answer. The rain came down hard again. People scurried into the station's mouth, obscuring her from my sight. I went on.

"Somehow I didn't think the word *kill* would bother you, Prosper. So how would you 'get rid of' me? Another convenient push? Another—"

The screech of the car tyres came first, then the shouts, then the whistles. The crowds milling round us stopped. Above their heads I saw the flashing lights. I pushed through, almost to the front.

Three police cars, boxing off the crossroads.

I heard a loud hailer—and then the press of the crowd forced me back. Again I pushed through, this time right to the front.

Nathalie! She was struggling between two uniformed policemen, one wrist already handcuffed...

I stood, transfixed—and then I felt the steel grip on my arm. Prosper's voice was a grating whisper.

"Away from here! Now!"

I shook away his hand—I couldn't just leave her! A fourth car arrived. Its doors opened, disgorged a clutch of blue uniforms. In the middle of them I saw the unmistakable figure of Christian Gwernig. Again the steel grip came.

"They have her. There's nothing you can do." He spun me round. "Make no fuss. Turn around and follow me. Slowly. Walk, don't run."

We went out into the pouring rain. One turning, two... I walked, unseeing. Did they have Riou as well? What would they do to her? Prosper stopped beside a rusty Transit van with faded lettering on the side. I saw a flash of key. I got in the other side and slammed the door.

"What happened?"

He ignored me, started the van, moved out into the traffic.

"What the hell happened!" I shouted. "It was supposed to be safe—"

He snapped round. "Calm yourself! Immediately! If you want to get out of this without being taken as well."

He stuck in the slow lane, driving sedately.

"Listen to me, Fraser. I hate your guts. I hate what you've

done to my party, to my chief—but it makes no difference to my orders. I'm responsible for getting you clear. I don't know why, but I am. So just sit there, nice and safe, and let it happen."

We were on a main road, now, the A1, going north. He slowed down, pulled over into a service station forecourt, found the diesel pump beside a line of used cars.

"Act normally. Fill up, take your time about it, pay cash." He handed me the keys and a thick roll of notes. "Then meet me round the back, in the toilet."

I did it, filled, paid. With the change in my pocket, I went round to the brick building's rear and opened the toilet door.

The punch hit me in the stomach and sent me flying backwards, sprawled me across the wet concrete apron. And then he was on my chest, his blade at my throat.

"Was the meat good, Fraser? Was it worth it all?"

My anger seared, white-hot, on the knife point.

"You're a piece of shit, Fraser. I knew you were trouble the minute I saw you. I should have killed you then, shouldn't I? If it was my call I still would, but you're going to be allowed to walk away from this. So this is what you do. You stay here for fifteen minutes. Here, round the back—you stay away from the forecourt. I'm leaving here now, and I don't want you knowing the slightest thing about how I do it. There's more money in the glove compartment." He stood up. "Roll over. On your stomach."

One eye on the knife, I did it.

The kick was vicious, in the kidneys. For a long time I lay on the wet concrete, retching, the rain pouring down on my humiliation—and then I levered myself up on the brick wall. Unsteadily, I walked round into the forecourt's light.

The van was still there. A lorry was parked at the other side of the pump. The driver was screwing his fuel cap back on. His voice was cheery Yorkshire concern.

"You all right, mate?"

I nodded, took the keys from my pocket, opened the van door and got into the driver's seat. Just as I was about to start, he spoke again.

"Your pal get it fixed, then? The fault?"

Key poised above the ignition, I paused. "What fault?"

"The electrical one," he said. "Under the bonnet. Up to his arse in wiring, he was. Little chap, beret, just a minute ago. Starter motor, he said. Buggered off in a red Fiesta like a shot from a bloody gun, soon as he was done."

Slowly, I let the key hand fall. "Yes," I said, "it's fixed."

He nodded happily and swung himself back up into the cab. As the lorry roared off he gave me a wave.

I sat there, unwilling to believe it—and then I forced myself to turn. Builder's clutter; planks, scaffolding pins, picks, shovels, pails...

And sacks.

A pile of them, full, right behind the driver's seat. The labels said ammonium nitrate. Fertiliser... My mouth dry, I knelt to investigate the messy floor around them. It only no time at all to find what I was looking for; wires, a junction box stuffed under the seat...

Careful to disturb nothing, I got out, closed the door and looked round. The girl at the till was counting change and there were no other customers. Behind the station and the parked cars I could see houses, lights, a phone box. I walked over to a gap in the perimeter fence and squeezed through. Again I scanned. There was nobody watching. I trudged across a muddy piece of wasteland.

In the phone box I put the keys down on the ledge and dialled 999. A bored voice asked which service I wanted.

"Police," I said.

I was connected, immediately. A man began to speak, but I cut in.

"Listen. There's a Ford Transit van in the first filling station out of London on the A1 north. Blue, lettering on the side."

"Is the vehicle yours, sir? If—"

Again I cut in. "There's a bomb in it."

I slammed the receiver back down in the cradle, got out, and started walking.

19

LEARNING

THE SEA AT Portobello was a flat calm the colour of dirty milk, its surface the reflection of a sky caught between morning mist and cloud. There was an eerie opacity to its colour, a thickness that seemed to permeate the air as well. Along the promenade it felt ozone-heavy, compressed, an unwieldy medium that hampered. Plastic bag in hand, I ploughed my way through it, until the futility of what I was doing could no longer be ignored.

A plan. Until I had one, there was no point in just going on. Determination had got me this far—determination and the need for purpose, the need to label my escape from London as more than mere flight. But now, after a day and a half, I needed something more. I sat down on the sea wall and surveyed the expanse of promenade to either side. Deserted... The only other living thing in sight was a greyish poodle, absurdly manicured and ribboned, sniffing at a discarded bag of chips by one of the lamp posts, its tartan leash trailing.

Scotland... Why did it never feel like home? Since crossing the border I hadn't felt like a fugitive, I'd felt like a stranger. I pushed the thought away. A plan...

But hunger was stronger than concentration. I unwrapped the single sandwich that was the last of my food. It was hard, stale and tasteless, but I ate it gratefully enough, for as things stood it could be the last meal for long enough. As I ate, I took out the bundle of notes Prosper had given me—the bluff money, the money that had been meant to lull me into security until he blew me up. It amounted to less than a hundred pounds. Even if I was frugal, it wouldn't go far.

No, if I was to stay free I needed help, and I could only think of two sources. The first I'd already tried to phone from Stonehenge. I wasn't happy at the thought—it involved calling in an old favour, a debt from my Barlinnie days, a debt I'd always sworn would never carry a price tag. But if I had to...

The other was Angela Holcroft—much less predictable. It hinged on this premise; if I found McPhie, I'd find the blackmail pictures. Would the promise of that be enough to make her back me? And just how risky would it be to make either call? The first would be to a known contact, the second to a house where my presence had been very public indeed. Phone taps? Surveillance? Or was that just paranoia?

From the plastic bag beside me I pulled out the morning's paper and checked it again. Nothing. No fugitives on the run, no bomb-rigged vans, no arrests outside tube stations. There hadn't been, in the thirty-six hours since the incident, not in print, anyway—and if television or radio had picked it up, none of the drivers I'd hitched a lift from had mentioned it. A good sign or a bad one? Bad, I decided. Such silence argued a security blackout, a continuing hunt. With or without backing I could afford no relaxation of my vigilance. The thought trailed away in frustration, because it got me no further.

The problem was that there could be no plan until I understood what had already happened to me. I stared out across the water, trying, for the hundredth time since getting out of London, to work it out.

There was only one real fact. Prosper had tried to kill me.

But why? And how had the police known how to pick us up? Had we been somehow traced from her green van in Shropshire, or had the PSB been infiltrated? And what would happen to her now? Could her brother hold her, charge her with anything? I took a deep breath—the loss of her was sharp, physical. I forced myself not to dwell on it. Now was what mattered, the present. I looked round at the promenade's damp emptiness and forced myself to concentrate. Measured by any criterion, the lead I was following now was almost non-existent, but I could think of nothing else. Sylvia and McPhie had come to Scotland, Angela had said, and the blackmail note confirmed it. I thought back to

McPhie's hotel room in Rennes, to the message that had been pinned to the door—*Call me. S. 6287298.*

An Edinburgh phone number with the 0131 missing, I'd already established that much in Brittany—and from the city phone book I'd stolen the night before I knew the six two eight narrowed it down further, to here, to Portobello. But I couldn't match it to a name or an address, the operator would give neither out—and when I'd tried to phone again, the number had simply gone on ringing, unanswered. Had the woman I'd spoken to from Brittany decamped? And if so, was it as a result of this business? She had recognised McPhie's name, from her response to my first call I was sure of it. So what now? Ask questions, quarter the town? And ask what, exactly?

Who owns a piano, an out-of-tune piano, in Portobello?

And who plays Scottish tunes on it, very slowly?

For that was my only real lead—the tune I'd heard down the phone line from Brittany, the traditional strathspey, *Orange And Blue.* My eyes found the wandering poodle. The idea was as absurd as its ridiculous finery.

No, the only way I could see was the longest one. I reached into the plastic bag, found the thick phone book I'd stolen. How many numbers did the Portobello code have? How many—

And as I opened the book, the sound came. I stared at the rows of numbers, wondering if I was hallucinating.

A single high note, repeated over and over again, somewhere in the middle distance.

A piano. Someone was tuning a piano.

*

I abandoned logic. Logic said that there were a thousand pianos in Portobello, but obsession said this was the one I sought. The sound's behaviour confirmed mine as I moved. It disorientated—every time I thought I had its direction, it became an echo compounded of mist and mortar. I would find myself staring at the damp moss of a stone garden wall, suddenly aware that the high plink was behind me. And it taunted as well—when I stopped, so did the sound, only to start again as I moved, a maddening high plink, its endless repeat the bleep of some disconsolate sonar. Was it seeking me or was I seeking it? And when we found each other, would something from the low sky reach down, hook us, reel us in? The fantasy was the surrealism of fatigue—it had been too long, far too long, since real rest. At a leafy corner I closed my eyes, tried to banish it. It was nearer now, I was sure. One street away? Two? I came to a narrow lane leading away from the beach. Big houses, Victorian, detached. The sound changed, intensified—triads, three-note chords, major, minor...

I had it, now. The house at the far corner, behind the beach front hotel. As I reached the rusty iron railings, the sound stopped again. Was I right? I scanned the house's front. It was huge, rambling, in bad repair. The heavy front door was open, revealing a modern frosted glass one behind. I turned to the worn wooden sign on the railing beside me.

The Thistle School of Dancing.
Ballet, Tap & Highland.
Proprietor Mrs. J. Lamont.

Dancing... Yes. Of course—the low, shuffling sound I'd heard on the phone, behind the music...

In confirmation, the piano played a single grandiose chord, then launched into melody—the same tune, *Orange and Blue.* So, no further doubt. My eyes went back to the sign. A piece of white card had been pinned to one side of it. I smoothed out the damp edges that the sea air had curled. *Room to let.* I opened the creaking gate, went up to the door and rang the bell.

The woman who answered was thin to the point of emaciation, her frame so spare that her swollen stomach seemed more like an African child's hunger than a Portobello pregnancy. One bony arm held a bundle of sheet music, the other, the half-eaten cheese roll which had left a clown's mouth of white flour round her lips. The traditional high-laced pumps on her feet marked her as the dancing teacher. She removed a pair of glasses with pebble-thick lenses before speaking.

"Sorry. Essential for seeing the dots, crap for seeing people. What can I do for you?"

She was the one I'd spoken to, I knew it. I fought to keep the knowledge from my voice.

"The room," I said, "the one on the sign."

She gave a doubtful glance at the plastic bag that was my only luggage, then motioned me to follow her. As she turned, she bit into the cheese roll, then shouted, her mouth full.

"Simmy!"

She got no answer. Impatiently, she flung open a pair of double doors on the left of the hallway.

It was where she taught. Bare-boarded, its only furniture was the polished wooden rail that ran the length of one wall, and the rickety upright piano which had led me here. A heavy Victorian tuner's key with a wrought iron handle lay on it. At the window, a fat man in a suit, his hair tied back in a greasy pony tail, was talking into a cordless phone.

"Simmy—" the woman began again. His placatory hand only pushed her voice up into a louder shout. "Simmy, for God's sake!"

She marched across to the piano and slammed the music down on its keys. The blare of discord worked. The call finished on an abrupt goodbye, the phone went down. The face that turned to me was acne-scarred. As the piano's notes died, he fixed a glib smile of interrogation to it. The voice was polite Edinburgh.

"And how can we help you?"

The reply came from the piano stool, acid. "The room, Simmy, the bloody room!"

The smile widened into a full-blown hustler's grin. "Ah, the room. Well, yes..."

As he ushered me out and up the stairs, the piano's angry plink started again. On the first landing, out of breath, he pushed past me and flung open the first door he came to.

It hit me as soon as I walked in.

The perfume.

Sylvia Holcroft's perfume—after Belle-île I knew I'd never forget it. Behind me, Simmy was still talking, but I no longer heard him. The craziness which had driven me to stalk the piano swelled. It seemed entirely appropriate that I should walk into her presence without her being there. I fought for logic—I'd been thrown a better chance than I could have hoped for. The perfumed spoor was fading, but she'd still been here very recently.

But her, in this? I looked round. It was hardly the luxury of Holcroft House; candlewick bedspread, threadbare carpet, plywood wardrobe, a bedside cabinet hieroglyphically scarred with cigarette burns. Behind me, the talking came to a halt.

"...spartan, of course, but very reasonable. Considering the sea view."

I moved across to the window. Action was everything now.

"I'll take it," I said.

"Oh." He concealed the surprise immediately. "Good. We only do complete weeks, of course. So that'll be fifty. Plus fifteen deposit. In advance."

More than half of what I had... He saw my hesitation and broke in quickly.

"Of course, if you could do without a receipt, er, we could probably waive the deposit." The hustler's grin returned, conspiratorial now. "What the tax man doesn't know, eh?"

I counted out the money. Lovingly, the pudgy hand took it.

"Right then," he said, "it's all yours."

I waited until I heard his laboured progress reach the bottom of the stairs, then turned and surveyed the room. First things first—a search.

The wardrobe yielded only a handful of wire hangers, the bedside cabinet was empty as well. I checked behind the curtains—nothing but dust. I got down on my knees, lifted the bedspread's edge.

A metal box. I drew it out. A tool box. Still on all fours, I began to empty its trays out on the bed. Good tools, old—screwdrivers, soldering kit, a battery tester, a large spanner. Maybe under—

Without warning, the door opened. "My wife says to tell you the bath's—"

I scrambled up. We faced each other, me holding the spanner, him holding the phone. When he spoke, the voice was no longer genteel Edinburgh.

"Just what're you after, pal?"

He advanced on me—and then his eyes fell to the heavy tool in my hand. Abruptly he turned, ran for the stairs. I saw the hand stabbing at the phone and rushed after him. Halfway down the stairs I jumped, caught a handful of fat shoulder. We both went down, but I managed to grab the bannister. He thudded to a rest at the bottom, at the woman's feet. The phone bounced away and the hair burst loose from its pony tail in a shaggy cloud.

It was the loose hair which brought recognition.

A fat man in a hawaiian shirt...

He was the man I'd seen getting into the lift outside McPhie's hotel room in Rennes. I watched the memory become mutual.

"You were in overalls," he said hoarsely. "You had a tool

box."

I nodded.

"What do you want?"

"Information."

His eyes found my hand, still holding the spanner. Slowly, I put it down on the staircase. He got to his feet.

"The woman who was here before," I said, "in that room, how long ago did she leave and where did she go?"

They looked at each other. His face was troubled, hers, inscrutable through the pebble-thick lenses. Finally, Simmy turned back to me.

"Exactly who wants to know?" he said, softly.

Before I could answer, the doorbell rang. Through the frosted glass door I saw small silhouettes. Children. The woman's head whipped round; of course, her pupils…

"Shit!" she hissed.

Simmy began to speak. "How much—"

She broke in with an angry hiss. "God, Simmy, not now!"

He was ready to protest, but again the doorbell insisted. He bent to retrieve the precious phone. Some of the Morningside composure returned to the voice.

"Tonight. Calton Hill—you know where that is?"

I nodded.

"Ten sharp," he said.

He wouldn't meet my eyes. He began brushing at the suit's dirty knees.

"No cops."

The hand stopped at my words. Both of them looked up at me. The silence was reappraisal.

"Right, no cops. Fine by me, pal. Absolutely fine," he said.

I came down the stairs and walked out between them. On the doorstep I found two fat little girls in kilts. One of them held a sword in its scabbard. As I headed for the gate I heard Simmy's voice behind me, Edinburgh once again, fully genteel.

"Angela! Sharon! Come away in! Would you like a biscuit before your lesson?"

The door closed. I turned and walked away into the mist. Now it was me who needed the phone.

*

By afternoon the weather had cleared to a semblance of summer, but it wasn't allowed to penetrate the public library's reading room. I paused at the door; damp, vast, dispiriting… I looked up to find myself under the scrutiny of Andrew Carnegie at his most sanctimonious, daring me or any of the other patrons to protest. Carnegie, America's steel-edged soul, Scotland's moral monster… I pushed on into the clammy half-silence he had deemed the right atmosphere for self-improvement.

The big reading tables were like shallow-roofed Greek temples, each with room for four supplicants. Avoiding the middle-aged librarian's eyes, I passed through the varied catalogue of worship—coughs, snores, mutterings. Occasionally, a broadsheet page turned, a spade shifting soil in literacy's graveyard. As I moved to a free chair, I felt eyes examine me, but without interest. Good, I fitted in to hopelessness and despair... The thought was reassuring but not pleasant. I sat down at one of the wooden altars.

There was a newspaper before me, open at the jobs page. I peered at it, scanning its border of careful ticks and asterisks. Whoever had made them had been determined. A crumpled ball of paper lay on the desk beside the newsprint. I lifted it, smoothed it out, looked down the list of what the writer had been prepared to try. Waiter. Car park attendant. Machine tool salesman... But why abandon the list? Had he found work? As I wondered, a hand reached over my shoulder with a pen. An expensive fountain pen. I barely heard the whispered words.

"Don't look."

I obeyed. The pen's fine nib reached the sheet of cheap paper, added to the job list in a fine copperplate.

Vehicle redistribution consultant.

The pen hesitated, then came down again.

Watch.

Out of the corner of my eye, I did so; a slim figure, check-shirted and jeaned. He went across to the reference stack by the far wall, took out a large red tome and consulted it. Then he turned his back to me. I saw the red book slide back into its place in the rack, but it stuck out a little. The message was clear.

He walked back out to the entrance, turned. For the briefest of moments I saw his face below the shock of wiry black hair; blank, its features finely chiselled, its rebellion implicit—and then he was gone. I waited a few minutes more, then rose and made my way, casually, to the stack he'd just left. The tome he'd chosen was *The Oxford English Dictionary.* Only Carnegie watched me open it. A single sheet of paper lay inside the front cover. Again, the copperplate handwriting, immaculate.

Dark blue Escort. P125GRU. Glove box.

I slipped it into my shirt pocket and made my escape.

*

The car was round the first corner, keys in the ignition. I got in and opened the glove compartment; an envelope, with my name on it. It contained thirty-five pounds in greasy old Scottish notes and two credit cards in the name of Roberts. I opened the folded sheet of paper that came with them.

I wandered lonely as a cloud that over heaven and earth did stray—well, I didn't, actually, but just to show you it wasn't all wasted.

I've never heard of McPhie, but your friend Simmy Lamont's well known. A musician once, like your good self, bass player in local bands, not bad but never got anywhere. Young Heroin Dealer Of The Year about a decade ago, made enough to go legit. Managed acts, bought a bookie's, went belly-up. After the receivers were done he still had enough salted to buy some kind of export business—tartan garbage, dolls and such. Sends them to the States by the containerload. Not the kind of company you should be keeping, if you shake his hand, count your fingers after.

Sorry there's not more cash. The cards are OK, they belong to a friend of mine. The limit on each of them's a grand. Use them as much as you like, then pay him later, with interest, when you're back in funds—the going rate's thirty per cent. Careful with the signature, though, it's tricky. The car—before you ask—is clean. My own, taxed, insured, paid up. I've spread the word that it's being repaired, but questions'll be asked if it's gone for more than a week.

And there's enough asking going on. The word's out. The cops want you, nobody knows why, but there's a description doing the rounds and a lot of heat hanging around behind it. Big man in charge, I hear, foreign. Anyway, watch your back and go near nobody else you know.

With me, nothing's changed, but business is good.

Do not go gentle into that good night...

C.

I sat back, pondering the information and the warnings. The big man in charge could only be Gwernig. Did he have a lead on me? Or had he simply second-guessed me back to Scotland, decided that I'd go to ground where I had contacts? I stared at the single C of the note's signature. Slowly, the past swamped the present.

Barlinnie. Midnight in the cell, the stench of the buckets, the screw's eye at the spy hole, the echo of the keys in the locks...

And through the lonely night noises, the furious, whispered patience of a teenage boy's voice.

...Janet and John went to the, the hall—no, fuck, the hill behind...

Con Cassidy, recidivist... Con the Keys, an old lag of nineteen. My cell mate, the only success of my teaching career, an illiterate who had learned to read and write in two months. By the end of six his fanatic progress had taken him through half the prison library, through Burns, Dickens, Stevenson, Owen, Sassoon.

And Dylan Thomas. *Do not go gentle...*

I folded the sheet of paper and stuck it back in the glove compartment. Later I'd burn it—he'd taken a big enough risk. I sat there, savouring the smell of the vehicle's newness—and the irony.

Vehicle redistribution consultant...

In my naiveté, I'd thought literacy would help him go straight. I felt an unfamiliar sensation at my mouth and looked in the mirror. I was smiling. I reached out, started the car. The engine came to life with a smooth purr. I pulled out onto the street.

Con the Keys... A professional car thief had lent me his car.

20

ATHENS

EDINBURGH, ATHENS OF the North...

It was dusk. The tired tourist tag reverberating in my head, I walked past the lightless classical facade of the Royal High School. Once, the sons of the middle classes had been educated here, but they'd long since abandoned it. Now it seemed lifeless, dead. I stopped.

Athens of the North, in everything but democracy... For years, this building had been the main contender to house a Scottish parliament, but other plans had prevailed. What was its future now? As I stared at the blackened stone, the sound of a distant siren pulled me back from the question. I checked around me; no signs of anyone following. I went through the iron gate that led up to Calton Hill.

By the time I reached the flat hilltop, the twilight was almost gone and the floodlights were on, highlighting the monument that gave the city's Greek pretensions their most obvious legitimacy. The Acropolis was Edinburgh's very own carefully manufactured romantic ruin. It had been begun as a memorial to the dead of the Napoleonic wars. An exact copy of the Parthenon was what the builders had planned, but the money had run out before it could be finished, and now it stood, a stubborn, perpetually misnamed folly, the empty facade of a half-hearted sentiment. I scanned the floodlit columns, but there was nobody within the circle of light. Would Simmy come? Where would be the safest place to wait? I walked across at a tangent to the monument, past a clutch of buildings gathered round an Italianate tower. A five minute climb brought me to the hill's brow, to the viewpoint over Scotland's capital city.

The last of the day's light pared the landscape down to its essentials. Up to my left, the untidy ridge of the old High Street's tenements made a long, ragged sleeve that culminated in the ugly stone fist of the castle. Down to my right, the new town, neatly squared and thoroughfared, the Georgian symmetry of its skirts unsullied by any hint of Scottishness, tried to ignore the implied threat.

Old town and new, fishwife and dowager... Ahead of me, on the neutral ground of Princes Street, Walter Scott's statue sat in its skeletal gothic moon rocket of a monument, a marble astronaut ready to blast off out of trouble when the quarrel erupted. To the North and East, the ugly urban sprawl of Leith and Pilton looked on and didn't give a damn.

"Aye, Big A city, eh?"

I turned. Him, Simmy. Same huckster's smile as this morning, same suit, the hair greased back into its pony tail. One hand held a briefcase, the other was in the suit pocket. A gun? Had I underestimated the danger? He was a quiet mover for such a big man, I'd heard nothing behind me... He came up beside me to the hill's edge.

"Athens o' the North. Auld Reekie." The silver toe of his cowboy boot grubbed at the earth on the gravel path's edge, dislodged a discarded condom. "An' the Aids capital o' Europe. Still, nice to see somebody's takin' care, eh?"

No trace at all of genteel Edinburgh, now... Another two figures appeared behind him, athletic-looking men in their early twenties, dressed in jeans and leather jackets. They surveyed us coldly, then turned and disappeared back into the darkness. Simmy's eyes met mine, saw the doubt.

"Nothin' to do with me, I promise you. I'm alone—not that I'd be stuck for company up here if I wanted it. A certain kind of company, of course." He laughed, jerked a thumb back over his shoulder at the monument. "Very Greek, if you get my drift."

Warily, I scanned the darkness behind him. Could I trust him? That was the place's reputation, I remembered now… After dark, Calton Hill belonged to the city's homosexuals.

"Never seen the attraction myself," Simmy went on, "but different strokes for different folks, eh? Be great business though, if it could be organised. Put a charge on that gate at the bottom—" His foot flicked away the condom. "—fiver a throw, say. Hand out a couple o' these." He turned to me. "A few free rubbers, a few free *Johnnies*." His voice mocked the name with relish. "That what you're interested in, *Johnnies?*" He paused. "Mister Fraser?"

So, my anonymity, my last protection, was gone. That could only mean one thing—he'd spoken either to McPhie or Sylvia. I made myself stay calm. Perhaps, just perhaps, it would be easier with everything out in the open.

"All right, you know who I am," I said. "I know who you are, too. You used to sell drugs, now you sell dolls."

He shrugged. "Commerce, Fraser—only language I understand, supply and demand, the marketplace. Information's a commodity like anythin' else."

"The woman who stayed in your house, Sylvia Holcroft. I want to know about her. About her and McPhie."

He gave me a look of theatrical disappointment, then made a great play of consulting his watch. "Like I said, Fraser, commerce is my language. You've got exactly one minute to start talkin' it. Understand?"

I understood all right. I'd known it would come to this. I reached into my pocket and found one of the wads of notes the Roberts credit card had got me. A hundred, in tens. There was more, but I'd no intention of letting him see it. I handed him the wad, let him count. As soon as the notes had disappeared into the inside pocket he spoke again.

"OK, it's a start. Buys you background, though, nothin' else. Deal?"

I nodded. "Sylvia," I repeated, "and McPhie."

"Sylvia." He repeated the name with a laugh. "Aye, she's come up in the world. First time I clapped eyes on her it was Sandra. Sandra Henderson."

"When was that?"

The fat hand came up, demanding patience. "Once upon a time," he began slowly, "all good stories start with that, don't they? Well, once upon a time there was a band. Not good, not bad, bit of R&B, bit of blues, soul, rock & roll when we were pissed. Bunch of white kids who thought they could sound black, get the picture?"

I nodded.

"The usual," he went on, "never enough cash for the right gear, for a decent van. Lot o' big dreams an' wee triumphs. Every time you got your leg over you were a star, the rest o' the time..." He shrugged. "Couple of guys takin' it seriously, the rest along for the ride. One-nighters, residencies, forty quid a gig, fifty tops. Social clubs when we had to, dance halls—Oil Can Harry's in Falkirk, Bonnyrigg Regal, supports at the Barrowland in Glasgow. *The Score,* we were called. Even had t-shirts printed, *Ah Know The Score."*

Something approaching affection came near his voice. He shook his head ruefully, as though the bad marketing of his youth was somehow sinful.

"Anyway, bands have roadies."

I remembered the photograph Angela Holcroft had shown me, the instrument cases, the gear.

"McPhie was your roadie?" I said.

He nodded.

"And her? Sylvia, Sandra?"

"Whispers. Old Willie Docherty's dive in Wishaw. She was a barmaid. Tough as nails an' the sexiest thing you ever saw, legs up to her armpits, looked like she was dyin' for it. Dressed like it, too, high heels, leather skirt halfway up her arse." He shook his head. "I tried—hell, everybody tried, but no go. It was an act, all of it, the only one she was any good at."

"What do you mean?"

"She'd been to drama school, Glasgow. Dropped out after a year, decided on a new career."

"What was that?"

He laughed, cynically. His free hand mimicked a fisherman, casting, reeling in.

"That's what all the come-on was about," he said. "It wasn't for the lads. She was baitin' the hook."

"Who for?"

The hand went back to the pocket, the acne-scarred face turned back to the view. "Old Willie was sixty if he was a day," he said. "Fat an' bald, ugly as sin, never had a bath from one week's end to the next. He used to stick to her like a limpet, always keepin' the lads off her—even when there was no lads, if you get me." His voice slowed with admiration. "An' she was pullin' him in, givin' him exactly what he wanted. Every night, in the stockroom behind the bar—just a wee taste, just enough to make him daft for more. Get the picture?"

I nodded. The familiar story, a susceptible male, ready to be milked... The first? Pattern for the others?

"He was a widower," Simmy went on. "He was goin' to marry her, cut his kids out o' the will. She'd've had the lot." He counted off on the pudgy fingers. "Dance hall, off-license, couple o' flats in the town, half share in a couple o' pubs." He turned back to me. "An' she blew it."

"How?"

"April '85. We hadnae been there for a few months, an' we were booked in for a residency." He smiled, mirthlessly. "Slave labour—three weeks, four sets a night. Anyway, as soon as we were in the door, the first Friday, she made a beeline for Johnny. Bonny Johnny, all cock an' no brains—all over him, she was, Willie goin' crazy every time he saw them together. The rest of us couldn't work it out, but one o' the other lassies told us. Willie's kids had found out, somebody'd spilled it to them, they'd started puttin' the pressure on the old man. So she started hittin' back—makin' him jealous, crazy, tryin' to hook him before the kids won an' put him off her for good. Johnny didn't have a clue—big-headed teuchter straight off the islands, thought she was daft for him."

"So how did she blow it?"

"She let it go too far, didn't she—let Johnny go all the way, just the once. Willie caught them at it, red-handed, threw her out."

"And then?"

He began to answer, then pulled himself back, shook his head. "Background's over, Fraser. I told you, I'm a businessman. Open to offers. Your ton's brought you the loss leader, showed you I know what I'm talkin' about. You want more, you make your bid. You start talkin' my language. Seriously."

I let the silence stand, pondering it. I had just under a thousand pounds...

"All right. Same again if you tell me where they've gone."

Briefly, the acne-scarred face stayed unreadable, and then he laughed. "Disappointin', Fraser, I'm surprised at you." The fat hand pointed along Princes Street. "I mean, if the price was right, I could show you."

I felt the adrenaline surge. "They're still here? In Edinburgh?"

"Not them, her. Bonny Johnny's no longer in the picture."

"Where is she?"

"Improve my cash flow situation, Fraser."

"Five hundred. Can you take me to her?"

His grin widened. "Oh, aye, I can do that, all right."

I caught the false note, but not fast enough. The blow came from behind and landed just above my right ear. His fat image jarred before me, doubled. I managed to spin round, lash out. My hand closed on something metallic, spindly. I heard a female voice shout *shit!,* and then I was on all fours on the gravel. One last moment of focus showed me the object I was holding in my hand.

Glasses, with pebble-thick lenses.

Shoes appeared before me. The sight of the piano tuning key dangling from a bony hand removed any doubt about who had hit me. Simmy's laughing voice came out of the vortex of darkness above me.

"Five hundred lousy quid? No comprende, pal, definitely no comprende. Not one fucking word."

Her voice cut him off. "For God's sake, Simmy, the needle!"

A hood came down over my head. Then the jab came, then oblivion.

*

I woke, but my mind refused to accept it. I was drowning, suffocating—the blackness surrounding me was hot, wet, scratching at my face, my breath was like thunder in my ears. I tried to shout, but my mouth was clamped shut. I forced back fright. Was this hallucination? Madness? The physical flinch that came with the thought saved me; hands and feet, I felt them move. Relieved, I breathed, deeply—and smelled.

Cloth, damp cloth. I remembered.

The hood.

The claustrophobia was immediate. Again I fought panic—*think, don't react.* What could I feel? Slowly, the universe rebuilt itself. My hands were behind me. Tied? Yes, but only loosely, my fingers could move enough to feel. Wood, a chair back...

I added it up. I was hooded. My mouth was taped. I was sitting, on a hard chair. Could I get up? Shakily, I tried. Nothing stopped me. I took a step forward, two. No constraints. I stumbled into something, an edge of furniture. I fell, heavily, felt the left knee of my jeans rip. I lay on the floor, waiting for the dizziness to stop. Somewhere near, a clock ticked. I made it to my feet again. Like a blind man, I edged sideways towards the sound. Nothing impeded me until my shoulder hit wall. New wall, through the hood I could smell the plaster—and new wood as well. Where was I? I turned my back, felt the smooth surface with my hands, shuffled my way round the room. One corner, two... A window! My hands searched for handles, catches, but I could find none. I continued my sightless journey—there had to be a door. Another corner, then I found it. I tried the handle. Locked. My heart was pounding. How much more of this could I take? I launched myself forward again, back into the room's centre—and then the noise came.

The lock. A key. The door opened. A new smell permeated the hood's dankness. I stood rock-still.

In the dirty Portobello room, the perfume had been fading. Now it was heavy, animal, musked. It approached, much more real than the footsteps which accompanied it, then circled me, a leisurely tour of inspection—and then it came closer, enveloping me through the rough cloth of the hood. Through my own breathing I could hear hers now, close up against my cheek. What now? Would she—

A hand touched me. Lightly, between my legs. Once more I flinched, then checked myself. Fear came. In the hood's tight darkness the blood roared in my ears. Sweat began to pour from me. The hand traced my penis through the cloth, rubbing. I would suffocate! I was sure! She was gripping me now, manipulating. My heart pounded—and despite everything, I felt myself respond. Her laugh came, easy with victory.

"That's my boy."

Dizziness, humiliation... I was going to faint—and then I felt the hood loosen. The dark mantle came away, the light dazzled. As I shut my eyes tightly against it, the tape was ripped from my mouth. The pain was fierce, clean and sharp. I clung to it for sanity as I gulped air. Finally I could see.

She was seated on a high stool opposite me; grey two-piece suit, silk shirt, pearls at her neck, silver at her wrists, the red hair a hanging halo. On the table beside her lay a handbag and a small pistol. I recognised its blued barrel—it was one of the ones she'd had on Belle-île. My eyes rose from it to find her mouth twisted in a cool smile.

"So you're human after all."

I flushed. She watched me, her amusement returning—and then the smile died abruptly.

"Why are you following me?"

Whatever rationed argument I'd thought to use with her was gone. "Ewen," I said, hoarsely. "Ewen needs his violin."

One eyebrow raised itself in a mixture of cynicism and surprise. "Nothing for yourself? Not even a grand, like the last time?"

This was her real voice, I knew—unmistakably Scottish. No pretence, no artifice, no forced accent of any sort. I shook my head.

"Just his instrument and my own, whatever state it's in. That's all I want."

She eyed me thoughtfully, then nodded her head, slowly. "You know, I think I actually believe you." She snorted her laughter. "Jesus! A knight in shining bloody armour, a Galahad with bruised knees! Where the hell were you when I needed you, all these bloody years ago?"

Her merriment faded into blankness. In the silence that followed, I knew that all I had left was the plea.

"Without his violin, Ewen doesn't stand a chance."

Her anger was measured, cold. "Don't talk to me about chances. Ever since he was born that little bastard's killed every chance I ever had—ever since he was damn well *conceived*, up against the back wall of a cheap bloody dance hall. You'll never know what that's like, will you, Galahad? To get caught—to be in the club, up the stick! To be set to marry a couple of hundred thousand and lose it all—everything, for one drunken Saturday night screw with a pig-ignorant roadie." The voice came down to a vindictive whisper. "So don't talk to me about chances!"

Roadie... What she had told me registered, slowly. I calculated, ages, dates. Yes, it fitted.

Ewen's father wasn't Michael Barrington, Ewen's father was John McPhie.

She watched it register. "Well done, Fraser, ten out of ten. Johnny Gorgeous, straight off an island full of tinkers, never held down a job for more than a month in his life. Great breeding stock, wouldn't you say?"

"But you kept the child," I said, quietly.

"Ah, it's the merciful mother scene you want, is it?"

The back of her hand came to her brow in perfect parody. The voice became stage English, Victorian melodrama.

"Oh, miserable sinner that I am, I could not bear to be parted from my darling child!"

Again, the laughter came. She took a cigarette from the bag beside her.

"You're like Barrington, Galahad, you know that? Just as sentimental—" As she lit it, her eyes dropped to my crotch. "—and just as easy."

Her contempt was palpable. I closed my eyes, felt myself redden. Through the confusion I realised she was speaking again.

"...on the train to the clinic, the cheapest I could find, in London. I ended up in the same carriage as him out of Glasgow, practised my best English accent on him, just for devilment. Michael Terence Barrington, a half-cut village headmaster, coming back from some cousin's wedding—an innocent, Galahad, just like you, far too busy eying my legs to dream I might already be pregnant."

I opened my eyes to find her staring at me in frank amusement.

"Public schoolboy. Private income on top of a teacher's salary. The consolation prize—but still, a step up for a failed drama student, wouldn't you agree? And it was child's play—a nice, easy come-on, then trousers down and skirt up. By the time we got off at King's Cross I'd had him twice, and he was drunk enough to believe he'd had me. After that all I had to do was keep my nerve. I waited another month, then turned up on his doorstep in Cornwall and announced that he was the father of my child. And of course—" The smile mocked. "—he did the decent thing. We were married within a fortnight. Seven months later I had the baby, severely premature, of course—" The mockery deepened. "—but the whole village understood."

The smile died. She watched the curl of cigarette smoke, then looked at me, calmly.

"So don't tell me I did badly by the brat—he could have been flushed down the toilet of some London clinic." The voice came back to its normal contempt. "No, Galahad, Michael Barrington was the best deal on the table, Michael boring Barrington—the man who couldn't even come back from the dead without being boring. Wrote me a letter."

She rose, walked round behind me. The voice's mimicry deepened to pompous maleness.

"'Dear Sylvia, I wasn't on the Morbihan, I am still alive. I cannot go on without seeing my children.'" She laughed. "One brat who could hold nothing but a fiddle, another—the one he insisted on—who could hardly hold a pencil. The village idiot."

I felt my anger snap. Nick was a fine child, a good human being. I didn't dare turn back to her—I couldn't keep my feelings from my face, I knew. But she didn't need to see me to guess them. Behind me I smelled the perfume as she approached again.

"Oh, dear, Galahad—not your cup of tea at all, am I? Don't make any of the right noises, don't coo over the cradle. What would you fancy? A little mouse who does it with the lights out? Got one hidden away somewhere—a nice wee gingham wet-dream, all demure and blushing?"

I felt the gun's barrel between my bound arms. It began to trace a line up my spine. Without warning, the hood came down over my head. I didn't dare move.

"Except it's only one bit of you that wants that, isn't it? We know what the other bit wants... Not that it matters."

The barrel stopped at the nape of my neck. The fear came. In the hot darkness, I closed my eyes. I felt her breath at my ear as she spoke.

"You know it, don't you? You know I'm going to kill you." She gave a whispered laugh, then went on. "That night, on the island, I made love to Barrington. Gave him the ride of his life. A mercy fuck." Her voice seemed to surround me. "He didn't know he was going to die. You do. I wonder what it's like with a man who knows?" She laughed again, gently. "The kind of man who likes a firm hand, we've already seen that... Do you think that kind of man could get it up, Galahad? If he knew he was never going to get another chance? What do you think?"

My eyes were tightly shut, now. The gun caressed my neck. Her voice was by my ear.

"Down."

The gun barrel ground into the back of my neck, forced me to my knees. The perfume moved. She was standing before me, now.

"Ready, Galahad?"

I felt the hotness of tears. What now? I heard her move away. The silence filled with noises I couldn't understand—and then the heel of her shoe was a sharp pain in my chest. As I sprawled away backwards, I heard more laughter, then the door's slam, then the key.

A moment's paralysis, and then I made it to my feet. I found the stool she'd sat on. My hands were shaking, but I managed to pick the thing up. I scrambled round to the window, turned the stool, then rammed the legs against the pane. The glass shattered. I felt wind at my throat as I edged myself up against the frame and brought my bonds down on the shards. In seconds I was free. I tore the hood from my head, gulped in air—and saw the lipstick scrawl on the bare wall.

Forget me. Forget the fiddle. Next time you really are dead.

The roar that came from me was anger and pain in equal measure. I listened to its echo round the bare walls—and then just ran at the door. It gave. Breathless, I found myself in a corridor. There was a table with leaflets... I read, quickly—I was in a show house, on a new estate in Colinton, on the city's west side.

The next two doors were unlocked. I stumbled out into a deserted building site.

Rubbing my shoulder, I stalked off through the mud towards the city centre, the tears still stinging my cheeks.

21

PURSUITS

OUTSIDE THE VILLAGE of Dullatur, just before dusk, I found what I needed, a phone box in a quiet lay-by. I pulled over and looked at the Escort's dashboard clock. Nine o'clock. Fifteen minutes to wait. I got out, checked the road behind me for following lights. None, good. I surveyed my surroundings.

To my north stood the blunt massif that was the beginning of the highlands, to the south, the urban sprawl that was its soft underbelly. My only company was a heron, perched on a rotting lock gate, waiting for the stagnant waters of the Forth and Clyde canal to present him with his supper. There was a small hillock behind me. I climbed it, found a convenient rock and sat down.

I was tired now, but calmer. In the fourteen hours since my encounter with Sylvia Holcroft, I'd had a chance to think, and though the humiliation still burned, perspective had returned. I had a bad bruise behind my right ear and rope burns at my wrists, but otherwise I was uninjured. I could get more cash from the credit card and I was still mobile—I'd found Con's blue Escort where I'd left it, untouched by vandal or traffic warden, in George Street.

So I was still free, I could still fight. I'd lost a battle—an important one—but it wasn't the whole war.

But there was one thing I definitely had lost. Ewen's violin seemed unattainable, now—I'd driven back out to the Portobello house, only to find it locked, and, I was sure, empty. Simmy and his wife had vanished, just as Sylvia had done, and I had no doubt that the Strad was gone with them, beyond my reach. I tried not to think of the peacock's cry, or of Ewen's answer.

No, from now on my own loss had to take precedence, and there was still an outside chance that I could do something about it, for along with pain and humiliation, the last twenty-four hours had brought information, one important piece which changed everything. Once again, I went over it all in my head.

McPhie was no longer in the picture, Simmy had said. I had no reason to doubt that. She had dumped him, I was willing to bet, just as soon as he'd outlived his usefulness. It would be entirely in character—and it made sense of something else as well.

The second ransom note Angela Holcroft had received—the scruffy, almost illiterate handwritten note that didn't dare demand the big money of the first one... Two sets of prints could easily be made from the same negatives. Cut off from his promised reward, had McPhie simply gone into business for himself? Did that mean I could track him down? And would that get me to my fiddle?

My lost fiddle...

Pain came on the thought's wings. I looked north, to the wall of hills. The mossed edge of the plateau stared back at me across the canal's reeds, a scarred and crenelated bulge, thrusting up from the plain's flatness like the cerebrum of some vast brain that was just beginning to think for itself. The land beyond was in every note she and I had ever played...

For that I loved it, but was it really my land? I turned, surveyed the other direction. Council estates, blue-hazed with smoke. Factory and warehouse, industrial debris, weed-covered railway sidings, the black cancers of the slag heaps. If the mountains were the land of my music, then this was the landscape of my disillusion, pit-wheeled and rusty-craned, raw with the memories of promised futures which had always been stolen.

This was the country which was, in the end, mine. I was of it, perhaps I even loved it, and I knew I'd never escape it. And I knew I'd never be able to call it home, except from afar. This was the Scotland which had imprisoned me, the Scotland which no Celtic ideals could ever encompass, the Scotland which had taught me, by harsh example, to show allegiance to no republic other than my own.

It was time. I rose, went back down to the phone box and

opened the door—and then, as my hand reached for the receiver, I paused. All perils had to be measured, now. How dangerous was it to ring this number again? A few hours ago I'd spoken to an answerphone. That had been luck. Who would check the machine?

Not him, not a high court judge—no, she was the house's secretary, she would do it. I picked up the receiver and rang.

Angela Holcroft answered immediately.

"You got my message?" I asked.

"Yes." Her voice was a terse whisper. "Another note came yesterday."

"To tell you where to send the money?"

"Oban. Church Street, number 27, someone called Samuels. I've done everything he said, sent old notes."

"When did it go?"

"This morning."

"And the tattoo?"

"Yes, you're right, that's exactly what it says. But listen—" The voice stopped abruptly, became loud, patrician to the point of parody. "No, darling, I can't, sorry, not now."

The realisation chilled—she was no longer alone. A false-sounding laugh came down the line.

"Some French policeman's just arrived, can't think what he wants with me. Terrible bore. Talk to you soon."

She hung up. My heart beating wildly, I came out of the box.

Gwernig, at Holcroft House...

Had Nathalie talked? I didn't believe it. No—it probably meant they'd found the green van in its hide, across the river. But if Christian Gwernig was on to Angela, would she tell him what she'd just told me? Could he force it out of her? Gradually, logic reasserted itself.

In a sense, it was good news. Con's note had put Gwernig in Edinburgh—for the police, Holcroft House was back, not forward... If Angela could stall them for half a day, I was still all right. I walked across to the canal bank, saw the heron rise from the lock gate, launch itself into an effortless glide. The sight brought me back to calm. I turned to the north.

Oban... I'd get there tonight, be ready for the morning.

Ready to confront John McPhie, when he came to collect his blackmail parcel of old notes. Oban was the nearest big town, the nearest anonymity for him, only a few hours' boat journey from his bolt hole. My hunch had been right.

C-O-L...

I knew now what the purple patch was, beside the mermaid on his arm. It was the name of an island, a Hebridean island—the island of the tinkers, that had been the phrase of Sylvia's contempt. A great many of Scotland's travelling people bore the name McPhie, and one island was particularly associated with them. Whichever way I added up the facts, I came to the same conclusion.

John McPhie was going home, to the isle of Colrhanna.

*

I spent a cramped night in the back seat on the banks of Loch Awe and drove the last few miles in the morning sunlight. I wondered about leaving the car outside the town somewhere and walking in, but in the end I decided against. Instead I found a parking space outside one of the big hotels on the water's edge. I got out and looked over the choppy waters of the Firth of Lorn.

Scotland, Europe's Atlantic breakwater... A thought slipped beneath my armour, took me back to a shady Breton kitchen garden and a tired, contented girl's voice.

The Celts... Had they been pushed to the sea or drawn to it...?

Was Gwernig still holding her? And if this ever finished, would there be any chance for the two of us? And was that what I wanted? Poet's daughter and urban guerrilla... I hardly knew her, I saw that now. I turned away from the thought and faced the dour town behind me.

Oban.

It was a place that made me uneasy. I'd always found it strange, sour in its outlook, a jack-of-all-trades metropolis with a village mentality, perpetually at odds with itself—schizoid, even. It was at once the capital of Gaelic Argyll, and a solid red sandstone outpost of Victorian North Britain—and neither incarnation pleased it. The only real identity the place had ever had was as a fishing port, but the minute it became easier to hook tourists than fish, that died. Oban took to the new job with cold efficiency and even colder resentment. The tourists came, Oban served—but grudgingly, through gritted teeth. I locked the car and headed for the centre. A phone…

I found one, checked the ferry times and bought a cap and

sunglasses from a shop festooned with dreary tartans. Then, the rudiments of disguise taken care of, I went to find 27 Church Street.

It wasn't difficult. A brief enquiry and two minutes' walk brought me to a small red-doored house in a terraced row, not far from the sea front. It was decorated, like most of its neighbours, with a bed-and-breakfast sign, but there were no cars pulled up in front of it. I looked round. There was a cafe on the corner. I went in, ordered coffee, and waited.

Within half an hour the postman came with a parcel, the size of a couple of paperbacks. The red door was opened by an attractive blonde who couldn't have been more than twenty, her ample charms barely concealed by a skimpy dressing gown. The latest McPhie conquest? It seemed like a good bet—but I'd know, soon, anyway. I looked at my watch. The ferry from Colrhanna docked at ten. I felt calm, ready. I knew what I had to do.

Twenty minutes later, he came, striding up the street in his motorcycle leathers, unsmiling, suspicious, the sullen mantle of Oban's ethos on his shoulders. I felt a tiny pinprick of anger; Ewen's father, Nick's torturer...

And the blonde's paramour. I watched the eager, arms-round-the-neck welcome, and then the red door shut behind them. It was another hour before he emerged, a satisfied smirk across his handsome face and a plastic carrier bag in one hand. Its load was the right size. I paid, then waited inside the cafe door. He passed. I gave him half a minute, then donned cap and glasses and began to follow his confident stride towards the town centre.

Chip shop, draper's, chemist's... Admiring female glances clung to him as he walked, but if he was aware of the fact, he gave no sign. The pavements were crowded. He bludgeoned his way through, expecting people to move out of his way. Where was he headed? A bank? No, not even John McPhie would be stupid enough to lodge blackmail money officially... We were on the main street, now, facing the harbour—mill shops, butchers, cheap restaurants decorated with cartoon pipers... Where was he going? Back down to the ferry terminal? If that was the case, I had a problem. Here on the main street, the crowds could cover me, but as soon as we reached the quayside I'd be exposed…

And then I began to worry on a different score.

The leathers.

Were they just for show, or did he really have a bike with

him? If he did, that argued no intention to return to Colrhanna. Could I follow a motorbike in the Escort? On Highland roads, without being lost, or spotted? I didn't think so. He crossed the road, away from the crowds, following the curve of the front's railings, down towards the quayside. I had no choice, I knew. I pulled the cap down over my eyes and followed. Without warning he turned left. I ran to catch up—a pub door. There was a row of powerful motorbikes outside. Was one of them his? Was he inside?

I inched the double doors open. He was at the bar, laughing, surrounded by three or four other men of the same age, all in the same kind of bike leathers. I frowned. I had to confront him, I knew, but the odds here were too great and the place was wrong. I needed him alone, out of the town. My mind raced. It all hinged on whether he intended to return to the island. There was one way to find out. I heard him call for drinks for his mates, the others joke about him being the big spender. That decided me. A round pulled and downed, that would give me enough time. The Caledonian MacBrayne ferry office was a hundred yards further down the quayside. As I turned and ran for it, the wind snatched away my cap.

By the time I'd reached the counter I had the story ready. The girl on duty was pinning a poster to the wall. She turned. I thickened my accent as much as I could.

"Darlin', maybe you could help me. I've missed a pal o' mine, off the Colrhanna boat. Johnny McPhie. If he's goin' back tonight I might still catch him. Can you tell me if he's booked on?"

She sighed her boredom and reached for the computer terminal—and as her head bowed, my eyes found the poster she'd been sticking up. My heart nearly stopped.

Me. A grainy picture, a description. The words swam before my eyes.

WANTED FOR MURDER

...possibly driving a blue Ford Escort,
registration PG 25 GRU.
Dangerous, do not approach...

I realised the girl was talking.

"...yes, he's booked on. J. McPhie, motorbike, one passenger.

We start boarding at six, if you come half an hour earlier you'll catch him..."

I managed to get out a muttered thanks before turning away. If they'd tracked me to Oban, what did it mean? How did they get the Escort's number? They'd know it was here by now, they had to... I willed myself not to run as I went back out through the door. If—

A car drew up before me. My mouth went dry. A Jaguar, red... The driver got out; dark glasses like my own, hair tucked away in a scarf, but she was impossible to disguise.

Angela Holcroft.

Her tone tried to accuse, but all I could hear was fear. "You should have left it alone, Fraser."

I said nothing. She began to break.

"He made me do it, he made me come. He knows everything. He said he'd go straight to the press if I didn't co-operate..."

More blackmail... I saw the the cheek's ugliness, the dark bruises no make-up could disguise. Anger ripped through me. And violence! So Nathalie had been right, her brother was totally without scruple, he'd stop at nothing! Terror was overtaking her, now.

"...I had to bring him! I had no choice..."

As the distraught voice tailed off, the other door opened.

"*Bonjour,* Fraser."

He patted the leather jacket's pocket as he rose. The gun was unmistakable. He tossed something at me. I caught it. My cap, the one the wind had blown away.

"Luck, seeing you run down here like that."

Not Gwernig...

Prosper.

22

DEAL

WE SAT IN THE Jaguar in the station car park, him behind, Angela Holcroft and I in the front seats. His voice was dry, pedantic.

"The English have a saying about cards on the table, Fraser. Let me present mine. There is a violin here, worth a great deal of money. I want that money for my party. Thanks to *Madame's* obstinacy we didn't get here in time to pick up the trail of the man who can lead us to it. But you did. So you will now help us get it. Don't think of refusing, the consequences would be severe."

I found his face in the rear view mirror; expressionless, unreadable. I turned to Angela.

"You know, don't you, that he's not a policeman."

She nodded. "When he hit me..."

There was silence—and then a short bark of laughter. Only when her dark glasses whipped round did I realise it had come from me. As she looked away again, I felt a tiny gout of hatred towards her.

This flower of the aristocracy, this inhabitant of a cosy world where policemen never hit anyone... And then I saw Prosper's laconic smile in the mirror, and felt sick—with self-disgust at the thought of sharing anything with him, even a thought. I fought my emotions; calm was everything, now. I spoke to the mirror.

"All right, you've got the gun, but I've got the information. You need me, and nothing happens until I get some answers. Why the bomb, in London?"

"To get rid of you, Fraser. Just you, you understand."

For the briefest of seconds comprehension failed me, and then slowly, I began to grasp it.

He had been behind it all. Nathalie had phoned, set up the rendezvous at the tube station. Prosper had tipped off Gwernig. And then, with her safely arrested...

"Why? Why kill me?"

He leaned forward. "Just let's say I had no intention of letting five years of planning be killed off for a schoolgirl crush on a beggar. Her loyalties are back where they belong, now. That's why I'm here—and that's as much as you need to know."

Was he saying that Nathalie had told him about the Stradivarius? Willingly? Before I could think it through, he spoke again.

"Enough of this. The man with the violin, the man who has the photographs of *Madame,* where is he?"

I turned to Angela, saw the tears begin to edge their way down beneath the dark lenses. Suddenly everything was clear.

The Strad was gone, with Sylvia and Simmy—but violin or no violin, Prosper was going to kill us. He had to, to cover his tracks. I could only see one chance and I knew I had to make it sound real. The lie came easily.

"I already have the Strad," I said. "But I want a cut."

Angela rounded on me. "You bastard! That's Ewen's!"

Make it real, I thought. I closed my eyes and lashed out. My fist caught her jaw, slammed her head back against the side window and knocked away the glasses. As she screamed I felt the barrel of Prosper's gun in the back of my neck.

"Easy, Fraser, easy."

A trickle of blood ran down from her mouth. She began to cry in earnest now—violent, coughing sobs. Fighting shame, I twisted round, faced Prosper.

"The ten grand, the blackmail money. Give me that, let me get clear, and you can have the damn fiddle."

The cold interrogator's eyes stayed on me. I struggled to keep my nerve.

"Where is it?" he asked.

"My car. The boot. Ten minutes' walk."

The silence was filled with the sound of her sobbing.

"Don't think of lying to me," he said, quietly.

"Come and see for yourself," I said. I nodded at Angela. "Leave her here. She's not going anywhere. A hysterical woman will only make us conspicuous."

He reached over, pulled out the Jaguar's keys. As both of us got out of the car, I wondered whether she'd have the sense to run.

*

We walked, quickly, business stride rather than tourist stroll. Past the station, back towards the town. The pub came into sight. Was McPhie still with his cronies? The line of bikes hadn't moved. *Stay inside,* I willed him. We passed without incident. Good, first hurdle... We strode on, back along the main street, our passage heralded by the shoreline's screaming gulls and the synthetic accordion music of the mill shops. Would it work? If manhunt posters were up in Oban, then the manhunt must be here. I hadn't concealed the car. They had to have found it by now... Didn't they? If—

"How much further, Fraser?"

"Fifty yards."

Still keeping to the front's railings, we rounded the next bend. The blue Escort was at the end of the row of parked cars. I could see no one around it. Would this work? They must have it in their sights, surely... But if they didn't, if I had to show the man behind me an empty car boot, what then? Could I take him?

We passed a banner, tied to the railings, one loose end flapping in the wind. *Ceud Mille Failte.* I didn't want a hundred thousand welcomes, for the first time in my life I wanted a hundred thousand cops. *Where the hell were they?* As we reached the Escort I scanned the other parked cars.

"Open it."

I put the key in the lock, turned. Was I wrong? Was no one here? I tried to stall.

"It's stuck."

I heard the suspicion rise in his voice. "Open it, Fraser."

The metal flap flew up. One glance showed him. I saw the hand move in the gun pocket, closed my eyes. Jump him? Now? If—

"Freeze!"

"Don't move!"

"Drop the weapon! NOW!"

The shouts came from three sides—and then there were

sirens, flashing lights. A machine gun barrel hit me in the chest, forced me down into the open boot.

"Read him his rights!" someone said.

I twisted round. As the blue uniforms closed round Prosper I saw his brief look of fury.

"Alexander Fraser, you do not have to say anything, but it may harm..."

And then, as they turned him, spreadeagled him against the next car, his face settled back into its usual impassive mask.

*

The interrogation room was bleak, its only furniture a chipped formica table and three chairs. The Scottish detective by Christian Gwernig's side reached over and pressed the battered cassette recorder's play button.

"11th of August, 3.15 pm, interview with Alexander Fraser, conducted by DI McSween in the presence of Commander Gwernig of the..."

He faltered. Gwernig did nothing to help him. Frowning, he turned to me.

"You are Alexander Fraser, born the 6th of April, 1957—"

Gwernig turned. "Thank you. I would like to talk to this man alone."

The Scottish inspector frowned at the accentless English. "Highly irregular, sir, if you don't mind me sayin' so. Suspect's been the subject of an extensive operation on our patch. Normal procedure's—"

"I know all that. But the only offence he's committed here has been to drive a car that doesn't belong to him. Practically your national sport, from what I understand."

The detective flushed. Gwernig's voice was iron.

"My enquiries take precedence. Consult your superiors."

Bright red, McSween got up and left the room. Once the door had slammed, Gwernig reached out and pressed the recorder's stop button.

"OK Mister Fiddler, let's not mess about. I've a dead body on Belle-île, I've a van full of explosives in London. Your prints are all over both. I want to know what the hell this is all about. I would add that intelligence about the PSB might mitigate circumstances greatly at your trial."

I said nothing. He eyed me morosely, and then his hand went to his pocket. He pulled out a piece of paper wrapped in polythene; a parking ticket. He pushed it across the table to me.

"I want to be sure we understand each other. This is how we got you. In Edinburgh you let your car collect a ticket. The police computer traced it to a man who'd shared a cell with you. He claimed the vehicle was being repaired." He shook his head. "An elementary mistake. No terrorist trained by Prosper Gragnic would ever make it." He leaned across the table to me. "I know you're not one of them, but you've had access to them. You know how important that is to me?"

I knew I had to speak. "What're you trying to do? Finish them? Put them all behind bars, even your sister? Doesn't it ever cross your mind that they have a right to their views?"

He got up from the table, thrust his hands in his pockets, walked a few steps away. When he turned back to me, I couldn't read his face.

"A right to their views, yes. But not to their violence. No one has a right to that."

"I agree."

"Then help me."

I shook my head. "Not in that way. Riou's honourable, so is Nathalie. Even if I had anything to tell you about them, I wouldn't."

I watched his face become stone. I took a deep breath.

"But I'll help you get Prosper."

"I've already got Prosper."

"For what? Carrying a firearm without a licence? Even if he's got a record, how long'll that put him away for?" When Gwernig said nothing, I went on. "I can put him away for you properly."

He grunted his disbelief. "For what?"

"Murder."

It was a long time before Gwernig spoke again. When he did so, he couldn't keep the interest from his voice.

"Evidence?' he said finally. "Hard evidence—you have it?"

"Myself and one other eyewitness."

This time, the silence was appraisal.

"And the price?" he said, finally.

"A deal. You get to know all of it, but you take no action until I've had time to finish my business. Finish it alone."

On the clock behind him I watched a full minute pass.

And then he reached out to the cassette recorder, pressed the eject button, and handed me the tape.

23

ISLAND

THE LOUNGE OF THE car ferry Hebridean Queen rang with loud laughter—confident, carefully modulated, expensively vowelled. I looked at the source of it, the dozen-strong group who had claimed the bar rail for their own.

Bright young things, lantern-jawed chaps, prototype Peters and Angelas, rattling their silver spoons...

Was it just the clothes that made their division from the rest of us so obvious? That carefully dressed-down casualness, the ancient sweater so artlessly Cartier-pinned, the denim shoulder so indifferent to its Chanel bag? No, I thought, it was the voice, that one unbearable voice they all seemed to share, the crass, plummy bray that was incapable of softness or self-doubt, the victory song of the world where money ruled without qualm and servants served without question.

The world where policemen never hit people...

I raised my pint glass. Had she got clear? Without involvement? A full day now since the incident and I'd heard nothing... There was no reason to suppose she hadn't, I decided—they'd have found the Jaguar's keys on Prosper, but he'd never talk, I knew. The memory came, of hitting her. Before I could succumb to the shame of it, another burst of elocuted mirth rolled across from the bar.

I closed my eyes. When the Scots said they hated the English, that voice was what they heard.

As the ship's horn indicated we were nearing Colrhanna, I looked round the bar. Was it resented? The tourists didn't seem to hear, but then tourists never do. But the locals, the islanders travelling home? I found one face, in the corner, an old woman's, lined, weather-beaten long past any idea of mere suntan. A stone idol of a face, a face that would have fitted Carnac or Stonehenge. Impassive and unreadable, it looked about as affected by the chatter as flint by the breeze. Again I lifted my glass. There was comfort in that. No matter what they were to themselves, to her they were simply part of the landscape.

But was I? I looked down at my garb—army camouflage combat jacket and hiking boots. Yesterday's disguise hadn't worked, would this? Gwernig had let me keep Con's Escort, but it seemed wrong for the get-up—too new, too flashy. But the get-up would give credence to my claim to be a hill walker, I hoped. Again, the tannoy announced our nearness. I drained the last of my beer and headed for the fresh air.

The sea was glassy, its calm cut only by the white slice of the bow wave, and the deck was a jumble sale of holiday uniform—the cyclist's thigh-hugging shorts, the fisherman's multi-pocketed waistcoat, the ever-present anorak of the weather-wary. A quiet ruled, compounded of midday-sun laziness and awed appreciation of the Paps of Jura, clearly visible off the port bow—and as the ragged edge of Colrhanna's shoreline approached, I wondered; was the weather a problem? I'd have been happier with drizzle, with heads anonymous under kagoul hoods, with rain-spattered windows on the car. With anything, in fact, that made identification harder.

Would McPhie be watching? He had no obvious reason to, the day before's events hadn't touched him—but it wasn't impossible. With my binoculars I scanned the shoreline ahead; concrete pier, church on the hill behind, a white building opposite that had to be the island's only hotel. Apart from that, there was only a solitary phone box and a scatter of cottages—but still, plenty of places where the boat's approach could be watched in safe anonymity.

A minimal risk, though, I decided. Again the horn sounded. Around me people began to stir. I obeyed the metallic voice that ordered me to the car deck, and by the time I'd reached it we'd docked. I drove straight off, and parked beside the phone box.

It was the directory I was after—the one I'd looked through

in Oban had been vandalised, and there was one thing I had to check. I opened the book. Colrhanna might be the ancestral home of the McPhies, but there were only four of them listed. His family had to be one of them. As I wrote down the addresses, I saw an overalled man, obviously a local, eying me through the plastic panes. For cover, I lifted the receiver, dialled the speaking clock—and as the recorded voice told me the time I reflected; no one's business stayed private for long on an island. If McPhie was to hear of my presence...

I froze; an engine, not a car's—a motorbike, a big one, coming down the hill behind me. I buried the receiver deeper in my ear. Through the mechanical message I heard the bike stop, just past the box. Him, there was no doubt of it. Even though I'd only heard the voice a few times, I knew it. He was speaking to the overalled man. I risked a look. He was wearing the same leathers as the day before, in Oban. Should I beard him here and now? Even as I was considering, I heard the starter kick. As he revved away to the left at high speed, I came out of the phone box.

"Nice bike," I said.

The overalled man shook his head. "Aye, but how nice'll it be when it's lyin' on top of him in a ditch somewhere? Here to his mother's place at Balcreggan in two and a half minutes!" He shook his head. "Daft bugger. Big Time Johnny—you'd think he owned the bloody island."

I felt a surge of elation; my quarry's address identified... Still the man's head was shaking.

"Drives like he owns the bloody place," he repeated.

A khaki Range Rover appeared from the ship's bow, gunned itself along the pier. Both of us had to step back quickly.

"Seems he's not the only one," I said.

The vehicle's twin followed it, with a blast of horn. As they accelerated away up the hill, I heard more of the vacuous laughter, and a single word that could have been *pheasant* or *peasant*. The overalled man's features arranged themselves into the same stony expression I'd seen on the boat, on the old woman's face.

"Aye," was all he said.

*

I was lucky. The farm of Balcreggan was marked on the Ordnance Survey map I bought from the Post Office. It was up at the north end of the island—on paper, easy enough to reconnoitre.

But before I'd gone even a mile, the disadvantages of having the car were obvious. Only fourteen miles long by three wide, the island had, effectively, only one loop of road, with two offshoots to north and south. Already, within minutes of setting off, I was meeting people who had completed their first circuit, and who recognised my car from the boat. They waved to me like old acquaintances. If McPhie did spot me, the Escort would have me marked miles away—especially in a bare landscape like this. No, it would be risky to use it for long, I'd have to cache it somewhere. I came round the tip of the reed-edged pool called Loch Toraidh, along past the farm of Kilbeg and the gates of Colrhanna House, and took the turnoff that would take me past Balcreggan.

I quickly came into sight of it, fifty yards up the hill to my left—a messy grey stone affair, much run down, a stark contrast to the smug opulence of Colrhanna House itself, set in its immaculate gardens on the other side of the road. There was no sign of the motorbike—no sign of life at all, in fact. I went on. It was better not to stop, there was no point in tempting fate by being more visible than I had to be. The road bent round to the left, following a stream, then climbed up over a cattle grid. Past it I saw nine or ten cars at the road's edge—and behind the cars, a footpath leading down to the most idyllic bay I had ever seen. I parked the car beside the others and got out.

Half a mile or so of golden, almost virgin, strand... I consulted the Ordnance Survey; Kilbeg Bay. As I folded the map away, footsteps came from the path—a brace of yelling children, complete with traditional bucket and spade.

Two boys.

I stared across the sunlit expanse of beach, my head suddenly filled with the images of Sylvia's sons.

Ewen's terrible rage, Nick's burned and beaten legs...

What if I failed here, as I had with Sylvia? What if McPhie simply laughed at my threats? What if I didn't hold as many cards as I thought and had to deal? In my head, the laughing sounds of the two boys' voices mingled with the peacock's cry, and I wondered—how much of what John McPhie had done would I forgive to get back my fiddle?

*

The two cars at Balcreggan's gate were rusted into the landscape. An honour guard of cows surrounded them, facing different ways, unsure from which side attack would come. The circular chewing of their cud seemed rhythmically connected to the sea sounds I could hear in the distance, as though both were part of some vast, hidden rural machine. Behind the beasts, the grey disrepair of the cottage was dank and unhealthy, a defiant challenge to the early evening's pleasant heat—this was a place which endured the sun rather than enjoyed it. There was no sign of human life.

I scanned the crumbling walls; a barn, two tin sheds, a lean-to at the house's side. Through its open door I saw the motorbike, incongruous in its gleaming newness. I looked at the rear wheel and saw the panniers. Not big enough for a fiddle, I thought, but big enough for photographs... Before caution could drown the thought, I followed it.

Neither was locked, both were filled with the kind of mess I'd come to associate with him—beer cans, single gloves, loose tools, empty cigarette packets. At the bottom of the first one I found a plastic packet that was the right size, unsealed, but it was only a bunch of brochures for more bikes. But down the side of the second I found something more interesting.

An envelope, ordinary, letter-sized. I drew it out. Sealed, with a stamp, but no address. As I pondered it, a new sound added itself to the rural rhythm. I drew back into the lean-to's darkness until I identified it. Chopping. Someone was cutting wood. I stuffed the envelope into my pocket and came out, warily. The noise was coming from the other side of the cottage. I followed a damp stone path round it.

A cautious look round the last corner showed me McPhie, stripped to the waist, splitting logs on a stump with a large axe. As I watched he stopped. I followed the line of his gaze.

At the bottom of the hill, Colrhanna House basked in the last of the day. The two Range Rovers I'd seen coming from the boat were pulled up on the circular drive, and the lawn before them was bright with parasol and picnic. The designer scruffiness was gone now; the womens' dresses were brilliant cut-outs against the lawn's green, the mens' dinner suits their shadows, black and attentive.

And as clear as crystal struck by silver, the laughing, moneyed accents rolled up the hillside.

I watched him watching it all, the sweat glistening on his body, the axe in his hand—and then, somewhere behind me, one of the beasts lowed. He turned. As soon as he saw me, his body tensed. And then it relaxed. We both knew we had come to some kind of finality.

"What the fuck do you want?" he said.

I didn't answer immediately. For the last three hours I'd thought long and hard about this. What had happened to the boys burned in me, but I knew, deep inside me, that the cruelties visited on them would never reach a courtroom. No... Although the desire in me for retribution was so strong I could almost taste it, there was nothing to be done on that score.

"My fiddle," I said, "the broken one. I want to know what you did with it. And I want the pictures as well. Of Angela."

"Why the fuck should I give you anything?"

"Blackmail's serious. Even a cocky lad like you should've known better than to send a note in your own handwriting, covered in your own prints."

He laughed. "She'll never testify."

"Maybe, maybe not." I paused. "I will."

A furious frown brought the brow down into a single line. I saw his grip tighten on the axe handle.

"Don't even think about it," I said, levelly. "The fiddle and the pictures. Now."

His voice came, sneering, peevish. "What the hell's an old bag like that to you? Rich old cow—rich old *English* cow! She's got plenty, she owed me. She got the bit of rough she wanted, so why the hell shouldn't she pay for it?"

"And that's the only reason you slept with her? For money?"

Another peal of patrician laughter rolled up the hill from the house party below. I watched its taunt strike home, deepen the sneer.

"No. Not just for money." With one smooth movement, he twisted, arced the axe deep into the stump behind him. "You know what it's like livin' here?" he said. "On this island, in a dump like this?" He pointed down the hill. "Lookin' at that! Watchin' your old man touch the forelock. Watchin' him vote Tory because he's frightened the laird'll find out if he doesn't. Kissin' the factor's arse every time the rent goes up. Beatin' the grouse for the laird and his rich fucking friends. Yes, your Lordship! Of course, your Ladyship!" His voice changed from menace to rich satisfaction. "She was one of them, wasn't she? Same high-and-mighty manners, same snotty accent. A rich old bag wi' money to burn." The lip curled even further. "Jesus, Fraser, I used to make her beg for it."

I checked the red rise of my anger. "And did he beg for it as well? The kid whose legs you burned? The one you nearly crippled?"

"Fucking little half-wit," he said, "Couldn't even stand still and hold the damn fiddle for five minutes while I checked the address."

"Whose address? Where were you taking the Strad?"

The reply was a gloat. "Wouldn't you like to know, Fraser." He shook his head. "No, nobody's gettin' this one away from me—her and that bastard Simmy might think they can cut me out, but they can't. I'll get my money, every penny. A hundred half-wit kids wouldn't stop me."

He stood there, the insects buzzing round the sweat-covered shoulders. I looked at his body. It was magnificent, perfect. How could something so straight and strong be so twisted inside? Did he know that Ewen was his son, that he'd stolen from his own child? Somehow I knew that it would have made no difference—he would have beaten Ewen raw, just as he had Nick. The sneer became an open laugh.

"Little bastard," he said, "little English bastard."

My voice was hardly more than breath. "Jesus, you're pathetic."

My contempt broke something in him. He came at me in a low snarling rush. I had plenty of time to avoid it, but I didn't—and even as we hit the dusty ground, I knew I had him. All I felt was triumph—icy joy. I wanted an excuse to thrash him senseless, I wanted revenge for the peacock's cry, for every day Ewen answered it, for every burn and welt on Nick's legs. His fist thumped into my side, but I hardly felt it—any more than I felt my own punches as I smashed them into him.

And it was the coldness of my rage which prevailed. In seconds I was on top of him, pinning his chest and arms with my knees. My right fist was slick with blood from his mouth. I watched it drip onto his face. Slowly, sanity began to return.

"My fiddle. Where is it?"

He coughed, spat away to the side, but he didn't speak. Before I could hit him again, another voice intervened.

"Stop."

It came from my side, from the dank house.

"Get up."

The old woman, the one whose face I had seen on the ferry... His mother? It had to be. In her hands she held a shotgun. It was pointing very steadily at me. As I rose, the envelope I'd taken from the bike's panniers fell from my pocket. McPhie saw it. He rolled over, reached out for it.

"No."

The sheer authority in her voice stopped his hand. She turned to me.

"What are you doing here? What has my son done to you?"

The voice was the clear, precise lilt of the Gaelic speaker to whom English will always be foreign. It was at once wary with suspicion and weary with certainty—the certainty that her son was surely the root cause of the violence against himself.

"Lift your letter."

As I did it, I heard McPhie scramble to his feet, but I didn't see him. I tore open the flap and pulled out the contents.

Another blackmail letter, the twin of the one he'd sent to Holcroft House. Twenty thousand pounds, this time. To Angela Holcroft? Again, so soon? No...

A first instalment. When the Stradivarius was sold he'd expect more. When it was sold by—

I stared at the name I found—and then my eyes came back to the lined face above the shotgun.

"You should go now," she said, the barrel still pointing squarely at my midriff.

I nodded, slowly. I knew where both fiddles were, now—this letter told me. I had what I had come for. Only one matter remained to be settled.

"Your son," I said harshly. "He is blackmailing a woman. There are photographs. Here, somewhere."

"He will not use them," she said simply.

The shotgun never budged—until we both heard the sound.

An unmistakable sound—an axe being pulled from wood. I spun round. All I saw was the blade's gleam—and then the report of the shotgun came. He screamed, landed on his back in the dust, still gripping the axe, his hand a bloody pulp of red round the shaft. I turned to her. One barrel was smoking, but the other wasn't—and once again, it was trained on me.

"Go now," she said. "He will be looked after."

I had no choice. I turned, began to make my way down the hill. As I came through the bushes, I looked down at Colrhanna House. The guests on the lawn were all silent now, all held in the same expectant pose as they watched me descend, mud-streaked and bloody, towards the road which separated me from them.

And then, as though by mutual signal, they turned away from me. The bright laughter began again.

Nothing, pheasant or peasant, would be allowed to spoil the party.

24

FAMILIES

THE SUN SHONE, the doves cooed across the cobbles, the windows purred with the promise of purchase—and the smart women strolled from side to side, zigzagging between the *vitrines*, sizing up each others' outfits, comparing, criticising, measuring, laughing. I was back in Rennes, sitting in the shade of a café's awning, looking at the crossroads where it had all started, just over three and a half weeks ago.

It was different today. The women had more men in tow, and more children, too. The children were well-dressed extensions of their mothers' taste, and the mens' role was even more strictly defined—to carry the gold-and-silver-lettered plastic bags, to nod in agreement with the pointed finger. I drank, hardly tasting the coffee as I watched them, thinking about Sylvia Holcroft. What did men mean to her? Or children? One word came; *accessories...* Unconsciously, the voice across the table from me picked up the train of thought.

"The only thing I don't understand, Mister Fiddler, is why she took them both with her. The boy Nick, and this man McPhie. She was going to dump them both anyway, so why not simply leave them behind in England?"

As Christian Gwernig spoke, his eyes automatically checked the street. A smooth movement brought the walkie-talkie from an inside pocket.

"Any sign?"

I heard the faint *non* of his subordinate's answer.

"Check with the others. Contact with me every ten minutes."

An equally efficient sleight-of-hand returned the device as he turned to me for his answer.

"Nick's safe return was an additional lever to use against the judge," I said. "As for McPhie, my bet is, she thought she might need him to deal with Barrington. I'm only guessing, but I think the letter Barrington sent her, the one that told her he was still alive, came just as she was about to grab the Strad and put the whole plan into action."

Gwernig stirred the coffee, nodding. "And he had to be killed, of course—without being identified, otherwise her marriage to the judge was out in the open as bigamous." He lifted the cup, drank. "No marriage, no divorce settlement. So she built a murder into the plan—a realistic enough murder, too, if it had worked. A faked break-in at the Belle-île house, Barrington gets in one shot before he gets hit himself, the perpetrator's prints—yours—all over the murder weapon and a tidy bundle of thousand franc notes. Inconvenient husband firmly dead, you dead, plausible story, no need to hide either body. If you hadn't got away..." He shrugged. "A cool woman—the sign of a good brain, that, the ability to improvise."

He saw the revulsion in my face, and smiled. "Don't worry, Mister Fiddler, I'm not expressing approval. But in my job, you learn to recognise talent whichever side it's on."

As he eyed me, speculatively, I realised I'd been paid an oblique compliment.

"Galls me, though," he went on, "not going after her. She should be behind bars—I hate crime and I hate cruelty."

"I'm not wild about it either, but it's the deal I made," I said. "If we stick to it we get Angela Holcroft's testimony on top of everything else. Assault, demanding money with menaces. Not negligible, I'd have thought."

He nodded. "Don't worry, Fraser, I won't rock any boats. A bargain's a bargain." Again the spoon stirred the coffee, with pointed slowness. "No danger of you forgetting that, is there?"

A veiled threat? No, I decided, just a reminder... But the goods had to be produced soon, I knew.

"What about Barrington?" I asked. "Has anything come to light yet? Do you know why he wasn't on the Morbihan?"

Gwernig eased himself back in his chair. "Nothing definite,

it's difficult to go back five years—but it was no accident, I'm sure of that. He boarded the ship at St. Malo, we know from the booking records—he was issued with a boarding card. So that means he got off again once he'd seen all the kids onto the boat." The stirring stopped, he put down the spoon. "Exactly why he did it, of course, we'll never know. Perhaps there was something he couldn't face back across the channel," he said, quietly. "By the sound of her, I can't say I blame him—and if he'd had the sense to stay dead, no one would ever have known. The papers we found in the Belle-île house, passport and so on—I don't know where they came from, but they were faultless. There would have been no reason to believe that he was anyone other than *Monsieur* Michael Knight, an English expatriate living quietly on the island."

"After the disaster, though, living on his own, the guilt must have been unbearable," I said.

He carefully didn't look at me. "Sounds like you know what you're talking about. Hard thing to be expert in, guilt."

An invitation to talk, about myself... There was a brief instant of tension, wrapped in the cafe's comfortable noises, and then he accepted my silence and went on.

"Guilt, conscience... Someone like Barrington I can understand. But the ones like Prosper—they think they've got a higher morality that absolves them from it." He shook his head. "Ends justifying means, bombs in petrol stations..."

He sat back in his chair. A smile came to his lips, a cold smile, tough and cynical, the first thing I'd seen in him that divided his face irrevocably from Nathalie's.

"And all to keep hold of my stupid sister. All because he believed that with you dead she'd come running back and marry that fool Riou." He turned to me, his face grim. "Nathalie Gwernig, daughter of the great patriotic Breton poet, the martyr who died for the cause—to these people she's aristocracy, isn't she? Married to her, Riou would pull twice as many votes, and Prosper knew it." Again he shook his head. "Beware kingmakers, Mister Fiddler—they're a damn sight worse than kings. Especially when they decide to build dynasties. Even if Riou wasn't in love with her, he'd've had no choice."

The walkie-talkie bleeped on his sarcasm.

"Still nothing? Stay with it."

As soon as it was gone again, I asked the question. "What do you mean, no choice?"

He finished his coffee. "I probably shouldn't tell you this, but I will. When they founded the PSB, Prosper kicked in a lot of money. An inheritance, he said, plus his life savings. Two years later he told Riou he'd lied, that it was the proceeds of a couple of bank jobs pulled by earlier Breton groups. Every *sou* traceable—but by then it had been spent. Riou's claim to legitimacy would have been ruined if it came out. Prosper had him by the balls."

My mind went back to the market place in Concarneau, to the day when Nathalie had been told to take me to Carnac. So I'd been right, Prosper had been giving the orders... It seemed a lifetime ago. I sat back in the chair.

"So if you knew that, why didn't you arrest him then? Riou as well?"

"Proof, Mister Fiddler, evidence. Contrary to what my sister thinks, I believe in the law, and the law demands it." He leaned across the table to me. "And I'll be a damn sight happier when I have yours. So when?"

A brown envelope landed on the table top between us. We both looked up.

Nathalie.

Her face was strained, tired. I didn't speak, neither did she. Gwernig turned, fixed me with a look—a policeman's look, an interrogator's.

"*Her?* She's your other witness?"

I nodded. He lifted the envelope, pulled out a single sheet of paper. I knew what it was—a signed statement, notarised. It said that at Kergorff on September the 4th, she had seen Prosper Gragnic murder René Siberil by impeding his escape from the path of an oncoming heavy lorry. We had agreed on it the night before, in a brief, hesitant telephone call. Along with my own testimony, it would be enough to put Prosper away for a very long time. Gwernig's voice came, harsh, demanding.

"You'll swear to this? In court?"

The silence was awkward with their mutual distrust. Necessity might have made allies of them, but they still detested each other; they always would. Finally, she gave a curt nod. For the first time, Gwernig seemed lost for words—and then the walkie-talkie cut in again.

"You've got him? Good. Hold him." He turned to Nathalie,

once more the cop, once more in command. "Stay here."

Action was a relief. I followed his quick walk, watched the smart women give way with raised eyebrows and flustered smiles—really, men were so odd, so troublesome... Finally, over the stylish heads, the voice came.

High and querulous, petulant. It sounded as wrong now as on the first day I'd heard it.

"...outrageous! I'll have your jobs for this, my father's a personal friend of the *préfet!* And if..."

The bluster died as soon as we broke through the little crowd which had gathered round the violin shop's brass plate.

"Hello, Philippe," I said.

Immediately he saw me, his blotched face went pale—and then Gwernig's two men hustled him in through the open door. We followed, into the hallway. Philippe was leaning back against the wall's plaster, staring down at the ground. Gwernig reached out and gently lifted his chin.

"The Stradivarius. Where is it?"

There was no answer.

"Tell me!" shouted Gwernig. *"Now!"*

Philippe screamed out the answer as though he'd been struck. "Upstairs! It's upstairs in the workshop, at the back!"

Gwernig turned to the his men. "Let him go."

Philippe slid down the wall. Gwernig turned to me.

"Bargain kept, Mister Fiddler, he's all yours. Goodbye till court."

The three of them went back out into the sunlit street, the door closed. I stood in the cool darkness, alone with Georges Berolet's son. Suddenly his face was against my leg.

"Please..." The voice was a defeated whimper. "Please don't tell my father."

25

BRIGHTNESS

IT WAS MIDNIGHT. The pedestrian precinct was chilly, deserted, but the lit-up window displays still shone with undiminished fervour. In the darkness they seemed religious—altars of feminine desire, zealously keeping the night at bay, money their god, enticement their vocation. Apart from myself and Nathalie, I could see only one other human being, the driver of a parked car a few hundred yards away.

"So you were lucky," she said.

"Yes. Another two days and the Strad would have been gone."

"Where?"

"America. They would have hidden it in Simmy's usual monthly containerload of dolls. That's why they had to wait so long. The shipment always went at the same time of the month."

She stopped. "But if she had everything arranged with this man Simmy, why did she need Philippe? Why not go straight to Edinburgh with the violin?"

"Philippe had the only expertise she couldn't get from her past," I said. "He knew the market. He found the customer—a rich old man, a collector."

She stood, silent. "Why did he do it? " she said, finally. "Philippe, I mean. Was it just greed?"

Greed... Could the garbled hours of confession I had just listened to be reduced to a single word?

"Yes," I replied, "but not just for money. Greed for standing in the world, greed for independence from his father."

I reached into my pocket, took out the evidence I'd recovered from Philippe Berolet's workshop, the photograph I'd found in the lining of my battered fiddle case. It was the proof of my innocence of Barrington's death—myself and Sylvia, on the Belle-île quayside. My face was clearly visible, but it was the red hair which filled the frame. I gave it to Nathalie.

"And greed for her, as well," I said. "He really believed that if he went along with it, he'd win her, keep her forever. Don't forget he'd lived most of his life surrounded—" I gestured at the shop windows. "—by all of this. You know the kind of women who come here. Sylvia was like all of them rolled into one. She was exactly what he always wanted, to the power ten."

"How did he meet her?"

"In a bar. She was here on holiday, he tried to pick her up. As soon as she found out what he did for a living, she let him bed her—he was perfect for the Strad, child's play for her to handle."

"So they were both sleeping with her? Philippe and McPhie? And the third one, Simmy, the one who tricked you?"

I shook my head. "None of them were sleeping with her. She wasn't interested in McPhie any more, he was just a tool to her, the same with Simmy. As for Philippe, she just kept him on a string—after that one time, she never let him touch her again, she was far too clever. She used to make him come to the Hôtel Cabuchon. She had her own suite there, down the corridor from McPhie's. She used to tease him, let him watch her dress and undress, but he never got to lay a hand on her. She dominated him completely. When the Strad was sold to the American, she was to be his reward."

Shuddering, Nathalie handed me back the photograph. "Ugh, *c'est répugnant!* Sex as a price, sex to control people. The only weapon that's worse is love."

She stopped abruptly, blushed. She was thinking of Prosper, it was obvious. It was a long time before she spoke again.

"He listened to us, me and Patrik. For years, everything we did. Car, kitchen, bed—he had microphones everywhere. That's how he found out about the Stradivarius. When Christian let me go after London, I told Patrik everything."

For a moment, I tried not to think about the implications of that; car, kitchen... We walked on in silence, and then she stopped again.

"They'll catch her, won't they?"

"Your brother thinks so," I said. "There's some evidence she's gone to America."

I left my own doubts unvoiced. Nobody had come close to catching Sylvia Holcroft so far… Briefly, Nathalie seemed relieved, and then her brow furrowed again.

"The bargain you made with Christian," she said. "I know I agreed to it, but now I'm not sure it was right."

"Why?"

The anger I loved in her surfaced. "Because Philippe gets away with it—all right, he was a fool, but how much of an excuse is that? He was still part of what hurt Ewen—and part of the plot to kill you on Belle-île as well. He's just as much of a bastard as Prosper."

"Prosper won't ever change, Philippe might."

"I don't care, he deserves punishment!"

"And does his father?" I said, softly. "You've spent half your life trying to come to terms with what your father did. Your brother has as well. Georges Berolet's a good man, Nathalie, I care what happens to him. You told me yourself that you were nearly destroyed by your father's crime. I don't want to see Georges Berolet destroyed by his son's."

The anger faded in her as quickly as it had come. She stood, watching me, the wind whipping at her hair. I had never seen her more beautiful. Finally she spoke.

"It must be hard to live the way you do, Alex. To live in absolutes, to decide about people, to judge. I hope you never do it for the wrong reasons."

She reached up and kissed me on the cheek. It was goodbye, I knew it. As she turned away I spoke.

"Why, Nathalie?"

She stopped, then just stood, motionless. And then she opened her handbag and brought out a piece of red-edged white cardboard. I recognised it.

A rail ticket, from London to Edinburgh... Of course—it had been in the pocket of the jacket I'd given her in the tube station, just before she'd been arrested. As our eyes met, I knew she'd worked it out; one rail ticket, not two...

"Was it so wrong?" I said. "To want to protect you?"

"By leaving me behind? Yes, that was wrong. I was ready to

share everything with you."

Before I could say more, the driver of the car got out. Patrik Riou. He came up to her side, but he made no attempt to greet me. Or to touch her. I looked at Nathalie's face. There were a hundred things to be said, but the gaze between us locked them all out.

"*Kenavo,* Alex."

"*Kenavo,* Nathalie."

*

Once the noise of the car was gone, I stood in the empty street, fighting the bitterness, recognising the irony. Prosper had had his Machiavellian way after all, the perfect couple had been recreated... I looked round at the gleaming windows.

Would they charm her, seduce her, mould her into the perfect political wife? If her choice was final, she would have no illusions about the role, that much I knew. She would dress the part, survey the chic as she surveyed her garden, then make it a part of her. She would carry his spear—and she would dazzle while she did it.

But would she polish it as well…?

And what was to happen to me...? I looked down at my fiddle case, battered and bent, once again holding Ewen's quarter-of-a-million Singer. I turned, headed back the way I had come.

It was time to collect all I could really call my own.

*

The courtyard Georges Berolet led me into was another century, another world—half-timbered, rotting, thick with the stench of refuse and sewage. The moonlight seemed to hang on it in smears. At the open staircase he paused.

"He lives there."

He pointed up at the building's only light, a dim flickering from a third floor window, and then he thrust an envelope into my hand. From the feel of it I could tell it contained money.

"Give him this," he said. "The man was given your violin in good faith. He should be recompensed in full measure."

He spun round, made to leave. I caught his sleeve. The face that turned to me was haggard with pain and grief.

"Georges—"

"Au revoir, Alex. God go with you."

As I watched him go, I wondered—could we still be friends, or was the debt he owed me too great? Would the sight of my face always remind him of his son's failure? I hoped not. The footsteps receded. I was left alone, with only the stench for company, staring up at the strange light from the high window.

Pigez's window.

Our first encounter had made Philippe Berolet hate me—for showing him up, as he saw it, in front of his father. And after hate had come paranoia and fear. He'd seen me as a rival—he had been sure that I would supplant him in his father's affections. Which had been stronger, I wondered, hate or fear?

He had sought out John McPhie at the Hôtel Cabuchon, he had given him a thousand francs for the smashed remains of my fiddle—and then he had lovingly restored it to playing condition, night after secret night.

And then he had revenged himself on me by giving it to my enemy, the beggar Pigez.

Proof of a sick spirit? It smacked of witchery, of the denigration of an enemy by the casting away of his talisman, his soul. The more I thought about it, the less I was able to untangle the threads of pity and anger in my own mind. I began the ascent of the creaking steps.

The third floor showed me only one door. I knocked, twice; no answer. I could hear nothing stirring. Careful to make no noise, I tried the handle. Unlocked... The smell of sour wine wafted out at me as I pushed the door open. I stepped inside.

I was in the first of two rooms, separated only by an ancient screen. The light came from the second one—candlelight, the smoky, waxed smell told me. I looked around—bare walls, crumbling, one corner badly fire-blackened, bottles everywhere. An old army overcoat was the floor's only covering. Piled high on it were apples, potatoes, oranges, nuts, tomatoes, most of them rotten. Strewn around were cores, skins, peel, shells. I hadn't come into a home, I had penetrated a lair.

And then my eyes found it, in the corner, covered with dust.

Ewen's morocco leather case.

My heart pounded. Was my own instrument in it? I snapped the locks open—and found The Singer's battered and abused cousin, three-stringed, cigarette-burned. Pigez's fiddle. I shut the case and went to the entrance of the second room.

And saw my violin.

She had been placed with great care on top of a scratched dresser, her back against the crumbling wall. The St. Christopher was hung neatly over the strings, and the sheen of her pine top was obscured by the oily smoke of a dozen spluttering candles. I examined the other objects which surrounded her.

A broken shard of mirror. A wristwatch with a metal band. A bunch of keys. A bright green enamel brooch. A brass cup on a length of chain, torn from some drinking fountain...

The entire collection was surrounded by a jagged sea of bright, broken glass—shards and fragments of every conceivable shape and colour. Understanding came. Pigez—it wasn't a name, it was a nickname.

Pigez, the magpie, the collector of brightness...

Not a lair, a nest—a nest that glinted, gleamed, shone...

I looked again at the fiddle, at the silver medal. Had that been all he wanted, the St. Christopher's shine? Almost independently of my will, I felt my arm reach out.

The roar warned me—almost too late. I turned, saw the danger—and managed to throw myself backwards, out of the blow's path. I crashed against the dresser, fell into the corner beside it. Glass and candles showered down. Pigez loomed over me.

The hammer was a heavy one, a mason's, square and blunt. One blow with it and I was dead, I knew. His face was flushed and furious, but he made no effort to strike again. Instead, he reached out with his free hand and took my fiddle from the dresser. Slowly, carefully, I reached into my pocket and found Georges Berolet's envelope. I pulled out the notes, spread them out on the mess of glass beside me.

"Here, look," I whispered. "I want to buy it from you."

The face's expression changed—to greed. He reached down for the notes—and then, suddenly, his face was full of the look I'd seen in him before, on that first day on the street; terror, abject.

Before I could speak, he was gone—and by the time I'd made it to my feet he was already on the stairs, outside. I skidded after him across the mess of rotten fruit, clattering the bottles out of my way.

The courtyard below was all but lightless. Dimly I made out three openings. Which one? The sound of him seemed everywhere. I just chose an opening and sprinted. I came out into a narrow alley, empty except for rows of dustbins. He was about twenty yards in front of me, running like the wind towards a church tower. I hared after him, shouting.

"Pigez! Wait! Don't—"

In front of him, the church clock struck one. He faltered, stopped. As I reached him, he spun round—and I saw that he had changed again. No more fear! The hammer came round in a wide arc. I staggered back. It followed me, its wild swings barely missing me. I kept backing off, he kept coming, sweeping the weapon from side to side like a scythe at corn. I tripped on the kerb, fell backwards, headlong. The line of dustbins broke my fall. The hammer blow crashed down beside me, ringing the metal like a bell. I tried to roll away through the garbage. My hand found a bin that hadn't been overturned. I pulled myself up by its handle, then grabbed it with both hands and lifted. As hard as I could, I threw. I fell again, hearing the roar of rage as the contents hit him. Dust, ash... The cloud enveloped me. As I staggered up again, the air cleared. He was standing before me. I was at his mercy now. If—

But he wasn't facing me, he was looking away, down to the right. The hammer dropped from one hand, my fiddle from the other. He fell to all fours among the garbage, began scrabbling through it. His hands came up again, laden with treasure.

A bundle of discarded ribbon, bright scarlet.

For a greedy second he peered at it, then flung it away from him. Again, the hands delved. As the ribbon floated gently down through the dust to land at his side, they came up again.

A plastic doll, armless, its blonde curls matted with ash. Its dress was of some metallic material that shone in the moonlight. He began to clean it on his filthy sleeve. Carefully I skirted round him. My eyes never left his kneeling figure as I reached down.

Slowly...

If I disturbed him, would the mood change again?

Gently...

Shaking, my fingers closed round my fiddle's neck. I lifted it from its cushion of refuse and began to back away. Still on his knees, he turned.

I stopped. He was holding the doll lovingly, with both hands. Beneath the grime, his face was a child's—bright, puzzled, engrossed by something new, unable to understand what it was.

The St. Christopher's silver was a coldness on the back of my hand. I looked at it—and obeyed the impulse that came. Still smiling, Pigez watched me unwind it from the scroll, then put its gleam down on the scarlet ribbon beside him.

He laughed, indulgently, a tolerant man amused by an old friend's folly.

I turned and walked away with my fiddle.

26

WOOD

THE DAMP SMELL OF the leaves in the suntrapped corner of the rose garden was Autumn's beginning. It mingled with the smell of the flowers, for although they had begun to lose their petals, they still had their perfume. It was a step away from hope to leave the freshness and go back into Holcroft House.

The corridor was the same, weapon and trophy facing each other across the cold void that could only signify death—but the woman by my side was different. As we passed through the accusing darkness between muzzle and antler I examined the changes in Angela Holcroft.

They were not subtle. On the face of it, the situation was a reversion, butterfly to caterpillar, for the vamp was gone. A conscious decision or a repression? As we walked I wondered; it was as though the skin of sensuality had been sloughed off whole, as though all hope of carnality and its satisfactions had finally been abandoned. The heels were low, the clinging dress had been exchanged for a sober grey skirt and cardigan, and, most striking of all, the sexual flag of the silver hair was gone, cropped into a neat helmet that bordered on the masculine. My speculation lasted until we reached the door of the classroom. She paused, then spoke.

"I'm leaving here, Fraser. Despite your efforts, I find I can no longer share a house with my brother."

"And the boys?"

"When he dies, I'll be there for them. In the meantime, I've insisted on professional care. There's a new housekeeper, nannies, a nurse, a psychiatrist on call, good teachers. They'll have everything they need. I think that's better, don't you?"

Better than what, I wanted to ask. But the truth of it stopped me. Yes, for her it would be better—anything would be better than love so deeply rooted in desperation. My eyes came back to her new garb—a mixture of camouflage and armour, the judge's sister, the high-caste English spinster. That was the part she would play until she was gone from here, until she could find a place to decide what real self there could be for her. But it left me at a loss for words. I could understand, sympathise—but would the two children survive without her? I heard a peal of laughter from the garden, and recognised it as Nick's; perhaps it would be all right. It was money which had secured their future here—perhaps it could buy them warmth as well. She accepted my scrutiny in calm silence.

"I'm sorry I had to hit you," I said.

"I understand why you had to," she replied, quietly.

There was an awkward silence—and then a burst of electronic noise came from behind the door.

Shots, explosions, sirens. She turned, abruptly, walked away down the hideous corridor. I listened to her receding footsteps until they were gone—and then I entered the classroom.

It had changed. There were no posters of composers now, no instruments. I followed the violent sounds to their source.

Ewen was sitting, hunched and wary, before a huge screen. He was holding a gun.

The weapon was the same as the one I'd seen in the Bristol café—a futuristic concoction of black plastic, connected to a huge games machine by a luminous pink cable. The boy's hold on it was white-knuckle tight. He never saw me. The screen was all, the concentration involved in hitting the moving targets too intense to allow diversion. Every so often the index finger would jerk the trigger. Every hit brought a riot of colour, followed by a comic-book bubble of word.

Blap!

Pow!

Zowie!

But the gaunt face never changed. Holding the two instrument cases, I watched the painless fall of the bright little figures.

Was this why Sir Peter Holcroft had bought himself sons? To remake them in his own mould, refashion them in his own, soulless image? The boy probably didn't even understand what death was, but I couldn't help but link the trivialised slaughter on the screen with the repellent, formalised reality of the hallway outside.

Killing, still taught as an exercise in hand-eye co-ordination...

Slaughter, still the preferred metaphor for testing motor skills...

What had the old man said, that night in the pub? That the boy's talent could be maximised in some other way... Anger welled up in me. How long before he was taken to his first cock-fight? And what right did Angela Holcroft have to leave, to abandon him to this, even for a few years? I stood, letting the sounds and images mesmerise me, almost hoping the boy's unblinking stare would keep me invisible.

But as I watched, a different despondency found me.

Ewen was good at the game, frighteningly good—almost every shot from the electronic gun hit its target and brought its painless bubble of cartoon reward. That argued expertise, long practice. As I put my two burdens down on the workbench I wondered if I was too late, if the bond between the boy and his instrument had already been destroyed. There was only one way to find out.

"Hello, Ewen," I said.

The missed shot told me he had heard, but the dark head never turned. Was he afraid? What would be the best way to give him back his instrument? Familiar sounds, perhaps, merely let him know it was there... I opened the locks of The Singer's case, loudly, and lifted the lid. Still the electronic warrior refused to respond. I took out the instrument and ran my fingers across the strings—and even across the screen's noises, even without a bow, the light, nutty tone sang out. But still the boy remained in his world of ephemeral mayhem, still he would not hear. Perhaps if he was alone with it... Gently, I put the shunned Stradivarius down beside its case and made to turn—but suddenly the instrument held me.

The varnished sleekness looked opulent against the plainness of the bench, but wood always looks right on wood, and for a moment it seemed to be a shield against the modern world, against the electronic slings and arrows which had captured the boy—but only for a moment. The truth was at once more complex and less romantic. The modern world had fought over this violin with all the casual viciousness which the video screen embodied for me—and with a ruthlessness which no cockfight or stag hunt could ever have matched.

Money.

Only one person had really cared about this instrument for what it was, only one person had not had the slightest interest in its value—Ewen. And unless the boy still wanted his violin, The Singer's recovery was a charade, a farce. Standing there, listening to the painless barbarity of the games machine's noises, I felt how badly I wanted to see him and his instrument become whole again. Would it happen? No, it would be better to just go, to leave it, better—

The plastic gun swivelled round and pointed at me. The Singer might not have existed—Ewen's eyes were shifting furiously from my face to the other fiddle case in my hand, searching for some sort of cue. I could see he had no memory of me—and instinctively I knew that words would be wrong. There was only one other response I could make. I put the second case on the bench and took out my own battered treasure.

The tragedy was that my own fiddle looked better than it had done for years, for Philippe Berolet's repairs had been good and skilful, all but invisible. But still the instrument looked the older of the two, even though the Cremona violin predated it by two hundred years. Briefly I forgot the boy as I examined them together on the bench.

Strange sisters, pauper and princess...

Which would have the better future? My eyes returned to Ewen's—and something in my gaze turned the gun back to the screen. A frenzied burst of marksmanship began.

The truth came to me, slowly; I couldn't just walk away. Everyone else had abdicated responsibility for this child—his terrifying parents, the man who had bought him, the woman who loved him but could not love him here, in this house. I had to seize some sort of initiative, I knew. Two steps took me across to the screen. I fumbled buttons until the images died.

Fury inflamed the dark face—and even as I lifted the Stradivarius, I knew how much of a risk I was taking. This was a severely disturbed child, a child who threw things... The instrument's price tag didn't bother me—but the thought that the boy might destroy something he loved because he wasn't ready to take it back, that was a real fear. Shouldn't I let it come back into his life in some kind of measured way? Shouldn't I—

But all the arguments, all the voices urging caution, seemed worthless, unreal compared to Ewen's confusion. I found myself holding the instrument out to him, thinking, *love it. Love your violin again.*

At first, all that happened was a tightening of the fingers on the plastic gun's trigger—and then he simply dropped the thing. From then on it was feverish confusion—the left hand grabbed the precious fiddle, the right scrambled for the bow, and his eyes, still angry, never left my face.

Until the music began.

It poured out of him like a force of nature, a tidal wave of melody—Bach, Mozart, Telemann, all jumbled together, all wrapped up in a furious rush of technique that staggered me. The boy's brilliance was frightening—Brahms, Tchaikovsky, Greig, Bruch, the right hand controlling the bow with a master's confidence, the left flying through the positions with fluid ease. I stood before him, amazed, hardly able to credit what I was seeing and hearing.

But for all that, it was, at first, barely music. Only after ten minutes or so did the mathematical pace slacken into something like expression, only then did he begin to make The Singer sing. Handel came, then more Bach, and things I didn't recognise—and then, as though to place himself in some context of Englishness, Elgar. It was very moving—and suddenly I was no longer looking at the amazing technique of bow and fingers, I was staring at his face, at the beauty of the dark features, so unaffected, so unmoved by the beauty of what he was playing.

Beauty...

A monstrous talent and physical perfection—Celtic physical perfection... No wonder Ewen had it, the child of Sandra Henderson and John McPhie.

The thought stopped me hearing the music. Could a monstrous talent only be spawned by monsters? And could it only live in this monster's lair of a house, with its savage extended family? As if he sensed my unease, Ewen stopped playing as abruptly as he had begun.

And just stood there, holding the Stradivarius, looking at

the wooden floor.

The expression on his face was unreadable now. Confusion? Catatonia? The armpits of his shirt were wet with sweat. I didn't know how to begin to analyse his silence—but the conviction rose out of it, inexorably; it was something I had to fill. I lifted my own fiddle from the bench.

The piece I decided to play was called *Lady Livingstone.*

It had always been one of my favourites—an air which was Scotland's fiddle music at its very best, a melody of strange power, by turns regal and intimate. Hesitantly, I began the first notes.

Ewen's face was stone.

Was I was reaching him? Three times I played it—and not well, because for once I was playing entirely for someone else, with nothing in it for myself. I came to the last phrase, let the bow drop.

Nothing.

I had failed. There wasn't the slightest glimmer of light or appreciation in the boy's eyes. We both stood for a long time in total silence beside the wooden bench—until I could stand it no more. I turned and put my fiddle back in its case, telling myself that I'd at least tried, that in itself, that was important, that—

Behind me, the video game began again.

Bitterness descended on me. Once the case was packed, I couldn't even bring myself to say goodbye to him. I walked to the heavy door and closed it behind me.

But even safely closed, it wasn't heavy enough to mute the game's sounds—and now, in the corridor, my eyes couldn't escape the death row of animal heads. Barbarity behind, barbarity in front… I was trapped. I leaned back against the cold stone, closed my eyes and wondered if I could ever close my ears. The peacock's cry came like a final elegy, dying away alone, unanswered. I pushed my back from the wall. It was time to go.

And then, over the game noises, I heard it.

The peacock's answer, the tune called *Lady Livingstone.*

Every stroke of the bow was right, every cadence was clear, stressed exactly as I had stressed it. But the tone, the command—they were better than anything I had ever achieved in my life. Joy rose in me. I waited until the end, then turned, smiling, hand on the doorknob, ready to praise, to congratulate.

And then I stopped myself.

It was the boy's victory, not mine.

As the tune began again I took one last look at the rows of death—and then two steps took me to the other door. The door that led out, away.

To my own victory—or at least the chance of it. As Ewen began the tune again, the slim figure at the far end of the carpet of rose petals turned.

With all the vigour of Scotland's music ringing in our ears, Nathalie and I smiled at each other across the sweet decay of England's Autumn.

THE AUTHOR

BRIAN McNEILL, born in 1950 in Falkirk, Scotland, has long been acclaimed as one of the most creative forces in his homeland's traditional music. In 1989, not content with his roles as performer, composer, songwriter, music producer, teacher, musical director and band leader, he added novelist to his resumé with *The Busker.* His manic schedule in the late eighties meant that most of the book was written on aeroplanes. A second novel, *To Answer The Peacock,* based on the same character, the rootless drifter and street musician Alex Fraser, appeared in 1995. *...In The Grass,* featuring shape-shifting detective Sammy Knox, arrived in 2006. The next two instalments of the Busker series, *No Easy Eden* and *The Hawk That Swoops,* are now published for the first time in eBook and paperback format. His latest work, *The 90th Kill,* has also just been published in both formats.

His audio visual shows, *The Back O' The North Wind,* about Scottish emigration to America, and the sequel, *The Baltic Tae Byzantium,* which explores the influence of the Scots in Europe, have won wide critical acclaim, and his continuing connection with America's Lone Star State led to him being created an honorary Texan in 1998. In 2017 he was inducted into the Scottish Traditional Music Hall Of Fame.

From 2001 to 2007 Brian was Head of Scottish Music at the Royal Scottish Academy of Music and Drama. Recently his home town of Falkirk honoured him by carving two lines of his song *The Lads O' The Fair* in stone, at a viewpoint looking over the town.

A Note from Brian

Thanks for reading THE BUSKER. I hope you enjoyed it and if you did, I'd love to know what you thought of it. If you wish, you can send a review to:

www.brianmcneill.co.uk

If you want to stay updated about any of my fiction—or about any of the music I make—please go to the website above and join my newsletter list. It appears four times a year.

The current list of my other books is as follows.

*

THE BUSKER

Book 1 of the Busker Series

Alex Fraser is a rootless drifter who lives by playing Scotland's traditional music on the street. He makes his home wherever his fiddle might earn him a few coins. He's a man hiding from life, haunted by the death of his wife, which he caused. After serving his sentence in Scotland, he decides to try his luck in Europe.

In Switzerland he befriends another busker—Max, an old accordionist. Max tells him a story, a puzzle rooted in the Spanish Civil War. It's a tale of kindness and brutality, involving a German intelligence unit, a rescued child, a painting and a huge inheritance. Max, dying, charges Alex with solving the puzzle.

The maelstrom of violence and greed he uncovers is byzantine, daunting and ruthless. It pursues him across a continent, makes him confront love again, and ultimately forces him to believe in his own worth as a human being.

...The Busker is a fast-moving thriller in the Hitchcock mould,

sending its title character, Alex Fraser, on a desperate chase around Europe pursued by both the police and a ruthless gang of killers determined to prevent its hero uncovering a secret that goes back to the brutal Spanish Civil War incident which opens the book. Fraser, a loner with secrets of his own, makes an interesting hero, while Brian provides enough European atmosphere, intrigue and adventure, including a tense escape scene over the pre-reform East German border, to make for an exciting read. ...a fine debut novel.

Dundee Peoples' Journal.

You can buy *The Busker* either as an eBook or a paperback on Amazon.

*

NO EASY EDEN

Book 3 of the *Busker* Series

In Germany, Alex is given a lift by Abigail Eve, a black US Air Force captain. They stop at a fast food restaurant in the town of Rothenburg. A few minutes later, three junkies come in. After creating a scene, the kids run off, followed by a concerned nun, and then as Alex and Abigail leave, a bomb explodes, killing her and hospitalising him. He wakes to find Gunther Klein, a reporter, at his bedside.

After Alex is discharged, Klein investigates. Who was the nun? Why were the junkies in the restaurant? To keep Alex safe, Klein sends him to his ex-wife Sigi's family, but when Alex discovers Sigi is part of what happened—and that the US military want to arrest him—he flees. In Rothenburg train station, trying to make the price of a ticket to anywhere with his fiddle, he meets an elderly black man. It's Abigail's father, jazz trumpeter Luther Eve, come to see where his daughter died.

With Luther's help, Alex escapes to the old East Germany, where he uncovers a plot between ex-STASI officers, a cynical American soldier and an ex-terrorist who has assumed a startling new identity.

Drugs, misplaced idealism and family betrayals come to a

head in Hamburg's red light district, where Alex must make the hardest choice of his life.

You can buy *No Easy Eden* either as an eBook or a paperback on Amazon.

*

THE HAWK THAT SWOOPS

Book 4 of the *Busker* Series

Now a witness in the counterfeit drugs case which began in *No Easy Eden,* Alex is in Washington DC. He's had a letter from his father; his mother is gravely ill. Can he find an uncle he's never heard of, in Appalachia? Due to fly out in a few hours, his visa expired, Alex knows it's impossible.

A hotel bar fracas with a teenager brings him up against the girl's aunt, supermodel Rose Vannier. Then, while he's at Rose's side in a taxi rank, a boy on a scooter tries to kill her. Alex tackles him, breaking the boy's neck. No police, Rose insists. Why? What is she hiding? The idea of American authority's reaction to his criminal record panics Alex into agreeing.

At Rose's Virginia farm, he meets her entourage. They're suspicious of him. Is he in danger? When a rattlesnake is planted in his bag, he decides to run. He steals a van, only to find Lou, the girl who started the whole thing, hidden in the back.

The busker and the streetwise kid bond—but then she's abducted, and Alex's van is rigged to crash. Injured as a result, he only just escapes on a freight train.

An elderly, blind Appalachian fiddler, Jane McClintock, nurses him back to health, and her humanity gives him the strength to go on, to probe the long list of convoluted lies around Rose and Lou—and to solve the sad and terrifying mystery of his own long-lost uncle.

You can buy *The Hawk That Swoops* either as an eBook or a paperback on Amazon.

*

...IN THE GRASS

Book 1 of *The Sammy Knox* Series

In the deceptively sleepy Cotswold town of Cadisham, there's mischief afoot.

When Lady Letitia Moresby, the society stripper, finds that her python, Justin, has been stolen, she calls in Sammy Knox, glamorous private eye and witch's familiar. Sammy, who can change with ease between cat and human, is, as usual, broke, so she takes the case with alacrity. With the help of her teenage charge Libby (a trainee witch, but she doesn't know it yet) and Scrapper, a grizzled escapee from an animal testing laboratory, she begins to investigate.

The trail, which leads her through zoos, gravel pits, scrapyards, accountants' cupboards and assorted bedrooms, involves a resolute bunch of rescued felines, a languid tiger with ambivalent motives, a venal tax inspector with an individual take on rubber stamping, and a sweet but dim bloodhound.

Who would have suspected the leafy Cotswolds of harbouring so many dark secrets...?

Sometimes we like to mention the existence of people who shouted loudly and without getting tired „over here" when talents were distributed. Ex-Battlefield Band musician Brian McNeill is one of these people, but we don't want to use up precious space by enumerating all of his talents. Suffice it to say that writing is one of them... ...In The Grass is full of speed, funny and thrilling: highly recommendable.

Folker.

Sensuous, cunning super-sleuth Sammy Knox is unmatched in the detective genre. Brian McNeill's brilliantly crafted story and fantastic cast of characters will transport you to another dimension from the very first page. Pure magic!

Carol Hird.

You can buy *...In The Grass* either as an eBook or a paperback on Amazon. Book 2 of the series, *...In A China Shop,* is in preparation.

*

THE 90TH KILL

All the teenage Samuel Cadogan ever wanted to do was draw—but after the death of his father, a Pennsylvania coal miner, his family explodes in a maelstrom of child abuse and violence, and he finds himself on the wrong side of the law.

He runs. For the next six years he supports himself as a sidewalk artist in Boston—and then circumstances force him to flee even further. In the US military, under his new name of Lemuel Brecon, he discovers he has one outstanding talent. He's a world-class sniper, a natural killer.

Dishonourably discharged after serving in Iraq, burned out and barely existing on the street, he's approached by two high-ranking and high-minded ex-officers who want the re-election of a corrupt and controversial president stopped. They know Brecon's talents, and they lure him into their plot with the possibility of revenge against those responsible for his family's disintegration. Finally seduced by the promise that they will find his missing sister, he agrees to be part of their scheme. But for all their professed principles, the way these officers manipulate him is as merciless as it is cold.

This is a story about the cynicism and ruthlessness of America's elites, about the intertwined nature of its political process and its gun culture—and above all, it's about the stubborn courage of individuals and their determination to resist, to fight for their humanity as the juggernaut of American power does its pitiless best to grind them down.

You can buy THE 90TH KILL *either as an eBook or a paperback on Amazon.*

*

THE HORSEMAN'S WORD AND OTHER STORIES

A collection of shorter fiction, based mainly on the speech and dialect of Brian's Scottish lowland home town of Falkirk.

1913. Love, loss, inheritance, religion and magic; the simmering tensions not far below the surface of a lowland farm…
1958. A courageous schoolgirl's simultaneous discovery of her heroine's surprising secret and her own morality…
1966. The rough community of a working class pub coming together to protect one of their own from exposure…
1967. A teenage boy's complicated coming of age between bedroom and building site…
1972. A student whose moment of rebellion teaches him the painful difference between slogan and reality…
2016. A wronged and implacable cat taking revenge on mankind, only to discover the real depth of human cruelty…

The cover story, The Horseman's Word... ...is almost reminiscent of Thomas Hardy... ...You can tell from every sentence that the author of these stories is a musician. Every story has its own melody and it resonates.

Karin Braun, Writress Corner.

...a wonderful, unusual volume of stories. Definitely read!

Claudia Schmid, Kriminetz.

Includes a glossary of Scottish words and phrases.

You can buy *The Horseman's Word and other stories* either as an eBook on Amazon, or as a paperback from Brian's website. The paperback is also available from Songdog Verlag in Switzerland.

In English:

http://songdog.ch/buch-detail/the-horsemans-word-

and-other-stories.html

In German:

http://songdog.ch/buch-detail/the-horsemans-word-schottische-storys.html

An audiobook, read by Brian, is also in preparation.